Anon, Sir, Anon

A Vivi & Farnham Mystery

ANON SIR ANON

By Rachel Heffington

A
Vivi & Farnham Mystery

Ruby Elixir Press
United States of America

Other Works

Fly Away Home
Five Glass Slippers

ISBN: 0692301429
Published by Ruby Eixir Press

Cover design and interior formatting by Rossano Designs

First Edition

Table of Contents

The Part Where
I Introduce Things

I don't know what possesses a person to take risks; I don't know what made me want to take on the deservedly respected genre of the British Murder Mystery and succumb my work to the standard set by truly great authors like Agatha Christie, Dorothy L. Sayers, G.K. Chesterton, and Sir Arthur Conan Doyle. I feel there is a certain blind faith in the thing, like Shakespeare has it in *King Lear*:

"I will wear my heart upon my sleeve

For daws to peck at."

Be gentle, daws. Perhaps my decision was a shard of that insane irony that makes me believe that one must aim for the bulls-eye or put away one's arrows. Perhaps it was simply granite determination to break my own promise that I would never again attempt to write a mystery.

In my personal life, I am arguably the most un-mysterious creature to ever walk the planet. I lose every game of *Clue*, even when I'm allowed Miss Scarlet; I propose secret staircases in walls four inches thick; I began a mystery novel at the age of fourteen and so thickened the plot that I ended by befuddling myself and the characters with the fellness of its nature.

But for all these vague disqualifications, I have always adored mysteries. From the location of the lost Nazi treasures to what ending Charles Dickens had in mind for *The Mystery of Edwin Drood*, from who sent the anonymous check in our mailbox to whether there really is a Something in Loch Ness, I am fascinated. I may not be mysterious but I am deeply, profoundly, George-ly curious and curiosity is the element on which hinges the entire mystery game. Without curiosity, I would have no need to solve a mystery; therefore, I am qualified.

I must take a moment to straighten my proverbial tie and recognize several co-conspirators to this plot: author Elisabeth G. Foley for her expertise and advice in the mystery genre, my friend, Ness Kingsley, for her corrections to my portrayal of her native heath, Abigail (Taylor) Heffington for giving me the Bartlett book, Jeremiah Lorrig for his help in fencing terminology, St. Rachel for catching what I meant by 'lending itself to a series' and designing the ideal cover, and my wonderful editor, Rachelle Rea, whose unflagging patience with my favoritism toward semi-colons, my inconsistent British spellings and my knock-kneed em-dashes has enabled this book to have its face decently washed. And of course, I would be grossly remiss if I failed to thank William Shakespeare who —at the risk of a truism—is certainly the most quotable author in history and lends much to my library of borrowed wit.

Anon, Sir, Anon is cozy—made of toast and tea and firelight—but a vein of terror, like the Northamptonshire fog, anchors the characters almost uncomfortably to reality. For whomever the bell tolls, it *will* leave a hole. Life *won't* go on exactly as normal and those who knew the victim will be forever marked. That fact makes it all the cozier, for one is coaxed into wiggling one's toes deeper into the slippers and having another cup of tea if only to push away the feeling that such things can and do happen.

I hope you will let Vivi and Farnham into the ranks of the British Detective. I hope you will let them have a chance to win you over and, if you like them, I hope you will allow me to write more about their cases, their characters, and the little town of Whistlecreig. For I think my old saying is true: "All's well that ends with a cup of tea."

With All My Heart,

Rachel Heffington

For Daniel, who wins every game of *Clue*
and can extract anything out of anyone:
A mystery for you to winkle.

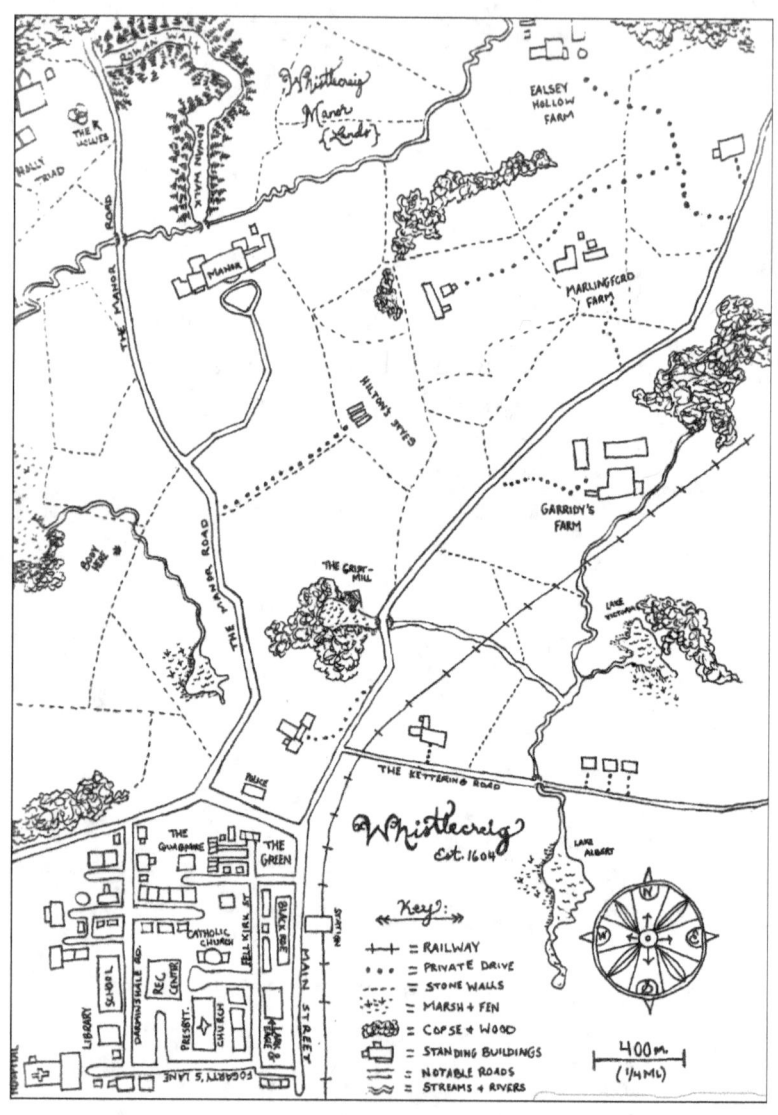

Available online at
http://inkpenauthoress.blogspot.com/p/my-books.html

Chapter One
At Whistlecreig

"Allen, a lady is coming; clear out a corner someplace."

The butler paused a moment in lifting Mr. Orville Farnham's coffee things, and Mr. Farnham took this opportunity to adjust his cuffs and avoid eye-contact.

"To *stay*, sir?"

Farnham glanced up. "Anywhere in the East wing will do."

"A *lady*, sir?"

Farnham felt the familiar clench of pain in his stomach. "A lady, Allen. Don't goggle; she's only a niece."

"Very well, sir." Allen stacked his master's cup and saucer beside the untouched breakfast from three hours past and departed.

Farnham drummed his fingertips along the back of the couch and grouched through another spasm of pain. A few rooks cawed outside, and their voices carried through the closed windows of Whistlecreig, peculiarly suited to Farnham's mood. He shoved his hand into the pocket of his navy cardigan and brought forth a letter he'd received in yesterday's mail.

Written in a round womanly hand, the direction begged leave to address Mr. Orville Farnham, Whistlecreig, Northamptonshire. It had not so much as arrived before Farnham knew it was from his relatives, not *so* strange a deduction when the only letters he received in general were from men of business or his infernal manager, Barth Melchior.

One does not write vague addresses in a sentimental hand unless one is a female relative; it simply isn't done. Thank heaven the practice was confined to that race of relatives one was allowed to dislike. How awkward, if it had been a letter from a brother, or cousin...for then it would have required a reply, and Farnham was none too keen on having the epistolary debt in his wallet.

Sentimental female relatives aside, Farnham had been expecting this letter since his collapse on-stage; people collapsed frequently on-stage when they make their living performing Shakespeare, but this occasion was rather special: Farnham—Farnham of *Whistlecreig*—had collapsed at entirely the wrong moment; fainted dead away, in fact.

It had all been in the papers—no one can keep something as dull as an actor fainting from the rabid clutches of bored journalism—and the relatives had wasted no time in descending upon him with the compunction of ravens on a birth-weakened lamb. He could not exactly complain that they'd come *en masse* as this saccharine letter was the first sign he'd had of them. The meaning of it, however, was plate-glass clear.

The Langleys (his sister's married family) were concerned for his health; he spent too much time alone. He kept odd hours and odder habits. He worked too hard. His "artistic temperament" was catching up with him. To comfort him in his "hour of convalescence," they were shooting off this niece, Miss Genevieve Langley, to play nursemaid.

Farnham read the letter over again with a sardonic grin. He sprang to his feet and paced before the shreds of red curtain that by some miracle of heaven had withstood six decades of moths. A regular bachelor's pad, Whistlecreig was, and though Farnham prided himself on feeling little but *physical* pain, a faint, resentful twinge cropped up toward this unknown female barreling toward him on the 12:55 out of Darlington.

How funny that they actually expected him to cooperate.

"Allen!"

The butler appeared.

"Fencing with me at half-one."

"Half-one, sir?"

"Inconvenient, Allen?"

"Only, sir, that is when the *doctor* has arranged to come up."

Farnham felt his chin then smiled. "Nevermind, Allen."

"Very good, sir."

Perhaps old Breen would be up for a match; personally, Farnham felt like stabbing something.

The train pulled to a stop like a hissing, dripping dragon at exactly thirty-seven past three. The conductor double-checked his big watch with a slight frown; fifteen minutes late, but who counted pennies and pence when it came to transportation? Do that and the working population would have a fit every solitary day. Working-population fits were not easily dealt with. It was better no one noticed.

The conductor passed an elegant lady wearing a blue cloche three times and each time he wondered why she sat like that—face glued to the window-pane—when there was nothing to the view but a soggy cord of wood and a half-dissolved circus poster and fat old Barnaby in his porter's booth. Maybe she was asleep.

"Madam?" he said quietly, not really wishing to wake her but fearing she would miss her stop.

The young woman didn't stir.

A different girl, a plain-looking one in a red tam o'shanter, watched him with interest, taking far too long to gather her things and get off the train. The conductor prodded the lady with the blue cloche and wished she'd wake up. They were almost always asleep, but...you know...there had been that *one* time and the police had come and then a private detective, and his wife had gone into hysterics and had never made tea proper since. The man shuddered a little and managed a tiny smile for the curious girl in the red tam.

She picked up her train-case and clutch and approached. "Is something wrong?"

"Wrong?" the conductor repeated, jiggling the blue-hatted form with more vigor than at first. "Wrong?"

With a moan and frown, the lady in blue turned, rubbing sleep and confusion from her eyes.

"*Nothing* wrong," the conductor informed the plain girl. He felt himself beam with fathoms-deep relief. There would be no trouble. "Is Whistlecreig *your* stop, madam?"

The sleepy beauty raised beautiful brown eyes and scoffed. "This town? Hah. Bad luck for me, I've gotta say yes." She shifted in her seat and began to sort her luggage. "Got a cigarette?"

The conductor obliged the goddess, and she took a light from him, thrusting her chin and keeping the cigarette pressed between her lips.

"Real dump, ain't it?" her voice was full of America and none too gentle. "But hey, I bring glitz to dumps. It's my specialty." She stood and exhaled a cloud of blue-grey smoke. "Know where I can find your bum hotel?"

"Ask Mr. Barnaby," the conductor said with a regrettable giggle.

"Thaaaaanks," she drawled and sprinkled her ashes on the polished toes of his shoes before stalking the length of the car and letting herself out the little green door.

The conductor watched, a bit stupefied by the smoke and the cigarette ashes on his Northampton-made oxfords. What a queen she must be to go around sprinkling cigarette butts on men's shoes! The lady wasn't nice, but she was lovely and the conductor felt terribly glad she hadn't been dead. He watched her elegant, skulky figure out the window and shook his head. What a story to tell Martha.

"Excuse me!" The girl in the red tam smiled at him and raised her bags to show she wished to pass his girth in the aisle. "It's my stop, too. Thanks a mil for the tea earlier."

"My pleasure." And though it was, perhaps, only his profound sense of relief at *not* finding another body dead on his train, the conductor thought that when the plain girl smiled, she looked just a little beautiful.

Genevieve Langley waited for thirty minutes at Whistlecreig Station—at least, that's what her watch said. It *felt* like three days and half, but she was a sensible girl and knew travel horribly skewed one's perception of time. For instance, that fifteen-minute delay in that obscure little market-town had felt an hour long. Still, as the time she had been waiting on the platform approached the half-hour, she grew restless. In reply to her mother's letter, Genevieve had received not a line.

By the end of this damp thirty minutes, she began to have misgivings about coming at all.

None of her family had answered her question, "What if Mr. Farnham doesn't want a nurse?" Instead, they had cheerfully explained that since she had helped now and then in the children's hospital since her uneventful coming-out, she certainly had experience enough to minister to an eccentric and very rich uncle suffering from stomach ulcers.

Well, stomach ulcers or not, Genevieve did not appreciate her current, rather damp position. Were it not for the round disapproval which would meet her back in Darlington, Genevieve thought she would be content to retreat without ever having set nose at Whistlecreig Manor. A demeaning breeze lifted her skirt and snatched at her red tam. Genevieve felt convinced that Mr. Orville Farnham in all his garish bachelor glory could be no more fearsome a thing than standing on a Northamptonshire train platform till someone remembered she was to arrive.

She would go after him herself, if need be. Genevieve took a space in line at the porter's window behind a young man in tweeds. He bought a ticket to Crowborough and moved off to the side. Genevieve stepped forward. The height of the booth required her to tip-toe to see through the window. Times like these, she thought it would chuff her to be a bit taller.

"Where might I find Whistlecreig Manor?" she inquired in her best attempt at a commanding accent.

The porter, a fat man, sipped a cup of coffee. He took his leisure looking her over. "What do you want wi' him? He's been bad-up i'bed this fortnight."

"I know that. I'm Genevieve Langley." She might have added that she was Orville Farnham's niece, but that would be groveling. Things hadn't come to so desperate a pass that she need grovel. "I've come to take care of Mr. Farnham. He is expecting me."

The porter sipped from his mug again and served a wall-eyed stare. "If he was a-gawn to send for a lady, blimey but I'll be demmed if he didn't pick a partickerly ugly one."

Genevieve was accustomed to being dubbed "plain," "drab," and even "commonplace," but this she would not suffer. "I suppose you think me Mr. Farnham's paramour? Perhaps a stage-girl with rouged knees? I am not beautiful, but I am a lady, which is more than most can honestly say."

"Well, y'needn't chelp at me."

Genevieve stepped back from the window, dropping mercifully below the man's line of vision. She was startled to find the young man in tweeds at her elbow. That he had heard her outburst seemed unfair.

His grin showed he had heard and appreciated it. "Looking for Whistlecreig?"

"Yes...thank you." Her confidence drained at a wasteful rate, and she wished she'd never left Darlington.

"Two miles West of here. I'm Jimmy Fields."

"Genevieve Langley."

They exchanged handshakes. That small connection bolstered her spirits to add, "Are you from Whistlecreig?"

Jimmy nodded and shoved his hands deep into the pockets of his coat, chin ducking into the high collar. "Grown up here. Love it, but I decided it's time to move on for a bit. I've a penchant for traveling."

Genevieve laughed and waved her train-case. "As have I. Well, pleasant to chatter like this, but I've two miles to walk with my trunk balanced on my back; I don't suppose you've anything as civilized as a handcart in Whistlecreig?"

Jimmy winked and took a key from his pocket. "I was going to leave my wheels here for a friend to pick up, but I've got a sec to run you down to Old Farnham's before I flee to Crowborough."

He dragged Genevieve's heavy leather trunk to his automobile, shoved it in the back, and hurried her into the passenger seat. He hopped in beside her with a grin. "Ready?"

They reversed, wheels spitting mud, and Jimmy pulled out onto the brown main-road, purring westward. Genevieve was more than a bit pleased to find herself spared the vexing prospect of a long, dirty walk—rescued by a charming stranger, no less. She could see that beneath the tweeds and mist-hoary locks, Jimmy Fields was a more than decent-looking man in the better half of his twenties.

"Why are you here?" he asked, breaking a rain-hushed silence and slowing at a turnstile.

She had been expecting this. "Mr. Farnham is ill, and I was sent to care for him."

"Ah, a little Florence Nightingale. Maybe you could advise me as how best to cure my toothache; my jaw is never this large most days." Without taking his eyes from the road, Jimmy brushed his fingertip against his strong jaw-line and Genevieve could see it was swollen and angry-looking.

"You could try oil-pulling," she suggested, "but honestly, I know very little about nursing." At Jimmy's curious glance, Genevieve settled in for an explanation: "I am actually a niece of Mr. Farnham's. The family elected me as the one best suited to be companion for an ill uncle."

"Do the rest of them shy at snorting dragons?"

She laughed. "Something like that."

"Are you married, Ms. Langley?"

He had remembered her name *and* he wondered whether she was married. Genevieve twisted the pearl ring she wore on her left hand and smiled. "*No.*"

"Called it off and kept the ring? Cruel woman."

Genevieve made to defend herself until she caught the laughter in Jimmy's eyes as he craned his neck to see around the curve and pulled onto a side-road bordered by boxwood. She swallowed a sigh. "The ring is just a trifle I've always fancied. The fact that I am unmarried has not gone unnoticed in my family."

She expected Jimmy would say something to this, but he continued to drive in affable silence.

"To speak it plain," Genevieve continued, "that is part of the reason they've packed me off down here where I can't offend them with my inability to make a brilliant marriage."

"Old cats." Jimmy slowed at a gap in the boxwood hedge and pulled into a private lane that gleamed with dusky silver mist in the uncertain funnel of the car's headlights. "Welcome to Whistlecreig."

Down the run of drive, so small at this distance as to look like a miniature castle, was Whistlecreig Manor. Genevieve clasped her gloved hands in her lap, well-pleased with the place from this vantage. At least it was not a hovel. "It's lovely."

"Oh, it has all the modern conveniences: mice, mold, damp, draughts. You name it, Farnham has sent off for the latest patented model."

They bounced over a rut, the car skittering to the left and right before settling back in the center of the drive, only to be driven back again like the ball in a game of tennis. Jimmy appeared to be little concerned with the state of the manor-roads and before Genevieve had time to decide whether she thought there were more stones or pot-holes, her driver had swung the automobile round the curve and parked before the front door of Whistlecreig Manor.

"Your journey's end, m'lady." Jimmy sprang from his seat and trotted round the front of the automobile. "Shall I run you in or will you be fine on your own?"

Genevieve accepted Jimmy's hand and stepped from the cab. "You've been fabulous. Don't miss your train on my account."

Jimmy deposited her trunk on the bottom step and swept his cap from his head, slightly breathless, eyes dancing. "Anytime, m'lady. Shall we meet again?"

"Shan't we? I am to be here for an undetermined length of time—are you off to Crowborough for good?" It irked her somewhat that she cared.

Jimmy shrugged. "Maybe, maybe not; see how long the wallet holds out." He held her eyes for a moment, and the rain came down between them. "Well, then. It's about time I shove off. See you in a bit?"

"Have fun with your traveling."

A salute. "Depend upon me—I will."

And like that, Jimmy was gone and Genevieve found herself quite alone—save the rain and rooks—with nothing between her and a new destiny but an insignificant bit of front door. *So this is how it feels*, she thought, *to be shut up in prison.*

She contemplated the forbidding knocker—a leopard's head with the teeth bared to admit an iron ring—and a certain stubbornness peculiar to her nature cropped up: she would not be put off by some jumped-up actor who went about nailing furious leopards to his front door. She straightened her jacket, rapped on the wood of the door, and waited. The house, at this angle, was a bit less beautiful than it had appeared from the boxwood hedge at the edge of the main road. A green hue suggestive of slime enveloped the stone walls and here and there a chunk of stone was entirely missing. What windows remained intact were, as a general rule, very fine indeed but this effect was lessened when one realized that there were but one third of the window slots filled with glass; the others had been bandaged with eye patches of plywood, giving the place a sneering manner.

Employed in these musings, Genevieve was startled by the front door falling in and the subsequent appearance of a respectable, hulking-strong butler.

She regained composure in a moment. "Hello."

"Hello, miss."

This was going nowhere. "I am Miss Genevieve Langley and I've come to stay with Mr. Farnham."

"He is expecting you," the man said.

"Is he? He sent no one to the station and, if a young local man had not acted generously, I would have had to walk."

"I was worried about that, but Mr. Farnham was not. Fortunate isn't it, miss, that there *was* a young man? I should have disliked knowing you had to walk here. Roads are not in the best condition this time of year. Rather wet, isn't it, madam?"

She swallowed a growing sense of indignation. "Very. May I come in?"

"Certainly, miss." The butler stood aside and let her pass into a large and amphibious hall glistening with moisture. "Would you like me to take your trunk inside?"

"If it isn't too much trouble," she said.

"None at all, miss." He rotated on his heel and disappeared down the steep front stairs, leaving Genevieve in the crypt, quite alone again.

Chapter Two
A Murder

It was a funny place with stone walls—quite damp—and mottled granite tiles on the floor. Once upon a time it might have been a fine hall, but now it reminded her of an abode more suited to frogs and salamanders than people. A steady, cold breath like a grave's whisper came from somewhere above, running fingers under Genevieve's hair and chilling her.

In a moment, the butler bobbed back up the stairs, briefly blotting out sunlight like an avenging deity as he passed through the doorway.

He slung her trunk to the ground and brushed grit from the shoulder of his black suit. "Mr. Farnham will be in his library, madam. Follow me, please." They went off a hall to the left, turned right almost immediately, then left again and came at last to a deep doorway. The door to this chamber stood open and a fire from deep within threw coral-colored shadows against the satin mahogany in an October dance. Here, at least, comfort dwelt. Just looking at the glow warmed Genevieve's spirit and whatever was in that room, be it dragonfire, it would be warm.

The butler preceded Genevieve through the doorway and announced her in a low but precise voice: "Miss Genevieve Langley, sir." He waved Genevieve into the room.

She settled her nerves with a deep breath before following the command. On light steps, she walked, making little noise in the deep carpet. It was a spacious room wainscoted with bookshelves, and here Genevieve felt she was on equal footing with this strange uncle; a man who reads can never be a total loss.

The fireplace, the butler, and a wing chair stood at the opposite end of the room: a tribunal of domestic comfort assembled to judge this intruder of their peace. In the wing chair sat a man she could take to be none other than Mr. Orville Farnham. He looked at her and fingered his chin, eyes slitted consideringly. The butler exited the room without making so much as one floorboard creak.

"You're a condolence piece?" Farnham asked at last.

"Pardon?" In her surprise, Genevieve took a few steps closer till she was quite near the tribunal.

"A condolence piece, sent here to look after me because the family's afraid I'll do something criminal or, what's worse in High Society, *odd.*"

Genevieve switched her bag from one hand to the other. "Is it true?"

With sudden movement, Farnham took his fingers from his chin and stared down the length of his remarkable nose. "That oddity is worse than crime?"

"Au contraire: that you're mad."

He almost smiled. "Aren't we all?"

Genevieve would concede no such thing; she froze him with her five-second glare and watched it take effect.

"Barring present company, of course," he said, making as much of a bow as he could manage while seated in a deep chair.

Theatrical. That thought reminded her of her uncle's profession and another person he'd dare not label 'mad.' She would see how this shaft burned: "And barring Shakespeare, you'd say."

"Oh no." Farnham smiled complacently, quite impervious to her suggestion. "Shakespeare was the worst of the lot— geniuses always are." Her uncle said nothing for some time after this and seemed to consider conversation accomplished. It lay upon her shoulders to make the next polite foray.

"I have had some small skill in nursing," she ventured.

"How small? Gout and croup small or 'pricked my finger on a hat-pin small'?" His pale blue eyes seemed to take her in at leisure, but unlike the porter's, formed no judgment. She almost wished he had shown what he thought, for then she would know how to look back at him.

"Hat-pin," he pronounced with a grim breed of gentleness in the tone. "No need to be upset; I'm not a great one for catching croup anyway—coughing is such a bang tedious business and my stomach hardly appreciates the gesture."

Genevieve was unsure how to respond; she grabbed for the topic quite literally at hand: "Where should I put my things?"

"In a corner." His response cracked out with militant alacrity and a passing frown.

"Which corner?" she pressed quietly.

His face eased into a waggish smirk. "Haven't the foggiest. House so bang full of 'em. Allen would know." He shoved his hands into his cardigan pockets and hunched his thin shoulders. "You hungry?"

"Always."

"I never am." He winced and shrugged. "Dodgy stomach. And don't tell me to take ginger; hate the stuff."

She smiled despite herself. "You ought to try."

"And you ought to have married well. Rebellious pair, aren't we? Bang it."

Genevieve set her bag on the ground and clasped her hands in front. "Why do you keep saying that?"

"Bang?" Her uncle's hand sliced through the air, dismissing the inquiry. "Used to swear—fond of the habit, actually. Found God, had to give it up. Such a trial fishing for adjectives when a good, solid, British 'damn' would suffice."

Genevieve found herself agreeing with that sentiment. "But why 'bang'?"

Farnham surprised her with a hearty chuckle that brought a boyishness to his gaunt face. "At the start, I tried slamming the table when the urge of an 'oh Hell' came on. Too startling for my friends, so I resorted to onomatopoeia: 'bang'."

"It's brilliant."

"Bang brilliant." He nodded his head slow and thoughtful, and his eyes flickered over Genevieve's right shoulder. "Oh, what luck. Here's the soul of Whistlecreig now. Hail hearty ho, Allen, what light from yonder window breaks?"

The butler came forward with a silver tray, in the center of which sat a card. "This just came for you, sir."

"Telegrams."

The way her uncle said the word with a sort of vocal wince made Genevieve curious. She waited as he read the thing and watched his eyebrows rise till his forehead was creased like a pug dog's.

She set her bags on the floor and tucked her hair behind her ears. "What is it?"

"Nothing interesting. Allen, is it time?"

"Time for what?"

Farnham did not answer. Her uncle seemed to fear small-talk and this was a thing that caused Genevieve's mind to race: she had been schooled from a young age that one could make conversation with an enemy if one could only master the art of small-talk. She *had* mastered it and spent the last several years talking small with everyone of her acquaintance. Now she found herself in a place where communication was dutifully carried out in terse remarks and enigmatic questions and, when the necessary information had been related, everyone fell silent. Whistlecreig wasn't like elsewhere...it didn't know how to behave like other places.

"It is time, sir." Allen tucked the silver tray under his arm, bowed, pivoted on his heel, and departed.

"Well, follow him. Dining room's just across the great hall. When I passed by earlier, it was making a very ancient and fishlike smell."

Genevieve's stomach balked. "Oh...my."

"No need to look so ill, Miss Langley. Quoting Shakespeare. Allen's made branzino. Off we go. I won't enjoy it, but you might." He stood, tugged the edges of his cardigan, and jutted his elbow at her.

She paused a second, wondering what he meant for her to do with it. Some odd gesture of gallantry, she supposed. Genevieve slipped her arm through his and suppressed a smile.

He cut his eyes at her. "You think me odd, Miss Langley? What a pass the world has come to when gentlemen no longer escort their ladies to table. Have you never been elbowed round?"

"Never."

"'Youth, whatsoever thou art, thou art but a scurvy fellow.' If ever I get my hands on a man of your acquaintance, I'll teach him."

Her uncle's arm was a warm thing to clasp as they made their way through the tangle of passages, and Genevieve thought what a sad fact it was that gentlemen no longer "elbow" their ladies, as Farnham had so bluntly put it; there was a certain peaceable respect in the gesture that made her feel like royalty as they hurried through the echoing hall and into another cell of firelight. The smell of baked seabass filled the room and through a curl of steam and candle-glow, Genevieve saw Allen pouring water into crystal glasses like a tee-totalling Bacchus in a three-piece suit. Farnham released her arm and pulled out a chair, waiting for her to sit before he pushed it in again. He took the place across from her, leaving the chair at the head of the table empty, though a place was set.

Genevieve had spread her napkin and thus exhausted any action that required no conversation. She looked at the third place. "Is Allen to join us?"

"No."

"Are we expecting company?"

Farnham laid his napkin across his legs with meticulous care and drummed his fingers on the tabletop. "None. The welcoming committee had gone to London to visit the Queen else they would have been here to pay you homage."

She felt the sting of his sarcasm and wished he wouldn't take everything she said as a personal insult. "I only wondered, as you weren't sitting at the head of the table."

"I've saved a place for Macbeth's ghost," he said tersely.

"I thought theatre-people refused to say the name of The Scottish Play."

Farnham speared a potato with his fork and passed the bowl to her. "I am not superstitious. Why should I use his name any less than I'd use yours? You're not going to give me bad luck, are you?"

Genevieve served herself and set the bowl before the empty plate at the head of the table and bowed toward it. "Then Macbeth, dear sir, would you take some supper?"

Farnham scoffed. "Silly girl. I was in jest. I leave a place at the head of the table because I hate to have my back to the gaping hall."

"You're afraid?"

"Curious. I like to know if anyone is looking at me."

"Oh, uncle, narcissism never did any man a good turn." Genevieve laughed at Farnham's befuddled expression and laughed harder when he flapped his elbows, looking like a crane whose fishing has gone awry.

"Perhaps we'd better bless the food and have done with ghosts," he said.

"Oui, monsieur, c'est une bonne idée."

Farnham bowed his head, and Genevieve did the same. She wondered where Allen had gone to and if he thought his employer's behavior in regards to the empty seat a bit odd.

"For what Thou hast given us, liege Lord, we thank Thee and ask that our lives might be of service to Thee," Farnham prayed in an elegant, soothing voice that seemed to treasure the holy words. "In Thy Son's magnificent name do we pray. Amen."

"Amen."

"One thing you will need to know, Miss Langley." Farnham turned his fork with the potato still speared on the tines and smiled at it. "We are often interrupted during our supper."

"By whom?"

"Or what? Or whither? Never you mind, for it changes every time. I thought you would like to be advised, though."

Puzzled, she shrugged. "Of course. Thank you."

Allen brought the branzinos on two plates and set one before each place, leaving the third place hungry. The whole fish in its crispy, salted jacket stared at her with a glassy eye, and Genevieve thought it looked at Whistlecreig and its inhabitants in a spirit of judgment and lemon-juice. "I incline to concur," she whispered.

"To whom are you speaking?" Farnham asked.

Genevieve snapped straight. "To my fish, if you must know."

"I could have gone a long time without knowing that." There was a bit of a silence—horrifyingly awkward—and Farnham smashed the potato he'd been turning on the fork since first stabbing it. "Tell me, Miss Langley, are you one of those nature-spiritualist people who eat nothing but dried fruit and hot water and apologize to the Earth for taking even that much from Her bosom? No? Good, because I was going to tell you that I'll have none of that here. We eat fish. We eat poultry and lamb and pork and whatever we take a fancy for. Allen raises cabbages and he doesn't weep a little weep over each plant as he decapitates it and takes its head to steam in a pot."

"Really, sir!" Allen's voice intruded.

Farnham stopped Allen with an imperious gesture. "I imagine we'd eat a horse if we decided it would taste any good. What I mean to say is that you'll find your feelings constantly trod upon if you insist on animals and plants having spirits and crying tears and marrying and owning property and all of that ridiculous brouhaha one hears so much about in this modern age. Animals have lives, and I like them to live their lives in comfort and decency. But I've got a life too and what's more, I've got a soul, and when the time is right I have no compunction about eating a bunny or two to keep body and soul entwined."

"Sir. Your potato," Allen murmured.

Genevieve passed a hand over her lips, praying she wouldn't dissolve into laughter as she watched Farnham stare at the shapeless mash that had once been a potato sitting cheek-to-jowl with the fin-tail of his branzino.

"Hmmm...well dear me," Farnham muttered.

Allen cleared his throat. "'I am a great eater of beef, and I believe that does harm to my wit', sir? Was that, perhaps, the quotation for which you were searching?"

Farnham drew himself up. "Oh fie on you, Allen."

Genevieve tried to keep her amusement inside, but the aggrieved expression on Allen's face and the surprise on

Farnham's as if he'd been an unlucky Jove discovering his Titanic strength was too much to be borne in silence. She laughed aloud—peals of it—and the idea of anyone laughing in a place like Whistlecreig only made her situation funnier. Farnham sat back, affronted. Allen whisked himself off someplace—Genevieve could only imagine where—and still she laughed. It was just too ridiculous, this house and these people and her uncle's passionate description of his butler merrily guillotining the cabbages in the garden.

"I suppose you think I'm joking," he said after she'd finally stopped laughing long enough to begin to feel embarrassed.

"No. That's what makes it so...so..." The hilarity almost burst out again but by a valiant sip of water, Genevieve saved herself from further disgrace.

"Now that your fish is quite cold," her uncle said, "shall we proceed with our supper?"

"By all means." Genevieve fanned her cheeks. "Branzino has given me permission to consume him as soon as he is cooled."

Farnham was furious, she supposed. For the next fifteen minutes, he flicked at the skin of his fish, making small cuts in the flesh but eating very little. He seemed to have lost all his appetite and when Allen finally came around with steaming cups of wassail, he beamed upon Farnham with a fatherly eye.

"I think a bit of company is good for you, sir."

"How so?"

"Look at how you've eaten. That's appetite there."

Genevieve fingered her napkin, curious to see Allen employing sarcasm which seemed to be his master's forte. But Farnham did not laugh—he even seemed a bit astonished and looked at the plate with a certain fondness.

"You know, Allen," he said, "I think I did make a good attempt."

"Enjoy your cider, sir." Allen rested his fingers on Farnham's shoulder for a moment then cleared away the dishes, leaving Genevieve and her uncle alone again.

There had been nothing said between them since Genevieve's unfortunate display of hilarity. It hadn't seemed so very inappropriate, but she had never been a judge of such matters. When it was all toted up at the back of the books, who would blame her for laughing over something as absurd as Farnham's monologue? But remorse crept in among the justification and spoiled it: she was a guest—an uninvited guest —intruding upon a bachelor-uncle's life and beginning her stint by laughing at a thing he appeared to take seriously.

She had been a perfect child about it. "Uncle, do forgive me."

"What?"

She seemed to have startled him out of a deep study. "For laughing earlier. I was out of place in doing so. I am sorry."

Farnham waved her off. "It was nothing."

"You aren't angry with me?"

He checked his watch, and his gaze wandered toward the darkness that was the hall. "Not. At. All." His words were measured as if ticked off by the second-hand of the great clock standing in the corner.

Preoccupied. That was his word in this moment. Genevieve waited. She would have left the room—ladies were expected to leave table before the gentlemen—but she had no idea where she ought to go if she was to depart. Customs and etiquette had prepared her very ill for everything she'd met so far since leaving Darlington.

"Should I...leave?" she asked, half-rising.

Farnham jumped again. "Oh—no. I want you to meet Dr. Breen."

"I thought we weren't expecting company."

"Company for *supper*. The doctor informed me in his message that he was eating at the Lark and Eagle." How strange her uncle acted...unsettled, distracted.

"Is this a social visit?" she asked.

"I call it that, but you'd probably not. Ummm...how are you around blood?"

"Oh my. Is there an injury?"

"It's a bit worse than that, Miss Langley: there's a murder."

Chapter Three
Take a Gamble

A murder? She counted their party: one, Farnham, two, Genevieve, three, Allen. Well *they* were all accounted for, so thank heaven none of them could be considered murderer or victim. Who then? And what on earth had a doctor to do with any of it?

Farnham's eye strayed out the door of the dining room into the bone-cold hall. "Where is the old man?"

"Here!" A robust voice caroled into the room and accompanying it, a tall, active-looking man with a shock of dark grey hair and a youthful face.

Farnham spread his hand to indicate the chair at the head of the table. "Won't you, Breen? Allen was about to bring in the pudding."

The doctor bowed to Genevieve and smiled, but Genevieve saw the quizzing, questing look he shot at Farnham.

"'I have been in such a pickle since I saw you last,'" Farnham said, not bothering to answer the unspoken question. It appeared to Genevieve that her uncle stared rather hard at his friend as if encouraging him to find some extra meaning in the words.

"Oh Lud." Dr. Breen pushed his chair away from the table and crossed his legs, resting rough boots on the white tablecloth. He stretched his arms behind his head and grinned in an amiable fashion. "I know this one. I *know* I know this one."

Rather than being puzzled or vexed with this new table ornament, Farnham pushed his chair back and did likewise. "You ought to know it. We've practiced enough," he grumbled, settling into the new position. His feet now blocked his face from his niece's view, but she could see Dr. Breen.

Breen worked his face into one big wrinkle. "Something about.....oh *Lud*."

"How—" Genevieve began, intending to ask a question.

Dr. Breen unfolded his arms and beamed at her. "Of *course*! 'Why, how now, Stephano?'"

Farnham applauded. "*The Tempest*. It's really quite simple, Breen. I give you all the Watsonizing parts, you know. The useless questions asked for decorum's sake. You shouldn't have trouble remembering stupid questions."

"So generous. *Unflinchingly* generous." Breen shook his head and his Scottish burr rolled the words richly. "Farnham, would you mind making introductions? I'm afraid I don't know this young lady."

Farnham's head appeared as he removed his feet from the table; he stood and cleared his throat. "Miss Genevieve Langley, Dr. Lawson Breen. Dr. Breen, my niece, Miss Genevieve Langley."

"I didn't know you had a niece." Breen nodded at her. "Pleased to make your acquaintance. Just stopping over for the night to see your old uncle? Nice girl. Wish my nieces would come visiting now and then. Takes me back to the days when I lived at home with my sisters."

Genevieve smoothed her knife's swirled handle and smirked. "I'm afraid he's stuck with me for a bit longer than that."

"Really?" Breen clomped his heavy boots one by one onto the floor, placed his fists on his thighs, and gave her a keen look. "*Really?*"

Why must everyone be so surprised? It was beginning to feel to Genevieve that she had made a horrible mistake in coming at all. There seemed to be nothing but bachelors from here to Battersea and these not even of eligible age. She wished there was such a thing as a housekeeper or parlor maid to be found—even a glimpse at a fellow female would ease her mind. But no, she was stuck among the uncouth male masses.

"I've been dosed to him like smelling salts, I suppose." Genevieve fingered the rim of her plate. "The family heard he was ill and wished to revive him and show their support so they sent me. Of course, if I'm the wrong brand, they might take me back again."

Breen put up a hand. "Didn't mean to sound so rough, I'm sorry. But I *am* curious. I've been trying to get Farnham to have an indoor companion all these years—even a bird would do!—he's always refused flat-down and now he's gone and got himself a...a woman!"

"A niece, Breen. A *niece!*" Farnham hissed, glancing around as if he feared some slight on his reputation would leak out of the house and into the papers. "And she's not company, she's..." He looked her over. "Well, she's *medicine.*"

"You mean you don't want to take her but it's for your own good?" Breen chuckled. "Ahhh me."

Medicine? Genevieve had more than half a mind to leave the table at once, extract her bags from Allen's care, and walk the two miles back to the station at Whistlecreig. Since coming to this mist-ridden land she'd met nothing but rough, rude men...and Jimmy. He was the one decent piece in this crummy afternoon.

What on earth had her mother got her into?

Farnham watched his niece's face and knew he'd said or done something wrong. Why must women be such bang tedious knots of complexities? He let his mind rove over the past few moments in search of any behavior that might warrant that scathing color on Genevieve's face. Nothing, nothing at all. He'd be the perfect model of a host: making conversation, making a valiant attempt at eating his dinner, leaving a place for the good Doctor Breen at the table's head...maybe she'd taken offense at them resting their feet upon the cloth. Well, if she was going to be so much of a woman as all that, she could go right back to Darlington; he wasn't going to have comfort uprooted for the sake of a niece who got miffed at everything and whispered condolences to her *branzino*. And there Breen was, toadying to her as if he was the Soul of Chivalry itself.

"This murder, Breen?" He cut in, quite fed up with it all. "What about it? Details? I must have them, you know. You can't expect me to investigate without details."

His old friend turned to him, mouth open from talking to that wretched girl, and smiled. "Oh, yes. I'd almost forgot about that in the fair presence of your niece."

The bowing, scraping fool! "Nonsense. Live women are dime-a-dozen. You're here to tell me about the dead one."

"Yes. Farm lad was walking his sweetheart home when they saw the body of the poor girl from the road—wait a moment, Farnham. How is it you know it's a she?"

Farnham, quite pleased at discomposing his friend, grinned. "You always sound rather congratulatory when it's a girl as if you'd finally found The Case."

"I sent a *telegram*, Farnham. How on earth can anyone sound congratulatory?"

"You can."

"*The* case?" Genevieve asked. "I'm sorry to be a clod, but I'm quite in the dark. Is my uncle on the police force, Doctor?"

"Ha!" Breen chortled and seemed to think the suggestion preposterous. "Him, on the police force? Ohhhh, where to start in the web of friendship?"

Farnham wished his niece wasn't there so they could get on with the facts of the case and Breen wouldn't have yet another chance to call him an amateur. But the doctor, his oldest friend and volunteer nuisance, was intent on having the whole, long tale.

"If you must explain, be concise," Farnham warned, and began to nurse his foot across one knee.

Breen winked at Genevieve and it was all Farnham could do to keep his temper when the girl smiled and turned pinkish in reply. What was it with the old fellow? He could charm a butterfly to swamp-muck with a summons of his pinky-finger. He could sell a bathing suit to an Eskimo and a waterproof hat to a Sahara-desert explorer. He ought to have gone into pharmaceutical sales and left the doctoring to someone with less charm.

"Your uncle, Miss Langley, is what the detective novels call an amateur sleuth," Breen explained. "It began over drinks one night, I believe. I'd had a pint too many but Farnham was still in possession of his wits. The police inspector burst into the pub and called my name, shouting something about a crisis. I staggered out, of course, and that obnoxiously curious uncle of yours followed me. By the time I got to the scene, the injured man was dead, and it wasn't till I came to the next morning that I realized I'd been attending the victim of a murder. I ought to have known, of course, by the fact that I was summoned by a policeman, but when you've got a few pints of bitter in your bloodstream you're none too keen on particular details."

Farnham decided it was more than time enough that he steered the conversation away from his 'obnoxious' curiosity. "You were quite wasted, Breen. I came along to be certain you didn't up with a cracked crown yourself."

Breen growled in mock anger and waved him off as if he'd been of no more moment than a midge. "The next morning Farnham began to rib me about attending a dying man while drunk—nevermind that he was dead before I got there—and in a temper I bet him he couldn't solve the murder before the police did. What were the stakes, fellow?"

"Ten quid," Farnham replied before remembering he wasn't interested in the story.

"Right. Ten quid he couldn't solve the case before the police."

"And did he?" Genevieve asked. Her color was still up but Farnham could see she was no longer angry. Excited, more like.

Breen winked. "Aye, he did. So we refreshed the bet. And over the years every time Farnham has been at Whistlecreig and there's been any sort of mystery, I remind him he stands to lose ten quid if he doesn't beat the police. I'm waiting for that one perfect case that baffles him."

Genevieve sat back in her seat. "I don't believe a word of it." She looked to Farnham as if she rather wanted to believe it. This made him feel slightly—and by that, he meant an increment—warmer to her.

"I swear on sweet Mary's knee, it's the truth," Breen pressed.

"But my uncle is always in the papers, and they've never said a thing about detective work."

Farnham snapped his head up. "This is youth. This is innocence. 'It's not in the papers and therefore it doesn't exist.' My child," he said, fixing Genevieve with what he hoped was a fatherly glare, "Don't make the error of believing the papers know everything, and strive to know *everything* the papers won't believe."

A pinch deep in Farnham's stomach reminded him he'd eaten too much supper and argued on top of it. And he hadn't even heard about the murder.

This stood to be a long night.

After dessert, Farnham led his guests straight from his reclining position at the dining-room table to his massive chair in the fire-lit study. Genevieve wondered if he was ever spotted anywhere else. Whistlecreig Manor was surely a waste on a man who lived like a mole, scurrying from one chamber to another, ignoring the dark passages between. They had visited for a time, had showed Vivi their prowess in playing chess blindfolded, and had discussed what Breen knew of the murder.

It was late by the time the doctor said goodbye and kissed Genevieve's hand with a grin for Farnham. Uncle and niece watched the doctor down the passage and Genevieve reflected that she rather liked the older gentleman. Of course he was a flatterer, but men of that age and countenance always were, and she didn't mind it; she was quite mature enough to disregard small attentions as mere foibles of bored men.

Farnham legged it back to his chair and cast himself into its leather depths, grunting. He sat up again, pulled a crushed silk pillow from underneath him, and returned to his broody position.

"Do you ever use the parlors? Or the ballroom?" Genevieve asked, turning on her uncle with studied innocence though she could guess the answer to come.

He hazarded an astonished glance in her direction and took his face from his thumb and forefinger where it had been propped. "Never. Well, seldom. At times in the summer I'll throw open one of the old bat-traps for a production of 'Much

Ado' or 'Midsummer Night's Dream', but hardly ever. People around here don't give much for Shakespeare. And the north parlor is where I practice swordsmanship—too bang cold for anything else."

"Do you get lonely here?"

"Lonely?" he asked, much as if he had no idea what the word meant, had never heard of anyone being lonely in his life. "You forget, child, that I'm not often at Whistlecreig...poor old abandoned place." He let his eyes travel across the room until they finally came to light upon Genevieve; she received a curious smile. "You've come upon me in a fit of poor health when I've had to throw open a room or two for recuperation's sake. I hardly *live* here. It's my home-base, but it's hardly a *home*."

"That is how I always felt about the summer-houses we'd take." Genevieve perched gingerly on a horsehair chair with her toes braced against the Aubusson carpet; she was good at this precarious variety of sitting but it hardly made for comfort. "Uncle, I did want to ask you a few things—about the murder, I mean."

"Ask away and I'll do my best to answer."

"The body was a young woman? And they couldn't tell whose?"

"'Death's a great disguiser.'"

Genevieve looked up. "Is that original?"

"Shakespeare's *Measure for Measure*."

"Ah, well, I suppose by that quotation you meant that the body was beyond recognition?"

"So the police told Breen."

"And has Dr. Breen been to see the body?"

"He was going directly after leaving here. Wanted to inform me first, of course. Try to weasel ten quid from me."

Genevieve felt a small horror in the base of her stomach. "It's so odd, the way it's a game to you."

They had a small silence then—the sort where one person has said something offensive and the other hasn't decided how to take it. In the end, Farnham shrugged.

"I don't mean to play at it," he said. "Forgive me if it seems so."

The silence continued and, to Genevieve, it was a silence in which her uncle mulled over things she had never seen, horrors he had helped resolve of which she had no comprehension.

"I think," he said after a space, "that you are misinformed of my character. Your family has probably represented me to you as an eccentric: a man who cares for nothing but his plays and Elizabethan speech and whiffing pipe-smoke to fill his vapid brain. Well...they're wrong."

Genevieve waited for more; one must be a poor debater if he is content refuting some evidence without putting forward any of his own. But Farnham said no more. He replaced his chin in his hand and stared at the fire with the abstract expression that fell like a shade over his countenance when he had finished his conversational duty.

In a few moments, Allen came to light her way to bed; Genevieve rose and studied her uncle, wavering between whether she ought to disturb him by saying 'goodnight' or simply leave him to himself. He looked sad and crumpled somehow, bony shoulders hunched forward, eyes brooding.

Lonely, her mind said.

And all the long way upstairs the halls seemed to echo the verdict in an ancient voice: *lonely, lonely, all alone.*

Chapter Four
Vivi

Farnham hearkened to the pattering of rain on the old, bubbled glass of his window-panes and turned a page in *Cyrano*. He had always liked the sound of a light-handed storm and reflected that, if he ever turned to poetry, he might work something about the rain into it. But poetry was unlikely when it was all he could do to keep from dying of stomach ulcers onstage; he had his health to think about.

Then there was this murder.

It took Farnham a moment to realize that the roiling in his stomach felt nothing like the pinching pain of his ulcers. This rumpled and mussed about like a fussy weanling and felt a horrible lot like...excitement.

He climbed out of bed and washed his face at the frigid tap; hot water was a thing concocted on the stove at Whistlecreig. He remembered with a guilty shrug that he had neglected to tell his niece. Well, Genevieve was in for many surprises, not the least of which was Antarctic tap-water. Was it terrible of him that he almost looked forward to hearing her complaint?

Flushed with anticipation? Farnham? It probably had to do with his digestion. The branzino hadn't sat well and was making him feel oddly chirky.

He was halfway through shaving his chin before realizing he was the one whistling "The Campbells are Coming" at a joyous pitch.

This was beyond curious. He glared at his cream-fluffed reflection and shook the razor at it: "There's a tenner at stake," he lectured, "and a murderer on the loose. Stop this."

Nevertheless, an unusually buoyant Farnham that strode into the dining-room at half-past eight. The room was empty and the table bare. Farnham checked his watch: he was quite on time and not a bit early. Where was Miss Langley? Perhaps she'd been delayed by the shock of the cold water. Ah, well.

"Allen?"

"Here, sir." Allen appeared, carrying a tray of the coffee things.

"Ah, coffee."

"Tea, sir."

"Nonsense. I'd like coffee. It's a day for the black brew."

"Miss's orders, sir."

"Where is the wench?"

"Kitchen, sir."

Farnham gave Allen an incredulous stare. He wasn't sure Livvy, his sister, would like her daughter in the kitchen. He wasn't sure *he* liked it. His niece in the kitchen? In the room where the magic happened? Food appeared. Food was not *made*. He didn't like food. He certainly didn't like his niece bothering with it. No, no, no. This would not do. Farnham slunk behind Allen and pushed through the heavy wooden door into the one region of Whistlecreig that interested him even less than ballrooms. It took him a moment to gather which end of the room held the stove, as the window across the kitchen flung a bald, whitish glare in his eyes.

"Genevieve?"

"Uncle Farnham, good morning." His niece's voice came from the close end of the room, perhaps three paces from where he stood.

Dear, dear, this Uncle *Farnham*ing would have to stop too. He shoved his hands into his cardigan and gripped the smooth stem of his pipe. At a slow pace, so she might not understand he was planning to interfere, Farnham covered the space between them and turned so his back was against the cold light. The butcher-block table, slumbering like a stone giant in the center of the flagged kitchen, let off a cold breath against his spine. "Sleep well?"

Genevieve turned from the stove. "Mmm. Featherbeds are delicious. I've never slept in one."

"Never?"

"Oh, heavens, no. Mama is very forward-thinking and the medical fashions of today declare featherbeds unhealthy."

This was an oddity. If featherbeds were unhealthy, lettuce was fattening. Farnham ran a hand over the top of his head, slightly disconcerted to feel his hair thinner than he remembered. Could it have happened overnight? So many things *had*. "Fie upon modern doctors. I have slept on a feather bolster my whole life and the only unhealthy bit I've ever found was the one case when the husband smothered his wife. But that, you'll understand, was not the fault of a mattress so much as a case of the wife's domestic intemperance that set off the husband's sense of outrage. Typical murder."

Genevieve had turned back to her cookery and did not appear very interested in the case; this led Farnham to wonder if perhaps murders were not the best subject with which to lead off the first morning's conversation with a perfect stranger of a niece.

He tried again: "Water too cold for you?"

She messed about with a fork in the skillet. "Mama always prescribed cold-water baths so I'm rather used to it."

"Good, good."

She looked at him curiously. "Why?"

"Well, it's good because if you were fond of hot baths I'm afraid I could do nothing for you. Cold water—we have that in abundance here and I would be delighted to supply you with it eternally."

Genevieve smiled but said nothing, and Farnham watched his niece at the stove, fascinated at the way she appeared to have taken up residence in the kitchen. He'd always heard that women transform a home, but he'd never liked the idea.

Genevieve wasn't a pretty girl—her mouth was too small and her nose too snub. Farnham knew that but somehow, as he watched his niece moving through the motions of making breakfast without a hint of the sense of imminent crisis with which he thought of cooking, the idea of homeliness dissolved.

"See that you don't burn the rashers," he offered by way of a compliment.

Genevieve took up a fork and turned the bacon in the pan; it gave a maddened sizzle. "There's no worry it'll burn—it is all fat and no meat. Where do you buy your bacon?"

What business was it of hers? "Garridy's."

"What is the farm we passed as our train pulled into Whistlecreig?"

Farnham considered. "Hiltons, I should imagine."

"I shall buy the bacon at Hilton's from now on."

"Why?"

"Their pigs look happier."

Farnham didn't have an argument for this—he'd wouldn't know what a happy pig looked like. "Are you my housekeeper now?"

"Someone has to do it, dear."

He resented this Rosalind for calling him "dear" in that motherly tone. "I have Allen for that."

"Allen is a butler." She smiled that curious smile of hers where the left side of her mouth quirked upward and removed a tray of puddings from the oven. "And butlers resent housework."

"He's never complained."

"They never do, but they retaliate in a million different ways. I know, dear. I took over household decisions for Mama on my twenty-third birthday. Ours invariably rubbed Father's black shoes with brown polish until we discovered that he'd been made to cook muffins for breakfast every Thursday. Put him right off his tea and the inner peace of the household was *intricately* bungled till I figured out where things had gone awry."

The smell of the frying bacon and hot puddings knotted Farnham's stomach, but from hunger or those bang ulcers he couldn't tell; the thought of eating meat turned his stomach to a hotbed of pain. "I don't think I can manage bacon this morning."

"Heavens no. This is for me." Genevieve forked the crispy rashers onto her plate and lifted a pudding from its tin bed, settling it beside two fried eggs.

Farnham resented girls with healthy appetites. "Where's mine?"

She nodded at the stove. "Just there. I'll fix it for you in a tick."

"Can't I have a pudding?"

"Not with your 'bang ulcers.' *Yes,* you've been speaking aloud. I'm putting you on a strict diet of porridge and chamomile tea with perhaps a *bit* of scone if you're quite an angel."

The *idea.* He drew himself up. "Farnham of Whistlecreig is never an angel."

"Then you'll have to do without scones."

"Bang it."

"Now about this murder."

Farnham felt his hackles fall. "Yes, I was wondering when we'd get to speak about that." He rubbed his palms together and felt the pain in his stomach fade as anticipation of exploring the thing rose. "We'll pop round to have a look at the body after breakfast, shan't we?"

"Your call. I'm not experienced in these matters," Genevieve said with a half-smile as she sprinkled the bacon with pepper and slid the plate onto a waiting tray. "What *is* the proper etiquette? Wait until noon and stay no longer than ten minutes, or don't wear white after Michaelmas?"

Farnham rubbed his jaw. "Do you know you're a menace? *'Better three hours too soon than a minute too late'*."

"You know best, dear."

"*Don't* call me that." His fist clenched almost against his will, and he shook out his fingers with a shaky laugh. "Umm...I apologize."

She made a face. "No, *I'm* sorry—I had almost settled in my role of maiden aunt before I was uprooted and sent here and I'm *used* to sweetening my conversation to suit fretful children. Well, if you are to tell me what to call you, I'm afraid I must have my preferences, too."

"You don't want to be called Genevieve?"

"Do *you* like it?"

He was shocked to see a shy, girlish look flit over her face as if she wanted to hear what he thought—really wanted to hear. "Oh...umm...it's a fine name. Fine. If you like it, that is. If you don't like it then...we'll call you something else."

"Vivi."

"Sorry?"

"Call me Vivi, please. No one *does*. It's always 'My eldest, Genevieve' or worse yet, 'Genevieve, the capable one.' I'm tired of being capable—it means they've given up on me. Call me Vivi."

He saw the set of her jaw and the weariness behind her eyes and, since he was not entirely heartless, he guessed the story of the battles she'd fought over the labels. "Vivi then."

They had a hum of silence now—an absence of conversation, rather—filled with the homely, comfortable sounds of bacon fat hissing in the cooling skillet and silverware against china as Vivi set out a few dishes on the trays and ferried them out to the dining room.

"I didn't know what dishes you usually used, but I like the china," she said, coming into the kitchen once more and hanging Allen's apron on a peg.

Farnham followed her goings and comings with his eyes and realized he had never scolded her for doing the cooking. He felt reluctant, somehow; besides, was there a guarantee that she'd listen? Vivi seemed quite an independent person. Not annoyingly so, but not the type to give up cooking because it wasn't the thing to do. Well, so long as Livvy didn't hear about it and come warbling at his throat...

He looked at the table she had spread, pleased to find it rather neater than usual with the addition of the china. "Family heirloom."

"Really?" She smiled and set his silverware beside his bowl of porridge.

Farnham was glad that he didn't have to explain that he had reverted back to the topic of china by saying "family heirloom." Some women forgot a conversation as soon as it happened, but not only could Vivi man the stove like a veteran, she appeared rather intuitive.

He still wasn't signing on for it, though; he pulled out Vivi's chair for her and waited till she sat, then pushed it back in before taking his seat opposite her on the other side of the table. Allen had disappeared again, but he didn't really need babying this morning; he would eat up without a row. Porridge steam curled upward and filled Farnham's nose with the wholesome scent of oats and milk. This, he thought, his stomach could handle, and it was nothing like the clods of rocky oatmeal Allen made sometimes.

"Shall we pray?" he asked.

"Mmm." Vivi folded her hands and bowed her head. Sunlight from the window at the far end of the table cast an aura over her head till she looked like the paintings of angelic children saying prayers before bed that he'd seen sometimes in the cheaper stores. All this Farnham took in at a glance, for he was accustomed to seeing and digesting a thing in as long as it took most men to straighten their ties.

He closed his eyes and let the rare peace fall over his shoulders like a vestment. "For what Thou hast given us, liege Lord, we thank Thee and ask that our lives might be of service to Thee. In Thy Son's magnificent name do we pray. Amen."

As Farnham dolloped honey on his porridge, he reflected on the beauty of rote prayers. Certainly he made up his own prayers—constantly—but there was a steadiness in the repetition of the same words he'd prayed every meal for the last forty years that the made-up ones lacked. It was the difference between stepping into a church under construction and a cathedral that had stood six hundred years, steeped in worship.

"The murder victim—who was she?" Vivi asked after a proper moment's pause.

Farnham grunted and flicked his napkin. "Most bodies don't come with calling cards. How should I know?"

"Doesn't anyone carry identification? I'd hate to be murdered and no one know it was me."

"Remind me to get Allen to sew a label on your coat-sleeve."

Vivi forked into her pudding and ate it while Farnham watched, idly swirling his porridge. He was thinking about what the Police Inspector had told him. "Vivi...it's...not going to be pretty."

"I should think not; it's a murder."

Farnham slapped the surface of his porridge with the back of the spoon. "Her face is...well...it's quite..."

"Quite what?"

"Bashed in. At least that's what Breen said."

Vivi chewed and swallowed then wiped her lips with her napkin. Her eyes flickered up for a moment before resting on his. "Poor darling."

"Wouldn't you rather stay here? As your uncle I want to protect you, you'll understand, but I'm not demanding you stay."

She smiled at him with a sort of modern sweetness. "You're a chivalrous old goose, but I want to come. Maybe I can be of some use."

He wouldn't go *that* far, but there might be something after all in what she said about butlers feeling resentment when forced to do work out of their proper line; Allen might not take kindly to waiting on a lady. "All right." He took a spoonful of porridge with the same dutifulness with which he took castor oil. "You can come along."

"Eat it *all*. I'm going upstairs to primp and I expect the bowl to be empty when I come back."

Farnham sighed. "Are you my nursemaid now?"

"Aren't I? I think it was in the job description."

Bang it. The girl was right.

Chapter Five
She Has a Name

When Vivi came down again after dressing in a sensible ensemble of brown wool, Allen was waiting at the foot of the stairs.

"Your Uncle Farnham was called away, miss."

"Away? But we were just—"

"To Whistlecreig, miss. He wanted to have a chat with the C. of P. That's Chief of Police, miss, if you were wondering."

"And did Mr. Farnham leave a message as to what I am supposed to do with myself while he's gone?"

"If it isn't overstepping my bounds, miss, I would say Mr. Farnham probably doesn't much care *what* you do so long as you don't spoil any of his books."

She had known her uncle was not entirely pleased at her arrival but she had thought they'd made some sort of breakthrough this morning at breakfast. Apparently, she had merely fancied the softening if Farnham felt no compunction in darting off without providing any sort of direction as to what a stranger might do to amuse herself in a house with half the wings and rooms shut up.

Allen shuffled and cleared his throat which reminded Vivi that she was not entirely alone in her awkwardness.

"I am sorry, Allen. I ought not to blame you for my uncle's caprice. Do you have such a thing as a garden here? I fancy a bit of fresh air."

"Only of the vegetable variety," Allen said a bit sadly. "But there's the Rowan Walk if you're wearing sturdy shoes and aren't afraid of getting a few burrs caught in your skirt."

Vivi smiled and squeezed Allen's arm. "Thanks a million. Where might I find this walk?"

"Out the back and down the slope. It opens at the bridge over the brook and heads toward the road to Whistlecreig." Allen studied her a moment. "I can show you."

In a short while, Allen had escorted Vivi through a hall off the great hall and down a passage into a stone all-purpose room with an eclectic mix of gardening tools, a chiffarobe, cobwebs, and a few pairs of cracked Wellington boots. Allen pushed several terra cotta flower pots to the side with his polished shoe and yanked the door open.

"Straight ahead of you and down in the cove. If you aren't back by one-thirty, I'll send old Belch to look after you."

Vivi had gone a step or two outside but turned around. "Excuse me?"

Allen laughed and shook his head. "Your uncle keeps a bloodhound. He's named after Sir Toby Belch from *Twelfth Night*. I doubt he'd be able to find his own shadow, let alone a person, but Mr. Farnham keeps him for atmosphere's sake. I'm only ribbing you though. There's nothing in the Rowan Walk to hurt a grasshopper."

Men. "Right. I'll try to save you the trouble of unleashing Belch. Toodles."

Vivi walked downhill, past an expanse of tilled-up earth which she took to be the garden. A few perennials whose deadened stalks kept a brittle promise for next year grew beside the unkempt turf; it had probably been a lawn in former generations, it dressed so green and weedless compared to the furze edging it about. The sun which had seemed amenable to shining at breakfast had since withdrawn in a pavilion of dark clouds; Vivi predicted that the day would end, as yesterday had done, in a soup of fog and mist. The idea made her glad she had got out while she could.

At the base of the hill, a brook chuckled and passed under a fading green bridge. It was a pretty spot and, when Vivi looked back up the hill and could no longer see her uncle's mansion, she felt a prickle of adventure. A strange feeling settled around her like an unfamiliar coat: this was the first time in her life in which she had been truly alone.

She took the bridge in a hurry, feeling the largeness of the land which rose up behind and before her. Her heels rapped on the wood smartly. Soon, Vivi had crested the next hill and stood at the mouth of the Rowan Walk.

The ancient trees locked limbs in rows on either side of a path that was still verdant and fresh under the shelter of its guardians. Vivi walked hard for a quarter mile or so before remembering she had no destination in mind, no reason to hurry; she dropped to a rambling pace and took notice of the primordial beauty.

Thrushes hopped over gnarled roots in the curling, fallen gold. The better part of the berries had fallen atop the leaves, but enough remained to give Vivi the cheering impression that the old rowans held flaming scarlet torches to light her way along the curving trail. Rustlings, twitchings, quiet whispers rose up in the deeper shadows beyond the trees, but where she walked there was nothing alive with her but the thrushes and the earth itself.

"I'm unchaperoned, Mother!" When she laughed, it was just a bit wicked and free. She drew deep, luxurious breaths through her nostrils and felt her soul expand with the old naturalness of the Walk. She quickened her pace at the wind's beckoning.

Rounding a sudden twist in the trail, Vivi found herself *viz a viz* with a red fox. She stopped short and it grinned at her, brushing its tale across a patch of somewhat trampled grass toward the side of the path. She took a step forward, intending to frighten the thing away. It tensed, drawing backward into a small pile of fallen limbs, but still grinned.

"Hello," she murmured.

There was no response from the animal and Vivi waved her hand wildly, rather wishing it would flee. Too bold, it seemed, too uncanny and unafraid of her presence as if it knew more about this rowan-realm than she ever could. The creature considered her a moment longer then burst away in an auburn snoot, more cat than dog. She watched a rogue shaft of sunlight jink on the fox's pelt before it vanished into the rowans like an amber spectre. Vivi was not quite frightened by the odd meeting with the creature; however, it did occur to her that not everything in the Rowan Walk must needs be friendly; there were predators among the woodland folk even as there were among humans.

This consideration brought to mind the victim of the recent murder. Vivi wrapped her arms around herself though the November morning had not been chill enough to warrant a coat. She felt small somehow in a manner she had never experienced even in the most awkward social situations in Darlington: Dr. Breen had said the victim was a young woman; young women were not supposed to die. Of course she had always known murder was wrong, but the baseness of it had never struck her in the way it did now, down among the rowans. Murder was the veniality of theft combined with the cruelty of ending a life; it was robbing a person of their story.

It was spilling blood over the best chapters of a book to purposely mar the sanctity of the tale.

A quickening wind hushed through the rowans, and blood-hued berries bounced to the ground like small artillery; Vivi walked on, subdued by the weight of her thoughts.

It was past three and oddly dark by the time Dr. Breen and Farnham swung round to Whistlecreig in Breen's lorry. Vivi was glad she had returned home an hour before, for the weather had taken a moist, sable turn. Angry winds buffeted Vivi as her uncle helped her into the back of the automobile. The men were not of a conversational mood; Vivi did not mind, for her revelation among the rowans had not yet loosened its grip and chatter seemed an idle thing. She rocked with the vehicle over the rutted roads and watched the vacancy of the fog-blinded windows.

After a drive of a couple miles, Breen parked at a long hedge, beyond which was a dry stane dyke and a bit of field. How far the field stretched and whether it ran uphill or down was a fact obscured by the fog. It was everywhere, the fog, wrapping them in woolen quiet.

"Watch your step." Breen's voice seemed both near and distant and strangely dispassionate in the cloud.

Vivi followed the dark grey swath behind Farnham's coat as he cut through a gap in the hedge; beyond him she knew to be Dr. Breen, beyond Dr. Breen a bit of a walk, and beyond the walk, she supposed, was the body. Funny, she wished she felt more than this vague horror. It was the strangest sensation, walking in a bit of cloud. Everything—even her thoughts—felt as if it had got a clog somewhere.

Farnham's back soon disappeared ahead of her and Vivi felt herself quite alone in the fog-ridden field. Her shoes made a tolerable noise in the crispy turf and her skirt picked at twigs and burrs, but it was oddly insufficient, all that noise. Nothing could out-scream the awful silence.

"To the left here."

The murmur came at Vivi's elbow. She twitched with the shock but did not shout—It was not her way. The voice at her side was Farnham; she could see him now that she thought to look for his heather-tweed in the shreds of grey. They walked on the palpable noiselessness for what seemed an eternity; surely the body could not have been seen by walkers this far from the road. Surely Dr. Breen had taken a wrong turn somewhere and had missed the site.

A brook gargled near Vivi's left foot and Farnham grabbed her elbow directly before she pitched into the water.

"Fond of bathing?"

She tried a laugh—more of a gasp. "Not in this weather, thanks."

"Keeping up?" Dr. Breen's head came into view on the other side of the burn, then his shoulders and a bit of coat. His legs remained in obscurity.

"Pretty well," Vivi answered.

He nodded. "Almost there. Jump the burn."

Vivi used her uncle's arm as a prop to aid her in getting over the brook, then tucked her hair into the back of her coat so she wouldn't have to feel the breath of the faint wind sucking at her neck. "How *could* they have seen the body from the road, Doctor?"

Breen's mouth folded into a smile. "You're unaccustomed to Northamptonshire fogs, Miss Langley. Makes a foot seem an acre; we're naught but two-hundred, three-hundred feet from the road—uphill, you'll note. Like a show-case."

Vivi had noted the slight incline as they walked. She tried to imagine the trek without fog—It was difficult. Now they wound through a sort of track—for sheep, Breen said—then paused.

The doctor ruffled his hair. "Dillon?"

"Just here, Doc."

Breen jumped and turned with a bitten-off laugh. "Zounds. This is the devil's fog. Almost missed you."

And we were looking for you. Vivi shuddered at the thought. That poor girl had not known her murderer was in the field. Perhaps he had lain in wait till she passed—all unsuspecting—on the road. Perhaps he—

"Miss Langley, are you quite certain you want to look?" Breen furrowed mist-hoary brows at her.

Vivi met his eyes, nodding. "I'm a nurse."

There was an aborted chuckle from the shape that was Farnham.

Breen shrugged and waved a hand at the body on the ground. Inspector Dillon stepped aside and pocketed his hands.

"How long has she been—?" Farnham asked.

"Since last night, I should think—perhaps a bit earlier," Breen's voice said.

"Cause of death?"

"Trauma to head."

"No sign of strangulation?"

"None."

"But you checked?"

"I did."

"How old?"

"About three-and-twenty. Young."

"Poor lass." Farnham had not touched the body—had hardly gone near—but he seemed finished with his assessment.

Vivi had hung in the background during this exchange, but now she stepped into the slit between Dr. Breen and her uncle. She wasn't accustomed to seeing dead people outside of coffins—there was something unhallowed about it. Vivi was quite certain her mother would have a conniption if present.

She looked at the prone form. It was almost beautiful in a horrible way, beaded over with a fine netting of mist as if the victim had been a princess sleeping beneath a silver fairy-spell. She would have passed for a very pretty tableau at Madame Tussaud's were it not for her face which was—

Vivi looked away, unwilling to see more of the wrecked features. One glimpse—bone and blood and bruises—had seared itself on her mind.

She closed her eyes and could still see it.

She opened them and it was there: lurid on a pillow of burgundied turf.

Farnham placed his palm against her back, and she leaned into it, feeling as if the fog had crawled into her bloodstream and was lifting her higher, higher, higher into the air.

"Whoap." Breen's hands were on her now, and Vivi felt quite awkwardly that someone had thrown his coat on the turf and lowered her into a sitting position.

"I'm all...right," she murmured, wishing the wooliness would give way.

"It's no shame to revolt at th'sight, miss," an unfamiliar voice said.

That would be the policeman...Inspector Dillon, was it? With concentration, Vivi made out a raw, red face beneath the octogonal hat of a country officer. He looked like a farm-boy dressed for play.

"There's not a lot nastier than that right there. A lady— and a pretty one, I'd guess. It's not right."

A truism, but what could one say? Vivi managed a weak smile for the baby-faced inspector and wrapped her arms around her knees. Ever so slowly, her wits seeped back into her possession and she felt brave enough to acknowledge the view of the body which she could obtain by peering between Farnham's legs.

"Any identification on the woman?" Farnham asked.

Breen grunted diffidence.

"No, Mr. Farnham." Inspector Dillon got up from his crouched position by Vivi and wiped his hands on his trousers.

Vivi's mind began to run in a dull, idle way over meaningless details of the corpse: the style shoe the woman had worn; the way her stocking twisted around one ankle; her red dress and brown coat; her blue-velvet cloche.

Her breath snapped short from a sudden recognition, Vivi's heart fell like a plummeting sparrow. "Lillian Bertois."

Farnham twisted her direction. "I'm sorry, did you speak?"

Vivi used the Inspector's proffered hand to stand and pressed damp fingertips to her temples. "The woman...I know who she is. *Was.*"

The men blinked at her, and Vivi noted Farnham's wince.

"How so, Miss Langley?" Doctor Breen asked.

"She was with me—yesterday. On the train."

"But isn't Lillian Bertois an—" Inspector Dillon began.

"An actress?" Farnham cut in. "Yes. On tour in England. She was due for an appearance in Northampton on...Tuesday?" He produced and consulted a creased billet. "Yes: Tuesday. Tomorrow."

"Where did you get that?" Dr. Breen asked.

"Picked it up in town three days ago—It's all over. You ought to have known."

Breen rolled his eyes. "Why did you bring it along tonight?"

"My dear Breen—famous American actresses don't come to out-of-the-way places without causing some stir."

"Did you think the corpse was she before you got here?" Breen pressed. He ruffled his hair. "You always do this." He shook his finger at Vivi. "He always does that!"

"Does...what?" Vivi managed.

"Asks useless questions to which he already knows the answers to make us feel ignorant."

"Could we just...focus?" This from Inspector Dillon. "What happened?"

Breen pulled his hands deep into his sleeves. "Mr. Orville Farnham has concealed his aces—he knew who our Jane Doe was before he left Whistlecreig. There was no reason to come all the way out here to make me look a dunce, Farnham."

"Nonsense." Farnham clapped a hand on the doctor's shoulder. "I wanted to see what my niece thought of the scenario."

"Women's intuition?" Breen asked with a deal of sarcasm.

"Women's intuition?" Vivi followed, quite curious now.

"Women's intuition," the Inspector said, marveling.

Farnham gave a short smile. "Of course I had *my* ideas but an unbiased opinion is always an asset. Miss Langley had not anticipated a row—she had not anticipated an actress. I assumed this...tragic young woman would make her appearance in town about the time of my niece and surmised they would have traveled by the same train. If Miss Langley could identify Lillian Bertois with no prompting, I could be reasonably certain of my hunch. The actress arrives and—evidently—is *killed* within a very short space of time yesterday evening. That makes for a very small pool of people that will have had any doings with her in Whistlecreig. It's bang brilliant!"

"Hmph," Breen grunted.

"Fascinating," Vivi whispered.

"But," Inspector Dillon said, growing practical, "Doesn't that make Miss Langley a suspect?"

Chapter Six
An Inquisition

"What bang good luck!" Farnham said, looking quite excited.

Vivi gave the young Inspector Dillon a scathing glare. "Are you suggesting I have something to do with the crime?"

He ducked his head, shoulders close to his ears in an exaggerated shrug. "I didn't say that, miss."

"You implied it; you said I was a suspect. How can you possibly think I had anything to do with this?"

Inspector Dillon reached out a hand to pat her shoulder, but Vivi jerked away.

"Do not touch me," she said. "If I turn up dead next, your fingerprints would be on me and *you'd* be a suspect." Furious, she saw Dr. Breen and Farnham exchanging amused glances.

She turned to them with somewhat of a vixen's fury. "Mr. Farnham. Would you kindly tell this dutiful public servant who I am?"

Farnham brushed a hand over his chin. "Well, Dillon, she's my niece."

Of all the idiotic things to say! Vivi drew herself together and looked down on Inspector Dillon from the snowy pinnacles of mental superiority. "I could care less about *that* unfortunate capacity. Inspector, I am Miss Genevieve Langley, daughter of Mr. Alfred Langley who is of the Topham-Langleys of Darlington. You won't have had much association with them, I'm certain, being a *country* officer, but I can assure you that there is nothing whatsoever in the idea that a Langley would commit a murder."

"Vivi—" Farnham broke in.

Interrupted thus, Vivi stopped and looked at her uncle. He shook his head slightly as if to discourage further explanation of the overwhelming virtue of their ancestry. It was meant to be a secret gesture, but Vivi noticed the Inspector marked it.

Farnham winced and spread his hands in an apologetic gesture. "There *was* your great-great-great uncle, Harold Topham-Langley...but he got off on a plea of insanity."

Breen turned a chuckle into a cough from the nether regions of their misty hollow. She saw the Inspector's mouth twitch as if he found this all quite a lark, and even Farnham looked more amused than concerned that his blood-relative was being collected into the paddy-wagon like a pick-pocket.

She scorned him with a flicker of her eyes. "Thank you, Uncle, for clearing my name. Chivalry is certainly not dead in Northamptonshire."

Vivi pulled her coat closer around her body and stomped off in the general direction of the car. She could not believe what she was hearing: Genevieve Langley, a suspect in a murder? It was idiocy. Not a person under the sun but that potato-fed, helmet-wearing fool would think to suggest it. Breen and her uncle were playing along because they were stupid bachelors who had probably not had this much fun in an eon; wasn't the whole idea of investigating a murder a joke to them? For one thing Vivi was grateful: she was young enough not to have to endure knowing Breen and Farnham as young collegians. The idea was insufferable. God help the professors who had endured their silliness.

Footsteps crashed through the grass behind her and someone pulled her elbow. She whipped about to face Inspector Dillon with a patronizing smile. "Am I under arrest? Heavens. The police are so efficient these days. I bet you hardly have any murders to solve in Whistlecreig."

The Inspector's face darkened, but he took off his helmet and clapped it to his belly in an abject mood. "I'm sorry for the inconvenience, miss. I'm sure it must be trying to your feelings."

Vivi regarded him a moment, feeling no softening toward him but a general animosity that mounted higher the humbler he looked. "Apology accepted."

"I know it isn't the proper way we ought to be introduced at all but...do try to cooperate."

"Cooperate? Why do you need my cooperation?"

"For going to the station, miss. To be quizzed."

"Oh, I'm to be quizzed, am I? Well, you needn't fear I'll run away and become a fugitive, Inspector Dillon. I'm quite willing to go to your superintendent and tell him anything you would like me to about this whole incident." She let him boil in that kettle a moment then graced him with a sweet smile. "Anything to help solve a case against one of my sisters. Men just don't understand the subtleties."

"Good, you caught up with her." Breen's voice and head appeared over Dillon's shoulder through the slowly-thinning fog. "Genevieve, my darling girl, we know you're innocent, but if you'll only go with the inspector I'm sure you can prove it quicker than standing here arguing with him."

Vivi sniffed and felt a tear leak out the corner of her right eye. She dashed at it, ashamed to be crying over something as silly as finding herself a murder suspect. Rough but kind, Breen brushed his knuckle across her cheek and caught the tear, lifting it away.

"Ohhhh, now, lassie, don't cry." He raised his hand a moment as if unsure how to best comfort her. He settled his palm on the top of her head. "It's nothing that terrible. You'll just tell the C of P what you were doing when and it'll all be right as rain."

"Are you certain?" Vivi asked, suddenly petulant and childish under the doctor's considerate palm. "They're likely to throw me in jail."

A short chuckle answered this observation. "Nothing like, luv. It'll just be a quiz and we'll be with you."

"What did she say to you?" The Chief of Police asked.

"I can't remember."

"Can't remember or won't?"

"You're not accusing me of withholding evidence now?" Vivi cast about for a look at Breen. He smiled encouragingly and her uncle, beside him, nodded.

"Are you?" The chief asked.

He was maddening, the way he seemed to strip her down as he talked till she felt clothed in less than a South American native.

"I can't remember what she said precisely, and if a thing is not accurately presented there is ample room for misconstruction," Vivi said.

The chief steepled his fingers, putting the points of his index finger against his nose, and stared at her over them. "And if there is nothing presented at all, the answer will certainly be misconstrued. Be a sensible little woman."

She saw the reason of this and thought a moment before speaking: "Miss Bertois seemed...haughty. Please don't make the mistake of thinking I speak out of jealousy because she is famous and beautiful."

"Are you saying she was haughty because she *was* or because you thought her to be so?"

"Your experience with women must be frightfully third-rate," Vivi said with a smile. "We're not all petty mongrels."

"No, you're not," the chief said with a smirk. "Proceed please."

"Her haughtiness seemed to keep everyone on the train far from her—probably the desired effect."

"Undoubtedly."

"But I've never been easily put off by airs and graces, and I fancied she might be nothing but a knot of nerves under that coldness. I had to pass her seat every time I got up for anything."

"Have you a weak bladder?" the Chief of Police asked, flicking through a pile of papers. When Vivi did not answer, feeling rather horrified, he glanced up. "Societal formalities go out the window in an inquisition, madam."

Vivi braced herself to crack out of every mold of carefully groomed society; she had never pictured herself chatting it up with a police inspector about her bladder. "A weak stomach," she managed at last. "The motion of the train began to make me queasy so I took several trips to and from the outer porch thing."

"The observation deck?" the chief suggested.

"That's not what they call it."

"I know. Proceed."

"Finally, Miss Bertois came out to the..."

"Observation deck..."

"To the bit of *porch* and lit a cigarette."

"Did *she* light the cigarette?"

"Yes. Well...well, no, actually." Vivi squinted her eyes shut to better picture the moment. "No, I believe she leaned in, and he lit it for her."

The Chief spun a pencil on the desk. "He? There was a man too?"

"Isn't there always? But she didn't know him; he was the conductor."

"How many bang people can you cram on a train's observation deck?" Farnham interrupted. "And why the blazes was the conductor out there?"

"My inquisition, Farnham," the chief said with a sharp look for Vivi's uncle. "Miss, why was the conductor outside the train?"

"We were talking. He offered me some tea because I felt ill. Miss Bertois didn't even bother speaking to him and a moment later he went inside and—"

"And you ladies regained use of your limbs?" Farnham mumbled from behind.

"Mr. Farnham, *please*," the Chief hissed. "Was anything said between you and Lillian Bertois?"

"I commented on the weather...and she said it was terrible. I commented on the countryside, and she called it dull. I commented on the season in London, and she said she'd been in America."

"Charming, wasn't she?" Farnham said.

The Chief grunted and faced Vivi full on so that she felt his gaze press into her soul as if daring her to tell a lie. "What transpired between you and Lillian Bertois after the train arrived in Whistlecreig?"

"Before or after I got off the train?"

He narrowed his eyes. "Both."

"She was asleep when the train arrived, and the conductor had quite a time waking her. She said Whistlecreig was her stop and that it was a dump...and that she specializes in bringing glitz to dumps."

"She's an actress," Farnham intoned from his dark corner of the room where he lounged, arms crossed, against the wall. "Of course she specializes in glitz."

"Farnham, really." This was Breen's soothing voice, and Vivi wondered if they'd ever held their tongues two seconds altogether their entire lives.

"And after you got off the train?" the Chief of Police pressed.

"She got off before I did; I had stopped to thank the conductor for the tea."

"So polite," the chief murmured, checking a few things off one of his papers. His eyes flickered up. "What next?"

"I waited at Whistlecreig Station for half an hour for my uncle's car."

"There are witnesses to this fact?"

"The porter would be able to tell you that I waited on that platform the entire time."

"And you didn't see anything else of Lillian Bertois?"

"Nothing. Until I attended my uncle and the doctor to see the body this afternoon."

The chief tossed his pencil into a drawer and stood. "Thank you, madam, for your time."

"What now?" Vivi asked, relieved for the ordeal to be over.

"Well, you can start by leaving my office, as I have no further need of you. I'm afraid you're no longer a suspect."

"Bang good of you to interrogate her and clear the air of it all," Farnham said, stepping forward to shake the Chief of Police's hand. "I'll be in touch and all that."

The Chief rolled his eyes and pinched Farnham's hand with the extreme tips of his fingers. "Likewise."

Vivi imagined the man took none too kindly to the fact that Farnham tended to solve quite a few of his cases before his men did. Oh well. That's what one got for being stupider than other people.

The trio exited the police station and crammed into Dr. Breen's car. Down where her legs ought to have been, Vivi felt nothing but a blur of exhaustion—she barely remembered how she had got to the vehicle at all. With a wry smile, she reflected that there had been a moment where she feared something would go awry and she would be pegged a murderess. Something to do with her mother's lessons that the guest was always right. The guest, in this case, being Chief McMulligan.

"Shall we celebrate?" Farnham asked.

Vivi came round to a sensation of imminent damp slithering down her neck, though the interior of Breen's car was comfortable and dry. "Celebration? Whatever for, uncle?"

"Your innocence, my child. Not many people go up for murder and come away clean as a copper penny."

"Not many people live in a small town with stupid policemen."

"Oh, you'd be surprised."

Vivi kept quiet, fearing that if she let herself speak, something more uncivil would come out. She hated Whistlecreig and everything in it so far, except Allen and Jimmy Fields and perhaps Dr. Breen.

Breen glanced over his shoulder as he pulled into the rutted street. "You made a sweet little confessor, though, I will admit. Pleasure to see you reciting your little catechism with so much conviction. Nothing like an easy conscience, eh, Farnham?" His laugh was low and purling, matched to the engine of his car.

Oh, he was out of her graces for the moment. "Have you any women in this town?" Vivi asked stiffly.

"Yes," Breen answered. The wipers made little improvement on the speckled windshield.

"Could we perhaps dig one up for company? Even a very ancient specimen would do. I'm afraid all this masculinity is wearing upon my patience."

"My darling girl, are you tired of being roughed around like a heifer tugged to market?" Breen asked.

"I have heard it put in more eloquent words, but yes."

Light and laughing, Breen turned his head away from the road and looked Vivi square on. "Hitherto you have been subjected to only the most uncouth bits of Whistlecreig: the fog, the mist, the damp, the cold, the bodies lying prostrate in fallow fields...shall we entertain her, Farnham?"

Farnham twisted to see his niece, and Vivi met his gaze squarely. Half of this was his fault and she wasn't going to be cowed into pretending it didn't matter to her that she had just been interrogated by a tight weasel of a man.

The corners of his mouth pinched decisively. "Yes, Breen. Vivi has done quite well so far. Let's give her the old rousing fun."

"Lark and Eagle or my place?"

"Where is the fire warmest? My blood is very snow-broth."

"Mrs. Froggle keeps a tidy blaze going at all times of year. The Quagmire is quite cozy, I am sure."

"Then let us de-muck our boots at your hearth."

"My pleasure."

Vivi leaned her head against the back of the seat, vaguely aware that they had turned off the main street of Whistlecreig and were pulling up to a stone house with lights cozily ablaze in the windows just visible through a hawthorn hedge.

The engine coughed to silence, and Breen climbed out of the driver's seat and opened Vivi's door with a flourish. "Welcome to the Quagmire, my dear Miss Langley."

She had to smile at the affectation, but it gratified her all the same that, at last, a man was being kind to her. "I forgive you both for being mules," she said.

Breen's dark eyebrows shot up, and he laughed. "And before we've even apologized? Oh, Generosity, your name is Genevieve Langley."

Farnham patted Vivi's shoulder. She was surprised at the friendliness, but in a trice her uncle had pocketed his hands and passed through the narrow gate between the hedges as if he hadn't meant anything she might have fancied. He opened the front door in his theatrical, flourishing way. A yellow rectangle of lamplight shone onto the cobbles as if the warmth inside reached out welcoming hands for its damp, cold guests.

Breen trailed behind Vivi into the house, and Vivi pursued Farnham up a malicious staircase and into a set of large rooms far more comfortable than she would have judged by the stairwell. A jolly fire chuckled in the hearth and rubbed elbows with brass andirons, and a kettle, quite suggestive of tea any moment, jiggled its lid like a set of castanets.

"Welcome, welcome." Breen unwrapped his scarf, stuffed it in a cubby-hole near the door, and hung his hat on a peg. His coat was shoved inside a closet hard-by a cluttered desk, and to this evil-looking hole he added Vivi and Farnham's wraps.

"Won't you take a seat, Vivi? There, in the red chair. Do you mind if I call you Vivi? I feel quite the uncle and this is a cozy party, is it not? Farnham, perch your ragged bones anywhere you've a fancy. Oh, not there—I just had that shirt ironed. Fine then, move the shirt. I don't mind. Oh, but this is jolly!"

It was a pleasant thing to see an active man making tea; his manner was not at all coaxing as a woman's would be: he commanded the accoutrements to do his bidding, and biscuit and sugar-cube bent to his will, finding homes in a Bakelite ashtray and an overturned turtle shell. He spooned tea-leaves into the bobber and plunked it in a pock-marked, ceramic pot into which he poured the contents of the singing kettle. A can of sardines was ripped open with the compunction of a polar-bear scenting a seal and, from some obscure cabinet in the corner, Dr. Breen produced half a fruit-cake.

"Brandy-soaked and baked by the fair hand of Mrs. Froggle."

Farnham poured a cup of tea and handed it to Vivi with two sugar cubes and a sardine on a toothpick. "Are you a mermaid, madam?"

Vivi took the cup from him, delicious warmth speeding into her fingertips. "Why on earth would you ask this question, O Triton?"

"We have consumed very little but fish and tea since you appeared. I feel a chicken is in order."

Breen carved slices of bread off a loaf with a rust-speckled knife and impaled them with a toasting-fork. "Unfair, unfair, Farnham. A man mustn't criticize another man for keeping a bachelor's kitchen. I don't have the benefit of a butler."

"Neither will I, if my niece has her way."

Vivi sipped from her cup; what a thing tea was! Like a magic spell, lifting one's humor from the deepest gloom to perfect satisfaction in a sip. "You may *keep* Allen as a *butler*, uncle, but I'm afraid as a cook he will not do. I shall try my hand at the food-stuffs."

She watched Breen hold the shavings of bread over the fire and twist the toasting fork this way and that in an impatient manner, as if even flame was too slow for his famished company.

"You will not cook," Farnham was saying. "Allen will."

Sleep, like chamomile, thickened her wits and made her yawn. "Allen doesn't like cooking, uncle-dearest."

"Has anyone asked Allen what view he holds?" Breen put in, testing the toast with his forefinger and yanking it back at the touch. "Perfectly browned. Allen himself could not have done finer. Cheese? Brie or Camembert? Agh, the lady has excellent taste; I enjoy a Roquefort myself, on occasion."

"My bang stomach is none too keen on it."

"Vivi, have you heard the tale of the Water Mouse? Vivi?" Breen rattling Vivi's elbow like a pump handle aroused her from a near-drowse in which she had been thinking of a more than pleasant-looking young man in dripping tweeds.

"Oh, my. Did I miss something?" She wrapped her hands around the warm belly of her teacup and tried to put Jimmy's face out of her mind.

"Nothing important," Farnham chuffed. "Breen was about to regale you with the most bang annoying tale to circulate Whistlecreig in the past forty years. Would you like to hear it?"

Vivi was not really interested in hearing about any mouse, water or otherwise. "What do you know—either of you—about Jimmy Fields?" she asked abruptly.

"What the..." Breen's spoon descended into his teacup with a splash and clatter. "Lor but your mind is far away."

Vivi tried not to blush. "Don't tease me. I only want to know because...he seems like a nice sort of fellow. Very pleasant to me on the ride over."

"Ride over to where?" Breen stirred a bit of cream into his half-empty cup.

"Whistlecreig Manor. My uncle had forgotten about me, conveniently."

"Convenience had nothing to do with it, Vivi. I purposed to let you wend your own way homeward. If you can't get from Whistlecreig proper to the Manor without getting lost you're not worthy of your legs."

"Well, I don't suppose you will have to worry I'll lose my heart to Jimmy Fields," Vivi said.

Dr. Breen winked. "And who said a thing about losing your heart? That is a suggestion purely your own."

Farnham crossed one leg over the other and nibbled the corner of a biscuit. "Why would you say there's no danger?"

"He won't be around."

"On whose authority do you say that, Vivi?"

"He bought a ticket to Crowborough...said he was tired of life at Whistlecreig, wanted to see a bit of the world."

Farnham's eyes brightened, and he took a sizable bite from his biscuit. A gale of crumbs blew onto his cardigan. "Bang good luck, Vivi. We have our second suspect."

Chapter Seven
I Suspect You Would

"Farnham, be reasonable!" Dr. Breen boomed. His friend had had many an odd hunch in years past, but this was the bally worst of them all. "Jimmy Fields is as honest and decent a lad as...as you and I were."

"Hardly comforting, Breen. *Were* we decent?"

"Damn you, Farnham!"

"Bang it, I believe the man is losing his temper." Farnham took a sip of tea and spread his mouth in that cat-smile used when he thought he'd had the best of an argument. Well, he hadn't. He hadn't for several reasons, not the least of which was that Breen would argue the case until he won and saw the grieved expression removed from that sweet lass's face.

"Jimmy left town during or shortly after the time in which the murder was committed," Farnham continued.

Breen glanced at Vivi and saw that her face was quite pale. Probably feeling faint but not likely to lose consciousness, being accustomed to the various stresses of Society life. "Preposterous. You are the worst detective in the history of detectives."

Farnham rolled his eyes. "Not what I'd call fair, seeing that it's a game and we're both playing. No different than chess, I'm sure and there's always someone worse than you in chess."

"Farnham, this isn't funny. You're making a serious claim on this young man whom we've only ever known to be honorable."

"No one has convicted him of anything, nor are we suggesting he is guilty."

"You don't know that he ever saw the deuced girl."

"I grant you that mark. Nevertheless, I should be very curious to see what he was doing within the hour of the train arriving at Whistlecreig and the time Miss Lillian Bertois was killed. Could be there are vouchers on every corner for his complete innocence; I will welcome it and gladly, if it is so."

Breen was about to say something cutting when Vivi stood and set her teacup on his cluttered desk.

"We need to be adults about this and stop arguing," she said. "The way to conduct an investigation is to gather a pool of suspects and begin to weigh their alibis against witnesses and see which hold water and which don't. Dr. Breen, I thank you for your kind hospitality, but I am rather tired and wish to go home."

What a creature this lass was. Couldn't pin her down like a normal woman; she was always popping up strong as a boxer one moment, quiet as pussy-cat the next. Breen extracted her things from the closet and helped her into them. Her arm brushed against his, and he felt that she was delicate and cold and unused to the rougher things in life. When she had stepped out in the hallway and started down Mrs. Froggle's narrow staircase, Breen caught at Farnham's arm.

"Listen, chap. Be kind with her."

"When have I been anything but?"

"She'll not be used to our ways. Dead bodies are part of my trade and you stagger down stage-murders thrice a week, but Vivi...she's not used to it. Be kind, blast you. Be kind."

He made certain he and Farnham met with their eyes, and when he had searched the pale depths he fancied he had extracted an unspoken promise from his oldest friend and comrade.

"Jolly good of you to spend the evening with me," he said quietly and clapped Farnham's shoulder. "Mrs. Froggle grows tiresome when quarrelling with her about rent is the best society a man has after toddling home at night."

"Tomorrow—early—at the station platform. Eight o'clock sharp. Don't be late."

Farnham plodded down the staircase and Breen watched from the landing, wondering how a man could be quite so placid over every mangled thing.

Vivi was waiting with her back against the hawthorn hedge when Farnham came outside. He paused on the damp step— cold and moist as a frog's skin—and considered his niece. Perhaps Breen was right: women can't always be expected to have iron nerves. He took the path out to the car-side and see-sawed on his toes. "I hope you—"

"I've been—" she started.

Farnham bowed. "You first." He offered Vivi his arm again and felt oddly gratified that she deigned to take it.

"Can we walk home?" Vivi asked.

"Only way; Breen would drive, but it's a habit of mine to get a bit of exercise walking back from town."

"Two miles, you said? An easy enough walk."

Uncle and niece ambled down Fogarty's Lane and onto Main Street, then past the village green where they held the agricultural show in September. The bad weather of the evening had cleared off with the springing-up of a light breeze, and cloud-tatters flitted over a half moon; the temperature was perfect for an almost-solitary walk: cold without being vampire-like. He felt the weight of Vivi's arm in his and was glad he was there to protect her if—God forbid—the killer was still in Whistlecreig.

The thought caused a prickling in the little hairs on the back of his neck. Farnham whistled one long, low note to break the silence between them. "What were you going to say before I interrupted you back there?"

"I was thinking about what you said...about Jimmy being a suspect."

"Ahh." Farnham cleared his throat and hummed a tuneless ditty.

"I want you to know that if he is, you don't have to worry that I'll let sentiment get in the way and obscure facts or something. I will help you in every way I can. I promise."

"I suspect you would."

"I like Jimmy, but I'm a sensible woman."

Her voice ended in resignation, and Farnham wondered how many times in his niece's life she had used that term, "sensible woman," to kill one or another of her hopes and dreams. A hare bounded across the road, and his eye glowed ebony in a stray moonbeam. Farnham watched it; he didn't go in much for nature—too bang many things that claimed his attention—but it was undeniably attractive to look at bits of it on occasion.

"'Truth is truth to the end of reckoning,' Vivi," he said at last.

Bang his clumsiness. That didn't sound terribly comforting. He tried again: "Tomorrow we'll get to the train platform and start quizzing folk. We'll likely come up with a dozen people who fit the criminal better than Jimmy. A local man doesn't leave town if he's just committed a murder. Too many questions asked, and Jimmy's clever." They walked on a few paces and, since Vivi still did not speak, Farnham sighed.

"I'd even be willing to bet the only crime he committed was stealing my niece's heart."

He had said it in complete jest, but a flush on Vivi's cheek showed Farnham he had hit a bit close to the mark. Lord in Heaven, he wasn't ready for this.

Morning. Morning coming through the window in an incessantly cheerful manner rather dazzling to the senses. Vivi lay in her bed for some moments, trying to remember if this was Darlington and why Rose-Lynn, the maid, hadn't yet come in. A notice of the mildew stains on the ceiling recalled to mind that this was Whistlecreig and there'd been a murder. Jolly good. Just what she'd pictured herself doing while playing nursemaid to "frail" Uncle Farnham.

Air colder than she'd expected took Vivi by the throat as she climbed out of bed. Her room on the west side of the house had not benefited from the sunshine she could see out the window. Quick as she could, Vivi pulled on a blue dress and bounced on the balls of her toes, willing her blood to return to life. She ran the brush through her hair, clipping a bit of it back with a bobby-pin. *Not* that she expected to meet anything worth meeting today, but one never knew when destiny would strike; she would hate to look shabby for destiny.

A smell of bacon and eggs filled the corridor outside Vivi's room, and she muttered to herself; old habits died hard at Whistlecreig. She would discuss the cookery question with Allen this morning—hopefully before her uncle awakened. She had better hurry, then. Vivi trotted down the staircase and through the dining-room. The table wasn't set, but the door to the kitchen was ajar. She went through, expecting to see Allen's round, loyal face wreathed in steam from the kettle, but it was not a round face that looked up at her....Farnham's countenance—pinched and slightly yellowed—turned several shades of red.

He waved a spatula and smoothed the baggy apron. "Hail hearty ho, niece."

"You cook? You hate food."

"I don't hate food, I hate eating. There is a difference."

"But...Allen?"

"Has gone to London. Left yesterday afternoon and shan't be back for a day or two."

Vivi wasn't at all sure that she could accept the evidence of her eyes. The great Orville Farnham in an apron, slaving away at a stove. A *butler* cooking was bad enough, but a Shakespearean actor? Absurd.

"Mysteries to be solved, deaths to avenge, people to arrest...puts the appetite back in a man."

He handed a plate into each of Vivi's hands and smiled at her as he portioned the eggs and adorned each fluffy yellow pile with two rashers of bacon. "I've been thinking about the mystery. I am determined we shall solve this before the police. Can you imagine Breen's glee if we didn't? He'd be insufferable."

"I agree." Vivi grinned at this amicable change in her uncle. "Shall we eat in the dining room?"

He took the plates from her and slid them onto the butcher-block table. "No bang time for that. We shall perch on the domestic slab and discuss this *au naturale.*"

Farnham put his hands around Vivi's waist and directed her to jump on the count of three. With his help she was able to wriggle onto the high table without much trouble. This was the strangest thing she had done yet since her arrival, but it wasn't so very much different than a picnic, if one came down to it. Farnham sprang onto the table and perched his plate on one knee, blessed the food, and dug in with astonishing appetite.

"I'm your nursemaid. Shouldn't I be monitoring your food intake?"

"Don't be a spoil sport. I'm hungry for once in my bang life; let my ulcers scream. We shall solve this mystery and we shall solve it in a week—no more. I shall bet Breen on that."

"And if we fail?"

"'We fail. But....'"

Vivi waited, eyebrows raised. Her uncle's eyes bored into her hopefully. It was quite obvious that Farnham expected some further speech. "But?"

"'But screw your courage to the sticking-place and we'll not fail.'" He passed a hand through his thinning hair and shook his head. "We'll need to work with you on this game."

"*Hamlet*, I suppose?"

"*Macbeth*, but at least you're trying. Listen, now. I know you told the inspector everything you heard, but if for some reason —any reason—you recall anything...tell me."

"Of course."

"And carry a pistol."

"Uncle!"

"You probably won't need to use it, but it would make me feel easier."

Vivi bit her lip and pressed scrambled eggs through the tines of her fork. She wasn't hungry at all. "Is it really so dangerous?"

"It's a case of murder, duck. He'd kill her, he'd kill you. Probably. If he took a fancy for it."

"So blunt..."

"I won't apologize for the truth."

She managed a thin smile and met her Uncle's sharp eyes. "No, I wouldn't ask it of you. Truth. Courage. One always necessitates the other. The way of life, right?"

But in her stomach a sparrow-fear darted up and beat its wings.

Chapter Eight
I'll be Jonnock Wi'you

Allen stepped off the train onto the platform at Paddington Station and shouldered past the opposing stream of passengers ready to take the places of those, like himself, who'd got to London and meant to stay. Rather damp crowd, he reflected as a wet wool arm slid across his hand. Must be raining out there, past the fine plate doors. He grasped his satchel-case tighter, keeping a bullish eye out for any of the vile pick-pocketing race, and stalked to the ticketing desk.

A walk would get the stiffness out of his legs in five minutes flat, but propriety forbade him to walk a long distance in the company of his traveling case. Besides, he could afford cab-fare if he wanted a cab, and looking like a countryman was not Allen's idea of *je ne sais quoi*. The role of butler he had left behind in Northamptonshire. In London, Bardwulf Allen was a man to garner respect. A man who no longer held those plate doors for other people but let others hold the door and make way for *him*. It gave a man dignity to walk through a door first. Was this how Mr. Orville Farnham felt in his day-to-day life? It was heady but rather blurring to the humble mind.

When outside and away from the crush at last, Allen put up a modest black umbrella. He hovered on the slick curb and waited. Presently, a bespectacled man who looked about as fond of rain as a rheumatic feline hitched up beside him and glared for a taxi.

"Messy day," Allen offered.

"Never wuss," the man croaked. "Shoes wet. Socks too."

"I heard newspaper helps...for drying." It was only by the best self-control that Allen remembered to leave off the habitual 'sir' in his address. This butler-ly piece of menswear advice administered, Allen shifted to his left foot. "Devil of a day to make for Harley Street."

Allen had never been to Harley Street, and he severely disliked the idea of carting his satchel for a regular steeplechase over London Bridge. With any luck, the man would give him some idea of the distance involved.

The man seemed bred of the worst London ilk with no trace of the Southern gentility in his manners. He sniffed and glared hard after a taxi that had passed without seeming to take his squint as a royal summons. "You've not got more'n a *mile* to suffer. I'm headed clear 'crost London. Be stuck in a cab for two hours, more'n likely."

Allen pursed his lips sympathetically. "The Government ought to address transportation."

"Everything's the demmed government's demmed fault!" the gentleman huffed. He hunched his spare shoulders and leaned off the curb into the rain.

"Surely not this weather?"

"Es-*specially* this weather! Pollution effects nature. Pollution pokes holes in the rears of the demmed clouds!" The man poked his umbrella skyward to illustrate the point.

Allen's eyebrows crawled up his forehead. "Even so," he said with a nice bow, "the medical district calls." And he left the high-strung stranger leaning into the street and himself pursued a puddle-avoiding course on Praed Street toward his clandestine errand.

Whistlecreig to Harley Street; doctors and young women; Allen sidestepped an over-eager muddy-faced boy hawking shoe-polish and reluctantly admitted the excitement scaling mountains in his deep chest...*scandal.* He'd been out of that market for quite some time. It felt invigorating, he noticed, like a dash of cayenne on an egg over-easy. If he took risks of this nature more frequently, might he always feel thirty years younger?

For he did feel so very young...

At this admittance, Allen rum-tum-tummed a bar of something very un-hymnlike and forged his way speedily down London-town, feeling even less like a butler than the average city-dweller.

The sky above the rolling hills of the farmland was almost too blue to be real. Field and copse had long ago turned russet and gold and there was no green to set off the color, but oh, it was gorgeous. Vivi had not known Northamptonshire could look like this. She thought of the Rowan Walk and how beautiful it would be on such a day; too bad she had stepped out the front of the Manor instead of the back. It just went to show her that one oughtn't to make rash decisions on staying or leaving until one had got to know a place. If she had stormed away from Whistlecreig as she felt like doing last night, she would never have known this Eden-pure morning.

"Do you keep horses?" Vivi asked as she and Farnham made their way down the mossy steps of the great house and took to the gravel drive.

Farnham stuffed his hands in his cardigan. "Do I look like I keep horses?"

Well, his humours were evidently less changeable than the Northamptonshire weather. She could take that as both a comfort and a concern. "I was only thinking, if you don't keep horses and you don't own a car, isn't there some quicker way to get to town rather than walking two miles each direction?"

He cocked an eyebrow at her with a sardonic grin and wheeled to his right, around the corner of the house. Vivi followed and saw that they were headed to the back garden. Down the hill would be the faded green bridge; across the ravine she saw the Rowan Walk, red and deep with its secrets. Farnham headed off toward the right to a shed cupped in a copse of apple trees at Manor's end.

"Have you met Sir Toby Belch?" he inquired.

"How creative; you ride your hound to the station?"

Farnham waved her off and yanked open the door, revealing a spacious shed with straw scattered in it and a dog-run behind. "I keep a pair of bicycles in here along with old Belch."

"Vulgar."

"Bicycles?"

"The name."

"Ah, well, he doesn't mind."

Farnham squatted within the doorway, and Vivi watched as he patted the inside of his thigh and whistled low and soft. She heard a scuffling of straw, and an excited drum-beat began against the side of the shed.

"Easy, there, old man." Farnham was smiling—an actual, delighted smile—and patting the head of a reddish hound. Folds of skin draped around the dog's neck like a Frenchman's cravat, and Vivi caught flashes of a black-brushed tail thrashing the straw, the shed, and Farnham's legs in turn.

Her uncle took a leather lead from his pocket and clipped it to Belch's neck, then brought him out and handed the lead to Vivi. "Hold him, won't you? I've got to check the tires of our little machines."

Vivi took the lead in her hands and had the wry thought that the massive hound weighed more than she and could probably knock her over with his energetic whip of a tail. "Hello, Sir Toby."

The hound knocked the palm of her dangling arm with his nose, and she recoiled from the unexpected moisture. "Oh, my. Yes, there's a good lad." She scratched behind each of his folded, drooping ears; Belch leaned against her legs and groaned.

"Good, good. You've made friends. Allen isn't here to give him his exercise so he'll come with us. You get the blue bike, I'll take the black."

Vivi handed off the lead and eyed the bike. "Must I dawdle round Whistlecreig on a blue bicycle? They'll think me odd."

"If that's the worst they think of you, you're a blessed mortal. Onto the bike. Come now, be a—" He stopped with an apologetic look.

"Sensible woman, yes, yes. When am I anything *but?*" If she had to keep proving herself to these men, she would do something irrational.

"I was going to say be a good chap, but 'sensible woman' does quite as well. Hurry now. We're meeting Breen at eight." Farnham threw one leg over his bicycle, knotted his pet's lead to the handlebar, and pedaled round the corner of the house, leaving Vivi to manage her bicycle herself.

It wasn't until her uncle had disappeared that Vivi wondered if she would remember how to ride one of these; she had spent hours riding her cousins' bikes on her frequent visits to London as a much younger girl, but it had been fifteen years since her mother had considered it anything like proper. This admonition in mind, Vivi experimentally straddled the bicycle and pushed off, wobbling around the back garden a moment before remembering to press hard and lean forward.

There. That was it. It all came back with astonishing ease and, for a second, Vivi half expected to see her cousins, Walter and Edward, racing past her and shouting over the popped-corn vendor in the park.

She rounded the corner of the Manor and set off down the drive, following Farnham and the hound trotting beside him. With a bit of effort, Vivi reached her uncle's side, and they were able to pedal together, eating up the dirt road in long, pleasant pushes; a few late larks sang in the hedges, and Belch's tether jangled where it connected to his collar. It was such a jolly, heartfelt morning—hardly the sort of a.m. on which one expected to round up a paddy-wagon full of murder suspects. Vivi dropped back a few meters and tried to forget about the murder.

"Left at the turnpike," Farnham called over his shoulder. "Right on Main Street. Steady on for a stretch and the station will be at the other end of town."

They reached the station platform, and it struck Vivi as oddly barren and much less forbidding than it had been two evenings ago. Forbidding, at least, until Jimmy Fields had rescued her. Prickles of indignation burrowed into Vivi's back, but she silenced them. She would treat Jimmy just like any other suspect, no matter what her more womanly feelings told her. Of course he was probably as innocent as she was, but never let it be said that Genevieve Langley fell for good looks and charm.

She hopped off her bicycle and strolled it next to the platform where Farnham had already leaned his. Up the four steps, and she was once again on the platform—almost the very place she stood last night when arguing with the porter. The man saw her now and his exaggerated expression of surprise annoyed her.

He hailed Farnham. "Mawnin' Farnham. Hear the police are flacking about like fliggers ower this mys'try."

Vivi could only guess what on earth the man was saying.

Her uncle seemed to have a better handle of the local speech. "Oh, no more than usual. They are doing their job thoroughly, I am certain. Lot of passengers come through here day before last?"

"Aye. I'll be jonnock wi'you Farnham. I fink I've found the man."

"We're certain it's a man?" Farnham asked in a delicately curious tone.

"What kind a' 'uman could craunch a gel's head like that and not be a bloke? Barnaby, says I, Barnaby, he's a nurker he is. Allus hotching about while waitin' for 'is train. Allus glining. He's a rum one, that'un."

A deep voice spoke at Vivi's elbow: "He's got hold of Barnaby, has he?"

Vivi stiffened at a voice so close to her side and whipped around. It was Breen; the doctor looked fresh and young this morning as if he'd had a fine night.

She smiled. "Mmm. Evidently he can understand a bit of what the man is babbling on about."

Breen chuckled. "What has he said so far?"

"Something about thinking he knows who committed the murder or such. Odd words. Hotching...glining...jonnock."

"'Jonnock' means to be honest...the rest is a lot of typical 'witness' bunglement. Fidgeting, glancing about furtively...that's all it means. All the classic signs of a passenger in a hurry that always gain such local interest and importance when there's a murderer to be found." Breen patted Vivi's arm and sidled up next to Farnham.

Farnham took the playbill from his coat pocket. "Did you happen to notice this woman two days ago?"

85

Barnaby took the picture into his box. He whistled. "Gaw, she's a looker. A bit ikey, looks like, but a beauty."

"Her name is Lillian Bertois—she's an American actress."

Barnaby snuffled loudly and seemed to wish he hadn't given the picture back. "Gaw, now I remember 'er. A blonde she was. And wearin' a sheeny dress just like that. She says to me, 'Mr. Barnaby, I should like a room at the hotel. You look like a capable man,' she says. So I says—"

"Did you happen to see anyone else of interest coming off the train between the hours of three and six, two afternoons back?" Farnham asked.

"Arra-one?"

"No, not yesterday, the day before."

"Well, thur was her." Barnaby pointed a finger at Vivi and chuckled.

Vivi felt the blood flame in her cheeks, but she looked straight into his eyes and tried not to remember their conversation. Farnham glanced at her, and Vivi rolled her eyes. Her uncle kept his face turned toward her but glanced at Barnaby, eyes slitted. "Yes, this is my niece, Miss Genevieve Langley."

"Th'one what chelped me. Got herself in a faddle for I called her plain. Well, plain hern might be, but hern has got a fine pair a'legs, I'll say."

It was not her imagination, she was sure, that her uncle winced, as if as pained as she was at the man's obvious ignorance of all forms of polite communication with ladies.

Farnham stretched out his hand and shook the porter's. "Thank you, Barnaby, for your help. I'll be in touch if I need any more information."

"Yezzir."

Barnaby made an absurd salute and winked at Vivi. She stiffened, glared him down for a full three seconds, and followed her uncle and the doctor off the platform.

"That was entirely useless," Farnham hissed between teeth clenched in a faux smile as he tied Belch's lead to his handlebar. "Of course I expected nothing but nonsense from the man. All that ridiculousness about Miss Bertois speaking with him. He said she wore a silky dress 'just like the picture.' It was wool, as you plainly recall. It's so disappointing when the locals begin adding wine to the water of their testimony. Completely discredits it. What a stupid man. I'm afraid he couldn't testify at a sheep-shearing let alone in court."

"So...have we any clues whatsoever?" Vivi asked as she pulled her bicycle away from the station platform and wheeled it down the road alongside her uncle.

"We can be certain Miss Bertois did not linger at the platform. No one of terrible note came across Barnaby's path —though since he considers only the most commonplace of travelers noteworthy, that isn't a terribly confident conclusion." Farnham's fingers picked incessantly at Belch's lead. He caught Vivi's eye and grinned sheepishly. "Next stop: the hotel."

Chapter Nine
At the Mill-Pond

Farnham slipped up behind Chief McMulligan, Inspector Dillon, and another young policeman where they stood at the hotel desk. Between them, cornered by the oaken counter and a shadow-box filled with flora and fauna of Whistlecreig, was a man with a brown hat and scarred chin. Farnham made certain to keep back from the others and watched without alerting any of the policemen to his presence.

"What was your client wearing when last you saw her?" the chief demanded.

"You think I notice things like that about a girl who owns a hundred different dresses?" The man gave Chief McMulligan an incredulous look. "I'm her manager, okay, not her costumer. Last time I saw Lillian Bertois was two days before she even left London."

"What was she wearing then?"

"A dress," he said testily.

"What color dress?"

"I'm color blind."

Charleton Burnes, the proprietor of The Black Roe, guffawed from his position at the key-rack. A jerk of Chief McMulligan's head silenced him.

"What did the dress look like?" the Chief asked.

"Look like?"

Farnham relished McMulligan's expression of utter fury. "Yes. Anything you noticed about it. *If* you can."

"You know something funny?" The man swung out of his corner and lit a cigar. "This dress had a skirt. And a top. And *sleeves*." He pinched the cigar between his teeth and stuffed his hands into his pocket. "I mean, what'll designers come up with next?"

"Mr. Owens, it is not my intention to inconvenience you," Chief McMulligan said, "but we are discussing the murder of a celebrity, here. I need any information you might have."

"*I'm* in complete shock. I'm the one who needs information." When he spoke, the tang of New York clung to his accents. "One of my more lucrative clients is lying in your little small-town morgue, and no one's apologizing to *me* about it."

The man saw Farnham and tossed his eyebrows then called over his shoulder: "And I thought you said you cleared everyone out of the place before quizzing me."

"I did!"

McMulligan and his men swiveled as one to follow their prey's retreat.

"*Farnham.*" His name had never sounded more like a curse than it did in Chief McMulligan's mouth.

"Chief McMulligan, Inspectors." Farnham bowed and shoved his hands deep in his trench coat pockets. "I came to see what news advanced with the dawning dew."

"You're not welcome. Official police investigation."

"Come now, good fellow! I've only popped over to ask Mr. Burnes a few questions. Can't block a man from a fair play, can you?"

Mr. Burnes turned from his work among the keys and gave Farnham a stolid glare. "Ent tellin' *you* anyfink."

"Nothing at all?"

"Naught."

"As you please." Ignoring Chief McMulligan's villainous glare, Farnham offered his hand to the brown-hatted man. "Mr. Orville Farnham at your service. Reenactor of the Bard's plays."

"Phillip Owens. Agent and manager."

"Manager? Perhaps you're acquainted with my agent, Barth Melchior."

"Haven't had the honor." He exhaled a plume of smoke to the side. "Lillian Bertois was my client."

"Lillian Bertois..." Farnham allowed a pleasant smile to drift over his face, followed by a manful try at melancholy. "I've an interest in this case for personal reasons. *You'll* understand."

"Ha!"

"Chief McMulligan," Farnham continued, cocking his head in the direction of the scornful laugh, "does not like interference in his work."

"Never seemed to bother you before," that person growled.

Still ignoring him, Farnham tossed his personal card to Phillip Owens. "I would hate to be canned on account of obscuring justice or some other quaint charge so, my good fellow, I'd be pleased to have you to my manor-house this afternoon. A man like you must be weary of traveling. Rest your feet by my fire for the afternoon, if you will. We can properly memorialize poor Miss Bertois and have a good meal at that."

Mr. Owens took the card... Chief McMulligan glowered, and to Farnham it was meat. "See you at two, then?"

A keen-eyed look clashed up at Farnham as a strong hand took the card. "At two."

"Good, good. And as I have no superfluous leisure...gentlemen."

Farnham bowed himself out of the hotel and onto the sidewalk. "Well, that was a horrific nothing from one end to the next," he said.

Vivi stood on the boardwalk outside with Sir Toby Belch's lead in her hands; he found her smiling and wondered why.

"Do you always get in the police's way?" she asked.

Vixen. *"Au contraire,* woman, they get in mine. Where's Breen?"

"Got a call and had to flee to the highlands. Did you get nothing at *all?*"

"Nothing. Mr. Burnes will not tell me what he has told Inspector Dillon. It is absurd how the locals take sides over these things as if we were sportsmen angling after the same fish."

Vivi handed him the lead. "Aren't you?"

"Tish. Lillian's manager, however, is in there at this very moment and seems anything but chuffed to bits at the idea of being interrogated by our noble police force. I invited him to luncheon at two."

"And I suppose I'm to cook? At least you gave me a few hours' warning."

Would the little woman never give him the peace befitting a man of his age and standing? If the bang proprietor of the town's only banged hotel refused to give him information, he would have to discover things himself. First, of course, would be to send Breen around to the hotel in a few hours. The police would have finished their work there and returned to that questionable realm of "Wanted" notices and burnt coffee. Burnes might talk to Breen.

Yes, Breen would be just the man for the job. Everyone liked Breen. Farnham had never been quite sure why the man was such a universal favorite—probably something to do with his hair. People liked men with hair. Did hair make an impression of trustfulness? Of decency? Perhaps it felt generous somehow. Perhaps people looked at a balding man and thought "Tight-wad" or, "Skin-flint" while a wigged man felt more....well...more padded. Less apt to take one's money or stare one down keenly.

Farnham ran his fingers across his head and stared down the sidewalk at the thing he had dreaded and expected since finding the body; a train had just pulled into the station— Farnham had heard the whistle and bustle from inside the hotel —and a pair of men with cameras and cheap city clothes were descending the steps of the platform. His gut tried calisthenics and managed to get in a cartwheel after a pair of ripping chin-ups.

"Looks like the hobble-de-hoy press has got wind of the incident," he muttered. He rather wished they wouldn't see Vivi.

She followed his look; her eyebrows folded in. "Oh dear."

"Come along—" He tucked her behind his shoulder. She was small. They wouldn't see her. "We'll walk toward the gristmill."

The press *might* be useful in one respect: they might badger Inspector Dillon and Chief McMulligan and leave him be. That is, if he managed to avoid detection. Badges ran both ways. For once, he was glad to be signified as lacking distinction.

With a bump, Farnham led Vivi down into the street. They avoided the sidewalk and steered round patches of mud, trying to look utterly inconspicuous. Anything to avoid colliding with a bang reporter. Farnham tried to keep in front of Vivi and let Belch have his lead. More than likely the reporters had come for the murder, but now and then a rogue member of the press had been known to attend him at Whistlecreig. Interviews. Farnham shuddered.

They had crossed the road and were passing the station platform. *Head low, shoulders hunched, talk to Vivi—*

One of the men hailed Farnham. "Any idea where I might find the scoop on the scandal?"

Farnham's stomach doubled up and bit him. "What scandal?"

"American Actress Meets Frightful Death."

"Oh, that. Try the police station—that's where one usually finds justice and horrors evenly mixed."

Resenting the fact that the press had come to Whistlecreig at all, Farnham plodded along faster and Belch broke into a lope. His pace forced Vivi to trot, but the good girl didn't complain at the impromptu jog. There was always a buzz around a murder—why wouldn't there be? Farnham had always been rather good about eluding the press when it came to his sleuthing, but the death of a celebrity was different. These were London men; they'd soon be followed by New York men. From then it was just one step down to infamy. His reputation had its limits. He could not last being known as the Actor Turned Detective. What a lurid headline for the papers. His stomach roiled like a young colony of vipers. *Bang* ulcers.

"Ulcers hurting you again?" Vivi asked.

Farnham bit his lip to ward off the uncivil expletive hovering over his temper. "I cannot *think*."

"Because of the pain?"

"Because of everything. 'I am in case to justle a constable.' I hate the police and I hate my bang stomach and I need a smoke."

Vivi said nothing, and for that Farnham was thankful. He continued the headlong pace down the center of town. Beyond the train station, the road narrowed and swept in a long, gentle curve to the left, bordered by hazel trees and blackthorn hedges. A fork ran to the right and crossed the tracks, continuing east toward Kettering. The city was some miles distant, but the road had been called "Kettering Road" from antiquity and no one had thought to rechristen it. Farnham and Vivi took the left sweep and were soon trotting down the rutted lane, putting a good distance between themselves and Whistlecreig.

"Is it legal to *ride* our bikes?" Vivi huffed.

Farnham stopped and felt a fool. "I never thought of that. Gristmill is just ahead. Mount up."

They rode the remaining few metres and stopped again at a broad wooden bridge with a wide stream running beneath. On the Kettering side of the road, the stream flowed their direction in blue kinks and ripples; on the left, it ran a few merry paces before hitting the mill-wheel and resigning itself with a peaceful sigh to a rest in the mill pond. Farnham felt a bit of that peace balm his soul. He could think. He could smoke. He would be all right, presently.

It was a pretty spot, Vivi decided. She liked it. The mill felt like a mother, gathering the rampant stream to her breast and hushing it with a chuckling murmur till it fell asleep in the cradle-pond. No wonder her uncle fled here. Vivi leaned her bike against the high rail and crossed her arms over the rail-cap, taking in the view. She would have liked to have her watercolors with her to capture the blues and browns of the water with the red mill-house reflected in its rings. Not that she could do it justice, but she would have liked to try. Perhaps Farnham mightn't mind her returning at some point. She would come back. Sometime later, when there wasn't a murder prostrate at the doorstep.

"It's the third day." Farnham's voice lazed through the heavy-eyed tranquility. When Vivi looked around, she saw that her uncle had gone halfway down the bank and was now stretched in the sage-colored grass with his hound at his side.

"Are you expecting a resurrection?"

Farnham took his pipe from his mouth and blew a puff of lilac smoke into the air. "Don't be an oyster, Vivi. Not becoming."

She rolled her eyes and ran her fingers through her hair. "Are we to look east with the light of the setting sun at our backs?"

"It is the third day," her uncle repeated, "meaning that the murderer is every day growing stronger in his hidden identity."

"Surely three days doesn't matter so much."

"Thank God she's a celebrity."

"Why?"

"So much easier to track a celebrity's friends and enemies."

"I thought they'd have more than the usual citizen."

Farnham blew another puff of smoke and settled back against the stream bank with a sigh. He had chosen a spot directly in the sunlight, and to Vivi it looked deliciously warm. Belch gave an experimental sneeze. Appearing surprised at himself, he sneezed again.

"Lillian Bertois was killed within an hour or two of her arrival," Farnham said. "We need to know whether she checked into the hotel and whether she spoke with anyone there. Any phone-calls, any telegrams, any visitors. I need to know her agent—and it's a blessed thing he's on his way to my doorstep.

I need to know why she wanted to appear in Whistlecreig. Bang it."

"What?"

"This might require me dragging *my* heels to London, though it shall be a last resort."

Vivi yawned. "God forbid."

Farnham squinted against his sunlight and shook his pipe at her. "You needn't be smug. London is a bang nasty city; it and I are on an entirely *professional* acquaintance."

"I like it."

"Then move there; no one asked you to come mud-daubing here in the sticks." He created a smile just to be sure she didn't take his sarcasm like a shrimp. "As I was saying, why Whistlecreig? Northampton has more theatres than it knows what to do with. Why a *country* town? That gives us a lead. Stupid of her, really. That means that she knew someone here, or had arranged a rendezvous with someone. Who?"

"Family, perhaps?"

"Oh, come now, Vivi. Would a woman go off to visit family members she knew to be dangerous? No. It is someone she did not know well enough to expect to infuriate."

Vivi shifted her weight from one foot to the next. "How do we know he was angry?"

"A blow to the head is enough to do the job. A cold-blooded killer isn't going to mutilate a face like that." Farnham looked out on the russet-rose flitter of a linnet in the rushes. "The murder was done in a passion by a man who had lost his wits to rage or fear—or both."

"Mmm. Who knew learning to keep one's temper could keep one from jail later on?"

Farnham gave her a sharp look. "Mothers, perhaps? There are reasons for common morality."

Vivi let her cheek drop onto her folded arms and settled into the warm caress of the sunlight. This bit of the world was so peaceful...She closed her eyes. "So our next step is to...?"

A pair of hands descended on the rail with a clap that made her twitch awake. "What-ho, Miss Langley? How does Whistlecreig treat the pretty wanderer?"

Chapter Ten
Ye Merry Gentlemen

Vivi's heart threw back in her chest like a horse rearing at the crack of a whip then thundered in a rush of blood to her temples. There was room for only one thought in that choking-second: Jimmy Fields ought to be in Crowborough.

Forcing her heart back to its place, Vivi mastered her emotions and raised her head with a bright smile. "Jimmy! What on earth are you doing back in Whistlecreig?"

He appeared gratified that she greeted him so, and his bright, easy smile soothed Vivi with its pleasant warmth. "Couldn't stay away when there were new people in town."

"'New people' meaning?" Vivi surprised herself with the degree of accidental flirtation in her response. She wondered if he would sense it too, and the thought burned hotter in her cheeks.

Jimmy pushed his cap further back on his curly thatch of hair and grinned. His jaw was trim; his toothache must have abated, poor creature. "Oh, naught but some pert young lady belonging to old Farnham. Thought I might look her up and try to make friends."

She was flattered by the fact that he had returned from Crowborough on her account; it was the most generous display of interest any man had given her—besides one wretched beast named Maynor—since Lord Lionel Darnell on her eighteenth birthday. And heaven knew Jimmy was a far better-looking man than the unfortunate earl.

Vivi shrugged. "I'm afraid I haven't seen anyone fitting that description around here. Of course, I'm new to the area. There *was* a young lady at Whistlecreig Manor—arrived a day or two ago—but I'm quite certain she belongs to *herself*."

Jimmy's grin broadened. He shook his head. "I'm glad to hear it." He leaned his forearms on the bridge-rail and winked. "Gives a man his chance to win her."

This was bold. "My uncle is here." Vivi nodded down the slope at Farnham who was fondling Belch's ears and viewing the young people with interest. "Come, drag yourself out of the greener pastures and do your social duty, sir."

Deep inside, Vivi feared Farnham would still suspect Jimmy of the actress's murder and say something ill-natured. She watched Farnham and his hound lounge up the bank with growing apprehension. He wasn't hurrying. He was barely smiling. But then, Farnham never did go in much for the whole amiable-expression thing.

When they were reunited on the bridge, Jimmy pumped Farnham's hand and Vivi watched his eyes closely. He met Farnham's with a direct, manly look, and her heart rested. Murderers don't look men in the eye with that much peaceful *bonhomie*.

"Mr. Farnham. Gorgeous day, isn't it?"

"Quite. My niece told me you had gone down South. What occasioned your return?"

"The reason that had me leaving in the first place. Thirsted for a change of scenery and new company..." Jimmy put his hands in his trouser pockets with a boyish shrug. "By the time I spent a day or two in Crowborough, I found I'd left the interesting company behind and...well...you know I'm a Northant lad through an' through." He thumped his chest, bringing on the thicker accent.

"'The courageous captain of compliments.'" Farnham's tone was dry but not unfriendly. In fact, Vivi rather thought he was pleased to see Jimmy. "We are glad to have you back around, lad. Your father is well? All right at Ealsey Hollow?"

Jimmy nodded, and Vivi noticed how his dark hair curled over the collar of his jacket. He was in need of a haircut, yes, but she thought the effect roguishly charming.

"Farm's doing right well. Fallow season, y'know, so Dad said I could have my head if I'd a fancy a bit of traveling."

"Generous of him," Farnham agreed. He rocked on his toes in the little space left by the conversation as it guttered out and streamed away like pipe-smoke. "Well," he said at last, a bit louder than their proximity merited, "my niece and I were just about to head back to the Manor. I wish you a good day." He tipped his cap and righted his bicycle, once more tying Belch's lead to the handles and throwing a leg over the bar.

Jimmy turned back to face Vivi and flapped his elbows, hands deep in the pockets of his tweeds. "Shall I be seeing you soon?"

"Of course. I'm sure Uncle won't mind if you drop by at some point." She followed Farnham's departing figure with her gaze for a moment. "We apparently don't stand much upon ceremony at Whistlecreig."

"Right. Well," Jimmy took her fingers and clapped his other hand over top, trapping them sweetly. "See you soon, then?"

"Soon." Vivi smiled, feeling that his inquiry wanted affirmation. Yes, she wanted to see Jimmy again; he needn't worry himself on that account. "I mustn't let myself go to cobwebs with only the old darlings for company, you know."

He dropped her fingers with a quick squeeze. "Indeed not. Genevieve Langley is a thing moth and dust doth not corrupt."

It was good to have someone to steady her bike as she straddled it and tried to keep her skirt from catching on the gears. Skirts and bicycles were certainly an invention of the devil's wife. If it wasn't the questionable modesty of hitching one's skirt up to one's thigh, it was the constant peril of being flipped stockings-over-collar off the front of the thing. *Oh* for a pair of trousers! At last Vivi was settled with tolerable decency on the seat, and Jimmy saluted her as she pedaled off. Vivi thanked God under her breath that she was past the waggle-waddle stage of remembering how to ride.

"Miss Langley," Jimmy called after her. "I'm ever so glad I came back."

Vivi only waved in reply, but the cool morning air brought blessed relief to the uncommon warmth spreading through her veins. *So am I.*

She drew up beside Farnham and the trio—dog, man and girl—rode through town and out onto the Whistlecreig road once more. The fields on either side rolled thistle-colored in gracious undulations, a deeper russet-purple where copses of oak overshadowed the edges. The sun shone, the earth was beautiful, and Jimmy Fields had returned to Whistlecreig for her sake. Vivi felt almost...excited. This worried her. She knew how unfounded her hopes always turned out to be. She must be careful; heartbreak was a wretched little thing, and she was not about to let herself grow too fond of a man she'd met twice.

At the quarter-hour mark, something had to be said. "Thank you for being gracious with Jimmy. I...I appreciated your thoughtfulness—for my sake."

Her uncle grunted and veered off a bit to the right to avoid a rut in the soft road; he rejoined her and gave a sidelong glance. "'I am the very pink of courtesy,' am I not?"

"Quite. You could have made it rotten."

Farnham chuckled. "Don't I know it."

"I want to investigate him," Vivi said. Her voice felt doubtful, so she tried again with a bolder tone: "I want to investigate Jimmy Fields."

His pale eyebrows rose. "Why this weathervane of purpose?"

"I want to help you solve this murder. If Jimmy was the murderer, we should be able to discover it quickly. And if he is not, we can clear him straightaway. At any rate, I would like to have it over with, whatever the outcome."

"And the sooner the better, my dear?" Farnham's glance this time was keen and comprehensive.

Vivi's bike wobbled into a pothole, and she pressed harder on the pedals, gaining speed. Farnham and Sir Toby kept up.

"Yes," she said quietly. "The sooner the better."

Fatherly fingers descended on her right shoulder and on and off her skin, as much a patting motion as could be summoned while cycling. Vivi noticed he steered with his right hand, knees bowing into the black center rod of the bike.

"I promise I'll do my best to clear him quickly," Farnham said. "He's an interesting chap. Ealsey Hollow is a fine farm and old Mr. Fields a fine neighbor. I would hate trouble for old Fields's sake alone, if not the lad's."

"Doctor Breen will get the information we need from the hotel?" Vivi asked. "He won't fail?"

"He'll not fail through lack of *effort*, no. I'll set him on it soon as we get home, phone Mrs. Froggle at his grand Quagmire and leave a message."

"You have a phone at Whistlecreig?"

"Of course we have."

Something niggled at the back of Vivi's recollection...something that made no sense if there was indeed a telephone. "Why did Breen send a telegram that first night? Surely it was a useless expense if a phone-call was possible."

"You're a sharp one." Farnham flagged a beetle out of his way before putting his left hand back on his handlebars. "You'll not like my answer, I'll warrant."

"Why did he *telegraph*?"

"It's part of the..."

"Ahhh, the game?" Vivi quizzed.

"The *system*. I put each telegram in my...." Farnham cleared his throat and turned right at the manor-drive, passing between the two stone posts marking a gap in the boxwood hedge. "In my scrapbook."

"That is positively morbid."

"It's a testament to our friendship."

"Friendships aren't built on blood!" Vivi protested.

Farnham braked suddenly and turned on her with a certain fierceness both unnerving and quaint. *"Aren't* they? Surely you've never stuck that aristocratic nose in *Henry V* or the Bible or any history of any war in the last two millennia if you think friendships can't be built on blood."

It was as if a short, fantastic gale had blown between them, and Vivi felt all the warmth of Jimmy's arrival swept away on an uncertain tide. She had been half in fun, but her uncle's reaction showed her that perhaps she had hit upon a spot sore within his very soul; surely it must be a deep-seeded plant to have grown so potent a subject in his eyes.

"I'm sorry," she said. "I didn't mean to insult you."

Farnham's lips pinched, and the skin around his knuckles on the handlebars was tight and yellow. He let out a slow breath, and the tense expression flickered. "You have my forgiveness."

That was it. That was *it?* Vivi watched, baffled, as her uncle cycled away toward the house as if there hadn't been a massive upheaval of spirits a moment back. She was accustomed to fleshing a thing out in all its nastiness before boxing it away as finished. Whistlecreig folk were different—

they didn't appear to enjoy lancing their carbuncles. She rolled her eyes and continued down the drive at a slow spin. Life here was an absolute puzzlement. Would she ever understand?

"You'll remember to offer him wine?"

Farnham's voice jogged Vivi out of a study of the brownest shade. "Pardon?"

He circled the dining room table with a cat-soft step. "If you're going to play the banged hostess of Whistlecreig–a thing no one has done in at least three decades–you'll remember to offer Mr. Owens a glass of wine with his luncheon?"

"I thought to offer him strychnine," Vivi said.

She looked at her own time-piece, checked it against the grandfather clock behind her, and returned it to her pocket. "Why exactly did you invite Mr. Owens to luncheon? Surely you can't imagine Miss Bertois' own manager would have murdered her?"

"Can and have, old girl. A man would have to have a terribly wonderful grudge to kill someone who pays him what Phillip Owens got paid for tugging on Fame's strings for Lillian Bertois, but he was in close connexion with her–closer than any of the suspects we have."

"And he might shed some light on her other acquaintances?"

Candlelight, though it was but afternoon, gleamed on the patches where hair had forsaken Farnham's head, for the windowless dining room was dim even at midday. "I hope so. It will, at any rate, give us an idea of the lady's character. First rule of the chase, my lady: the murdered must have raised a hue and cry. Somehow she attracted attention to herself. Somehow she got in the murderer's way."

"No wonder they teach us to look both ways before crossing a street."

"There are reasons for parental caution. A thing we've discussed before now."

The front doorbell jangled like the final trump. Vivi's whole body seized in holy terror—ceased to function completely for a moment. Embarrassed, she opened her eyes again slowly. What a high pitch her nerves were playing! Quite equal to anything achieved by the soprano, Lotte Schöne, and her like.

Vivi grabbed Farnham's sleeve and sent him toward the front door. "Mein worthy host, would you like to do the honors?"

"Nay, nay, we'll pluck this crow together."

He seemed in perfect possession of himself as he moved like a shadow through the shadows. A thin, bleak, entirely English shadow the color of the bland biscuits he refused to eat. Together, then, they approached the front door. Farnham straightened the edges of his eternal cardigan, flared his nostrils in a manner Napoleonic, and wrenched open the door.

Upon the step, damp like most men Vivi had encountered in Northamptonshire, stood Phillip Owens. He filled the steps nicely, none too broad nor too thin, but the thing that arrested notice were the canny set of his eyes and the scar running across his chin. It was the scar that moved him to the top of the suspects list in Vivi's head. She lifted her own chin in his presence, willing herself to feel every centimeter of her height.

"Welcome to Whistlecreig, Mr. Owens. Pleasant ride?" Farnham pumped his hand and extended a benevolent arm toward the hall. "Awful weather. Having just the *worst* dose of it we've had in this whole autumn. Nothing as eerie as Nature setting the stage for a tragedy. Not that it wasn't nice today. Terribly pleasant all around."

"Bad things happen in bad weather." Mr. Owens turned the hat he'd removed round and round and round in his hands and the mist dropped off in pewter slips.

"Oh, it isn't Mistress Weather's fault men are devils. Come in, won't you? I am afraid our butler popped off without notice—not dead, you'll understand, just departed—and we had to rely on our own deftness with the cuisine, which is not, I'll warn you, quite as deft as I'd like."

"When I've been traveling for a week solid, I'm not too picky about my feed. New York to London, London up to Glasgow, Glasgow down here soon as I heard about Lillian. Pint of beer and a joint of meat's enough for me. Kind of you to ask me."

In response to Farnham's elbow, Vivi hurried ahead. "I hope we can do better than that for you, Mr. Owens. There is wine and Beef Wellington, and a poached pear in syrup for the finale. No sense in discussing somber things over a ghostly table." She stationed herself at the door and smiled for the men as they passed. Mr. Owens' eyes caught hers, slunk away then roved back again.

He was not a bad-looking man but for that scar! With it, he looked a reprobate entire.

In a few moments, Farnham had arranged Mr. Owens at the table's head, himself in his customary place. It had been foreordained that Vivi would act as maitre'd, and to this end she slipped into the kitchen and arranged the finalities of the dishes. Too long since she'd last had occasion to cook an actual meal. She had enjoyed it, truth be told, and it was a pleasure still to garnish the Wellington with a few bright rowan berries and to bear it into the dining room under the grateful smiles of a hungry man.

"Miss Farnham, you're an angel of mercy," Mr. Owens said.

Vivi laughed. "My name is Genevieve Langley. I am *not* Mr. Farnham's daughter."

Farnham rustled in his corner. "Heavens, no."

"You must forgive me, Ms. Langley and you, Mr. Farnham. Shouldn't have assumed..."

"I am his niece," Vivi offered by way of explanation. The tell-tale cloud on Mr. Owens' brow cleared, and Vivi wondered what could possess anyone to suspect she was Orville Farnham's paramour. The bald idea!

She began to feel that playing hostess had its risks.

"We are here to talk about Lil's murder, aren't we?" Mr. Owens pushed away his plate after a third helping of Beef Wellington taken after his honeyed pears. The man possessed a Herculean appetite, Farnham noticed. "There was a reason I came so far."

"We are," Farnham said.

"Damnable thing."

"Quite so."

"Can't imagine what inspired him to do it."

"Many things move a man to murder." Farnham ran his pinky finger around the inside of his saucer, taking up a collection of the final juices from that quintessential poached pear.

The manager nodded. "Of course. What I mean is, who would do it in an out of the way place like this?" Phillip Owens stuck his tongue in back of his cheek with a knowing smile. "Man's gonna bother to do a thing like that, why not take advantage of the publicity? There's money to be made in notoriety as well as fame."

Farnham dropped his feet to the floor. "Who indeed?"

"Sloppy job. Sloppy."

"You mean to say you suspect Miss Bertois was killed as a money-making venture?" Farnham blew a tuneless whistle through his teeth. "What *will* men think of next?"

A heavy roll of the shoulders was all Farnham got as answer. He cut his eyes across to Vivi and her pale, puzzled demeanor. "Why did Miss Bertois wish to appear in Whistlecreig? I realize she had a show in Northampton... shouldn't that be enough? Whistlecreig is such an out of the way place."

Mr. Owens shrugged. "Maybe it was part of her new plan. She said she wanted to see more of the countryside. Maybe she had more friends than just you, Mr. Farnham."

Farnham shot a silencing look at his niece and prayed her to ask no questions.

"Now I'm not saying I know of anyone for *certain* she knew in Whistlecreig, but it seems to me her nerves were pitchy over this whole Northamptonshire tour. I took it to be exhaustion and excitement..."

"Do you have any idea, Mr. Owens, who killed your client? I realize it won't be pleasant to bring forth these topics, but it must be done somehow..."

For a moment, Farnham wondered if the rough New Yorker might refuse to specify, but Owens raised his well-filled wine glass in salute.

"Like you say, it has to be done and, between you and I, I'd far rather tell a mutual friend than the police. *I* am not looking for notoriety. The *time* involved...well, it's a bit much when you're trying to publicize other peoples' lives and make an honest living."

It was difficult for Farnham, trying not to look excited. "If you do have any ideas, Mr. Owens, justice would be much obliged to you. I am having Puck's job understanding a motive behind any of it."

Owens peered at him sleepily over the rim of his glass. "Look, Mr. Farnham, I know she was a particular friend of yours... but she was not without problems."

"Are any of us?" Farnham asked, right on beat.

"Gorgeous thing like her, Mr. Farnham...won't be hard for you to imagine how men reacted to her."

"No indeed."

"Or how she reacted to men. I might have been the only man she didn't fawn over in her lifetime–though I guess she knew better than to try it with an old fellow like you." He laughed. "She'd play with us like a funny little kitten. Paw at us. Tease us. 'You're ugly, Owens,' she'd say, 'so don't give me those looks.' Fine for me. Her style of beauty never brings no good with it. Believe me, Mr. Farnham, she thought no more of breaking hearts than that one gal...Helena Troy?"

Farnham wove his napkin through the fingers of his left hand. "Helen *of* Troy, perhaps?"

"That's the girl. And you know how men take to their favorite paying too much attention to someone else. Jealousy's the headline. Can't bear the thought of any man having what they once had. Better kill the stinker and have done with it, right? Least that's the angle *I'd* take if I were investigating."

Vivi looked alert, and Farnham smiled in her direction while his stomach flipped eagerly. "You sir, are an adept thinker."

Mr. Owens set his goblet on the table and passed a hand over his scarred chin. "I'm afraid I can't help you much over *who* did it. Like I said, could have been any guy she's caught in the past two years. And that list is longer than the roster at the Ritz."

"Rich men, poor men...beauty undoes them both," Farnham mused.

"Now, Mr. F, here's a thought..." The agent's eyes widened as he fixed them on someplace distant and nodded slowly. "Jealousy runs both sides of the river…no one says it's a *man* who killed Lillian Bertois."

"A woman!" Vivi breathed.

Farnham's eyes settled on Phillip Owens' scar, small and livid down the slope of his chin. "'Hell hath no fury like a woman scorned'…"

"But this varies the suspects *widely,*" Vivi protested as soon as they had seen the New York agent out the front doors and made themselves comfortable in Farnham's study. "If it isn't a man then it could be any woman in Whistlecreig. But I *know* it could not have been a woman."

"Why not?"

She bated a moment, scanning for some reasonable excuse. "Women don't kill other women in that bash-you-in manner. It's just not done."

Farnham smirked and threw a log on the fire. "Grant you, poison is generally the weapon *du jour* but there are strong women just as there are weak men. One of your Helgas could have done it and easily."

"Do you think it's a woman?"

"I think nothing except that we have the right scent: jealousy is a *prime* motive for murder."

"When it comes to that," Vivi said, scooting a log a bit closer to the flames, "I'd bet a fiver it was Mr. Owens himself. Did you notice his battle-plan for gaining notoriety? No one expends that much brain-power without having thought of it once himself."

"There's many a man who has *thought* to commit murder, but it's our lot to deal only with the ones who have done it."

"And you don't think Owens did?"

"In faith, lady, 'his face is the worst thing about him'."

Vivi rolled her eyes. "I beg leave to disagree. In all respects, he's an odious man."

"And here I was thinking you found him attractive. Why were you staring at him?"

"I like to take the measure of a man by watching his face. Helps me see character."

"And what do you read in mine?"

Surprised, Vivi turned round from the fire and met his cool grey stare. The shadows had filled in the gauntness of his cheeks with patches of dark amber and turned the remaining hair of his head to pale wisps. He seemed frailer than ever, which was an accomplishment. Behind him, the afternoon sun poured from the window and set his face in further darkness.

She took him in, studied him, turned him in her mind like a wooden doll to be examined at leisure. Long had it been since she'd been given permission to inspect a person thoroughly; for some time she had had to be content with snatches of observation.

"I am not sure you'll enjoy hearing," Vivi said at last, letting him go.

"Nonsense. I'm a man. I can take what a little chit like you has to give."

"You're prone to being disagreeable and selfish," Vivi began with vocal hesitancy. She was not at all certain she wouldn't throw him into his worst temper yet with her pronouncement, but he demanded and who was she to deny him? "Yet I think your ill humors are put on like a poorly cut jacket. You aren't truly intolerant, though undeniably vain. You like to be listened to, catered to, and thought much of, but for all your upper-crust airs, you're a warm-hearted enough creature and you *hate* for people to know it."

The saucy smile she had tried to quell came out in the end and flashed at Farnham. He stared at her like a thing carved, and the corners of his mouth tucked in an expression Vivi could hardly decipher. Was he angry? Pleased? Neither?

"I think, Miss Genevieve Langley, you had better get to work. Those maps I showed you in the dining room won't inspect themselves."

She got to her feet, still grinning, and made a curtsy. "Farewell, Heir of Whistlecreig. I promise not to spill your secrets to the world."

"I have no secrets!" Farnham called after her. "Not a one! Don't you dare tell *any*one my secrets."

Pausing in the hall, Vivi laughed and poked her head back into the room. "I cannot spill things you don't have..."

"'What! my dear Lady Disdain! are you yet living?' To work!"

Still smiling, away she went.

Vivi spent the rest of the afternoon in the dining room, encamped with a cheap tallow candle and a covey of worn maps. They were unusual maps of Whistlecreig, and to these Vivi applied herself.

"Where would I commit a murder?" Vivi murmured.

She traced a footpath denoted in neat, birdlike dashes with her finger and chewed her bottom lip. Too far South and the murder would be too close to the village. Too far West, the murderer would have been too near the road to make such a thing advisable.

"Come on, you," she hissed. "Out with your secrets."

The light, where it pooled in from the hall, had turned a liquid amber with the advance of evening; from amber to grey, from grey to plum. She had been alone in the dining room for some time. Faintly, through the echoing foyer, came the sound of lively footsteps.

"'How now, you secret, black, and midnight hags?'" a plummy voice caroled through the doorway.

Breen was here, announcing his arrival with that peculiar 'was-hail.' Vivi rose from the far end of the table and hurried to greet him.

"Good evening, Dr. Breen!"

"My dear." He kissed her cheek and allowed her to lead him to the back of the dining room

Vivi cast at it with her hand and laughed. "My endeavors of the evening."

Palms flat on the table, Breen leaned over her maps. The smoky tapers bit at the shadows in his face till he looked more than half highwayman, and a delicious worm of terror writhed against Vivi's ribs.

"Looks rather villainous," he growled, and his burr was thick and delightful with mock evil.

She stepped back and smoothed her skirt. "Doesn't it, though? I feel like a very dull variety of pirate queen."

"Was this your uncle's doing?" Breen straightened. "Where is he?"

"Yes, my assignment straight from the great Orville Farnham himself...I imagine he's lurking somewhere about—I really don't know. It has just been me and this great booming house since antiquity, it feels. Gosh, I'm starved." She plopped into the chair and pulled a map nearer, identifying the manor house with her forefinger. "I've been trying to discover where the murder was committed."

"In the field, obviously?" he puckered his brow.

"No...see..." Vivi moved her finger a few inches over to the field, some mile from the manor, where the body had been found. "Farnham says there was no sign of a struggle where the body was found. First clue."

Breen rubbed his jaw. "That's true...but there didn't have to be much of a struggle to inflict that injury: one blow to the head and the deed was done—she'd not be *wrestling* him. The other injuries...the disfiguration...that could just as easily have been done in the field. The police are certain that is the murder site. The turf was bloody, and the ground a bit trampled, so Dillon tells me."

Vivi smoothed the soft, old paper of the map with her fingertips as if she could conjure meaning from touching the places noted on its skin. She was not as adamantly against the police force as her uncle, but it had not helped her opinion to be taken to the station for questioning. Anyone with half a brain would know she was innocent. She dropped her chin into her hand, propping her elbow on the satin finish of the dining room table.

"I suppose one team will be correct in the end," she said. "Farnham does not think a murderer would commit the thing on a hillside within sight of a road."

"Even in the fog?" Breen asked in a tone that seemed to Vivi a cavern of skepticism. "You can't see three paces ahead let alone a few furlongs."

She smiled a secret smile, savoring the irony of her current employment. "My dear doctor, there is very little I know about solving murders except this: every little idea seems to count. Farnham asked me to come up with a list of five places the murder could have been committed."

"Number one: in the field," Breen said.

"Nonsensical man. I think it far more likely the body was carried to the field from another place."

"Within the time constraints we have?" Breen protested. "She never checked into the hotel. The murder was committed early on."

"The luggage..." Vivi pressed her fingers onto her eyelids to ease the headache that had advanced on her with the dusk. "Where on earth is it? It must be in the murderer's possession."

"High marks for effort, Harriet Vane, but you're wrong." He cast his still powerful frame into a chair and knocked on the table with his knuckles. "She left it at the station and said she'd send for it later. The police have it now."

"Bang it."

Breen viewed her with an expression of fond amusement in his eyes. "I wish I was a younger man."

"Heavens."

"Really, lass. You do a man good to know you."

Vivi folded her maps and pushed them back into the pasteboard box in which they'd come to her, burying a little snub-nosed pistol Farnham had stored among them. "That's certainly the first time a man has ever said any such thing to me."

"Young men are fools. You're sweet, intelligent, and pleasant. I don't know what their damn—*darned* problem is. Excuse me."

A warm glow of satisfaction rose in Vivi's core and thrust out the headache. She pushed away from the table and kissed Dr. Breen's cheek then deposited the map box on the sideboard. "Perhaps glamour and beauty is more in demand these days. At any rate, I think you're a duck and—"

A doorbell rang in the vicinity of the hall. Vivi grimaced and made to resume the conversation. It rang again, throttling conversation. "I forgot Allen wasn't here. Great Scot."

"Yes, I am a fabulous one," Breen quipped. "Fewer finer than I. In the absence of a butler, lassie, may this great Scot answer the door?"

"Please."

Breen bounced up from his chair, tossed Vivi a wink, and strode from the dining room. The room seemed far emptier without his buoyant personality. The candle-flames bounced in an erratic dance with some unseen spectre of a draft. Two dried petals from the centerpiece of roses fell to the table with a tick like mouse claws, one right after another so it seemed that a ghost's hand had quietly drawn its nails over the wood. Vivi wished Breen would hurry and come back. What was he so long about? She almost resented him coming at all, since his leaving again made the dining room so eerie a place to be alone.

Having nothing to do in the interim, Vivi unfolded and folded the maps and arranged them again inside the pasteboard box. Still Breen did not come. What had become of him?

At last she heard the deep-throated thrum of the hall echoing his voice, and in a moment Dr. Breen shimmered into view in the doorway.

"Vivi?"

"What on earth kept you?"

"I've got a young man in the hall who says he is looking for you."

"Jimmy?"

"Nope. New man. Never seen him before."

Vivi shook her head, eyebrows raised. What people would say to force their way into famous peoples' homes. "What is his name? I'm certainly not expecting any visitors."

"Michael Maynor."

Vivi sucked her breath through her teeth and fabricated her most pleasant smile. "By all means, show him into the study or drawing room or whatever it's called."

"But there's no fire or candles in there," Breen pointed out.

Vivi smoothed her hair, chin thrust upward. "I don't much care, seeing as it's Michael Maynor."

"You...know him?"

"I knew Mama could not leave me alone on the subject." Vivi tried to press the wrinkles from her clothes but it was useless—she'd been riding bicycles and pouring over maps half the day; an iron would be hard-pressed to take them out. *Hard-pressed...iron...*Groaning at her own quip and hating that she had gained that level of tiredness in which her mind automatically created puns, Vivi stretched her smile into enormous, fake proportions.

"I just love unexpected company," she said, and rolled her eyes so Breen might not misunderstand her scathing sarcasm. "Michael Maynor is a London man...one of the many with whom my family has tried to set me up over the years. Many would think it strange he hasn't found a wife yet. Those unfortunate ladies—like myself—who were forced to try to win him think it the most natural thing in the world."

"He seems perfectly handsome and mannerable." Breen threw a sympathetic glance backward into the hall.

"Yes." Vivi pushed past him and tossed a verdict over her shoulder: "And quite as stuck on himself as Narcissus ever was." Her eyes searched the cavernous hall for the familiar, dashing figure. Ah, there he was, surveying the family portraits on one of the dank walls. "Mr. Maynor," she called. "How lovely to see you."

Michael spun to face her with a smirk on his face. Mama swore he looked like the old Arrow Collar man, only blonde, and Vivi couldn't help but think she was right. He cut a magnificent silhouette in his tan traveling coat: broad shoulders, slicked hair, Grecian features. He came to her with both hands outstretched and took her coldly offered fingers in his. "Genevieve, Genevieve, my dear thing. You're looking lovely."

Vivi gave him the smallest curtsy. "And since when last we met, you pronounced me 'plain as porridge,' I can only upbraid you for a liar and hope you are more honest in your business dealings than in compliments."

He chuckled and kissed her hand, then released it. "Well met, my beautiful little harpy."

"Why are you here, Michael?" Her voice was tight and tiny.

"Have a friend in town I came to visit. Heard a Miss Genevieve Langley had come to stay at Whistlecreig and thought I'd take the advantage of being a good friend and announce my charming presence in person. So much chummier than sending a card."

Vivi smiled and folded her hands against her skirt, small, polite, impeccably distant. "My uncle is not at home right now, and I'm afraid our butler is away on business, but—"

Michael spread his hands with a free grin. "Butlers on business? What a modernist."

She bent her head as if into a stiff wind and continued: "But if you would like to wait in the study, I am certain he will not be long."

"Will you wait with me? It's been an age since we've seen each other."

"I'll get a light." Breen smiled and disappeared into the dining room.

Staying with Michael seemed dangerous; he was a profoundly accomplished trifler with women. Leaving him alone in Farnham's study did not seem the way to earn her uncle's confidence. Breen would be there. Dear Breen. He would keep Michael Maynor from anything...distressing.

"Of course I'll wait with you. I want to hear news from Darlington—have you seen any of my family?"

"I have not been much in Darlington of late. London's my native heath though my name's not MacGregor. Your cousin Edward has been at the Club pretty often, so I've kept up to date with the family happenings."

They had moved down a maze of hallways as he spoke, and Vivi groped for the doorknob of the study, hidden in the dusk. Breen had gone back into the dining room to fetch candles; it struck Vivi that she was alone in a dark hall with a man she no-wise trusted.

Just as she thought this, his laugh sounded close to her ear —too close. She stepped a bit more into the corner and ran her fingers frantically over the wood panels of the door, trying to find the knob. Where was it? Her heart raced, and she feared Michael might hear the panic that shook her breath.

"Some trouble?" he asked, too close again.

"None," she breathed. "The door's a bit stiff is all."

There. At least she felt the cold kiss of iron under her palm; the knob was situated peculiarly in the center of the door. Sweet relief flowed through her as she flung it open and motioned for Michael to go in. A humorous spasm passed through Michael's handsome face, and he winked.

"If you're my gaoler, I don't mind being imprisoned in a room with a door that sticks."

Vivi folded her hands again and hurried to the window directly in front of her. She felt in need of some escape, even if it meant pitching herself out a window into the thorn-filled arms of those rose bushes. Michael sauntered to Farnham's wing chair and sat down. He filled the space between the wings better, but he lacked Farnham's magnificence of spirit. The phrase "magnificence of spirit" had come into Vivi's head quite unexpectedly. She smiled. Her uncle was magnificent in his own way.

"You're smiling, sweet-thing. Want to tell me why?"

"Who is your friend?" Vivi asked. Would Breen never come with the candles? Dash it all if he thought she wanted a moment alone with this cad.

"A fellow by the name of Jimmy Fields," Maynor murmured through a pair of well-formed lips.

Vivi felt her cheeks go red. She had always thought them the lips of a young Apollo and at one time had fancied what it must be to be kissed by him. Now—oh never. Her insides tremored at the thought, so Vivi did what she always did when nervous: she folded her hands before her and met the problem head on.

"You know Jimmy Fields?" Somehow she was not as surprised to hear it as she might be.

"Do you?" Michael seemed discomfited by the idea.

"We've met."

Michael's lips spread in a rogue's grin. "You have a crush on him. Look at you turning red. Gosh, you're cute."

"How well do you know Jimmy?" *Why do you know Jimmy?*

"We spent some time at Uni together."

"Jimmy is a writer?" Why hadn't he told her? Then Vivi recalled that they had shared more words in her imagination than in their brief meetings.

Michael waved a hand at her. "I'm the writer. He switched to journalism after a few months, then quit it all for good and came back to the land of cow-dung and pig-slop."

"It isn't all bad here," Vivi said.

"Jimmy's a good fellow. I like him. He liked me. We shared similar interests."

Vivi had never been quite sure what interests Michael Maynor held besides women. The thought that Jimmy could possibly share that hobby with this man made her feel like she had stomach ulcers of her own. He probably liked boating and cricket; she remembered Michael's summer hobbies with relief.

She shrugged, tried to look natural. "Since I like Jimmy, too, you can't be too much alike."

Michael sprang to his feet and advanced on her. "Why don't you like me?" He took her cold hands in his, and Vivi's heart turned to a column of ice through her throat. His thumbs chafed the blood into her hands, and he bent his head over her. She felt as if each of his fingers was a hot brand, burning himself into her body. "What have I ever done to make you hate me?"

"Please...let me go."

He held her hands a second longer, then dropped them. "I thought you liked chivalrous men. Your hands looked cold."

Vivi thought of a great many things she could say in reply to that, none of which her mother would have considered appropriate. She stayed quiet and was more than joyous when Breen entered, balancing a large silver tray on one arm and a lit candle-tree in the crook of the other.

"Thought Mr. Maynor might like a bit of tea and a snack after his journey. If he doesn't, I certainly do." He clanked the tray onto the side-table near Farnham's wing chair and placed the candle-tree on another, then stretched his arms. "You'd never guess how much a half-dozen blazing candles weighs." He chafed at his elbow, hissing through his teeth.

"Mr. Maynor knows Jimmy Fields, Doctor."

Breen smiled. "Small world."

How very original. Vivi wished he's say something witty and useful that would draw Michael's attention away from her face. She wished Farnham would hurry up and come home. It was dark now and, if he was within the house, he ought to make his appearance. Hunger would drive him down if the cold didn't. Then she remembered his ulcers and cursed his lack of appetite.

"Don't you think it curious, Vivi?"

Vivi snapped back to the conversation, and a ripping pain tore up the right side of her neck. She rubbed the spot and disdained whiplash violently. "I'm sorry, I wasn't listening."

Michael narrowed his eyes and grinned. "Dreamy little thing."

"Not dreamy. Tired," Vivi muttered.

"No worries." Breen cleared his throat and looked between she and Michael as if trying to distinguish if he ought to step in and reprimand one or the other. "I was only saying, isn't it curious that you arrived just in time to see your uncle at work on this mystery?"

"Mystery?" Michael asked. "Tell me more. I like a good enigma."

Vivi would rather have marched into Chief McMulligan's office and surrendered herself for a second inquisition than to share the details of Lillian Bertois's demise with Michael Maynor. Breen, however, appeared to have found the subject on which he would wax eloquent. He poured cups of tea all round and handed one to Michael with a nod of his head.

"There was a murder three days ago."

Michael pursed his chiseled lips to blow on the tea, then sipped it. Vivi blushed again at catching herself thinking about his mouth. That was what she got for studying art. She studied faces too carefully, memorized too thoroughly every expression playing over the human canvas.

"A murder? In this quiet little place? I'll have to give Jimmy a thrashing. Naughty chap."

Michael laughed, but he was alone in his mirth. Vivi had a scorching desire to lacerate his fine face with her nails for treating it like a joke. What sort of a friend teased about his own friend committing a murder? Then again, what sort of uncle let his niece be quizzed by a rough police chief? She would hold her peace this once, if only to prove to Farnham that she could be a very sensible woman.

"You came to visit Jimmy?" she asked.

"Been planning it for some time." Michael's heavy gold ring beat against the side of his teacup with a bright "ting" as he moved his fingers. "Felt it was time to have one of the country larks he used to boast about."

Three days ago Jimmy had been headed to Crowborough for an undetermined amount of time. If he had been expecting a friend...Vivi watched candlelight gleam on the gold of Michael's ring like a bit of truth caught in a brass lie.

"For some time." She repeated his words in a musing tone, then looked up at him with a peaceable smile. "Isn't that nice?"

Suspect four, she thought with firm conviction. *Michael Maynor.*

Chapter Eleven
God Bless Breen

Farnham entered the dining room with a dozen things to tell Vivi. A brief glance into the pitchy room showed that not only was Vivi notably absent but the candles had gone too. In fact, he could not even tell if she had left the semiprecious maps out. She shouldn't have, for detailed maps of Whistlecreig were hard to come by. He had penciled in several notes of his own on that map beside his father's and uncles' notes, and if his niece was just going to leave them around for anyone to peep at...*well*. First he'd have to find where the niece herself had gone before he could quiz her about her carelessness with his maps.

A peek into the kitchen showed that she was not there, had apparently not had dinner, even. The room still smelled of the morning's bacon with nary a warmer scent to disperse the cloddish smell. Farnham drew his head back into the dining room and squinted at the pale moon-face of the grandfather clock. Eight thirty-ish. No, wait. Half-seven. He rubbed his eyes and glared at the stiff black hands. The last thing he wanted was spectacles.

He took to the hall and then the passages, assuming Vivi had installed herself in his study, a thought at which Farnham felt robust indignation. He didn't mind sharing things but having a woman usurp them was no jovial matter. The door to his study was ajar, and Farnham heard Breen's hale laughter and Vivi's light tones, too low to make out the words. And there was a third voice Farnham could not place. Was it Jimmy? Cheeky fellow if it was. No, no the accent was too refined, too Londonian. Guests in the study? Oh, this was worse than he thought.

Farnham popped and refolded his shirt-collar and straightened the edges of his cardigan. He pushed through the doorway then, because no one seemed to be paying him the slightest heed, announced his presence with a great clearing of the throat. It worked.

Vivi, who had been standing near the window looking not at all in high spirits, sprang forward with a glad cry. "And here is Uncle Farnham now."

A reprimand was on his tongue but, when Vivi hooked her arm through his and drew him forward, the stiff clinging in her gesture silenced him. For some reason she was upset and he thought it quite likely the fault of that young god-like creature in the chair. *His* chair.

He stared at the fellow, unwilling to initiate an acquaintance with a man who could sit in another man's wing-chair with a smile like that upon his face; Farnham felt he knew the depression of dispossessed lords when seeing Americans purchase and dwell in their family castles. As if there weren't years of blood spilled and blood shared connecting a man with his ancestral home!

Before he could concoct some excuse for throwing the fellow from Whistlecreig with a "stand not upon the order of your going but go at once" manner, Vivi tugged him nearer. Nearer, but not so near the man that Farnham could think her *eager* to perform the required introduction. This reluctance on her part somewhat mollified him.

"Uncle Farnham, this is Mr. Michael Maynor."

"A man of alliteration," he remarked drily.

Her fingers pressed into his arm. "Michael, this is my uncle, the great Orville Farnham."

Michael nodded to Farnham but never stood; instead, he sipped tea from one of the heirloom cups and winked at Farnham. "Nice little niece you've got there. Makes a sweet hostess."

"Excuse me, sir. Is there a reason for your presence? Some bond between us of which I was not informed?"

A blink was the only response before Michael's comely features stretched in a grin. "I've heard you were an actor of the dry plays; they said you quoted old William incessantly but I never believed it. He actually quotes Shakespeare, just like that?"

Farnham's spine shivered like a lance. "Pardon me, but that phrase was of my own invention."

Michael laughed and the sound filled the room like the scriptures' clanging cymbal. "Your uncle's not a theatre-man, Viv. He's a comic."

"Excuse me for not finding that funny." Farnham caught the half-pleading, half-acknowledging look Breen threw in his direction. He pursed his lips and willed the evil spirit down, down to the font of annoyance from whence it hailed.

Vivi released his arm and stepped between the man and himself, a bit to the right side, like a mediator. She twined her fingers together and rocked on her toes. Nervous. The girl was nervous.

"Michael knows Jimmy, uncle. He's come to visit Whistlecreig."

Farnham thought his stomach had just been lanced with a pen-knife. "You're staying here, sirrah?"

"In town."

With great effort, Farnham loosened his stiff fingers from a clenched fist and the pain in his gut ebbed. "Ah. And might I ask how you know Miss Langley?"

"Old friends," Michael said, drawing the first word out as if he was viewing several decades of memories through its sound. "I hope you don't mind me dropping by to say hello."

Vivi didn't seem too fond of the man—blond hair and all—but if they were old friends, he would try to behave. Social calls had always been awkward for him; maybe his niece felt the same. If this Maynor fellow had just arrived in town he would probably not have heard of the murder, which was just as well. Farnham was not interested in retelling every detail of the past several days for the benefit of this inquisitive young Apollo. No, Michael Maynor would have heard nothing of it. He would be spared that annoyance.

"I hope the doctor and my niece have not bored you."

"On the contrary." Michael crossed one leg over the other and spread his arms on the wings of the chair in a display of affability. "They've been regaling me with tales of the bloody happenings in this provincial district—if you'll pardon a pun."

Bang. He *had* heard.

Doctor Breen knew the signs of contempt in his most familiar patient as well as he knew the signs of pregnancy in a woman and croup in an infant: Orville Farnham disliked that boy and if an alkaline substance was not applied immediately, there would be pyrotechnics. This Michael Maynor chap needed to be removed from the premises as quickly as possible; Breen knew he had not given his report on the information he'd scraped up from the hotel-keeper and that Farnham had not had a chance to discuss with Vivi the whys and wherefores of her map-studies. Long friendship with the man had taught

Breen that Farnham's patience wore thin under prolonged suspense. The man was a bally ticking time-bomb.

Breen pulled his father's watch from his breast pocket and opened it to check the time. "Good heavens, already forty after eight. Mr. Maynor...have you been to the Lark and Eagle?"

The young man ran a hand through his light hair. "The Lark and...what is it? A pub?"

"Only the best pub in Northamptonshire." Breen watched Vivi watch him. "The owner is a bit of a friend of mine and the brew is always tapped fresh as a baby for me and my crowd. Shall we?" He closed his watch with a fine click and pretended to polish it on his sleeve in a thoughtful manner. Would Mr. Maynor take the clue? He prayed he wasn't one of those tee-totallers who caused such trouble in the world when you wanted to get them out of the way by offering drinks all round.

Michael placed his teacup on the tray and stood. "Don't see why not. Sounds like rather a jolly way to kick off an evening in the country. Do you have a telephone? I'll give Jimmy a ring."

Breen opened his mouth to direct Michael to the hall for that errand, but Farnham shrugged and raised his nose to that angle which indicated intense disdain. Breen winced. He needed to evacuate Michael Maynor before a tempest they'd all regret.

"Of course we have a telephone, Mr. Maynor." The skin around Farnham's eyes crinkled in a smile hideous to look upon, it was so full of effort. "You are quite welcome to use it. I do wonder, though, if it would end up a futile attempt; Ealsey Hollow Farm does *not* own a telephone. Farm folk and all that. But by all means, feel welcome to use our phone."

A look exchanged between them, miffed on Michael's account, innocent on Farnham's. Breen kissed Vivi goodnight and slapped Farnham's shoulder.

"We're off, then. Through this door here, right." Breen pushed Mr. Maynor into the hall and shut the door with triumph. "You remember the way down the hall? It's a bit convoluted, I know, but dear Farnham won't have a passage changed. Yes, just ahead there and into the hall. Where did you put your coat? Ah, yes. On the rack. Usually there's a butler but he's on business. Oh, you've heard? Yes, name's Allen. Good fellow. Very good. Never fear, Mr. Maynor; Jimmy often ends up at the Lark and Eagle. Everyone does. We're sure to find him or someone who knows his whereabouts. Now, lad, tell me more about what you do..."

Vivi could not relax until she heard the ponderous thump of Whistlecreig's massive door and knew for certain that the hellion of a man was gone. Her insides still quaked and she found herself trembling. She had kept her nerves but being affable to a man she despised had plucked all energy from her veins. Her mother had been right: she was not cut out for a Society woman; in polite societies, one must always associate with people one hated without letting on for a moment one felt other than complete delight in the acquaintance. She thought she understood why Farnham took himself away from his theatre on occasion to a place as lonesome as Whistlecreig. Thinking of her uncle drew Vivi's thoughts from biting the blood back into her lips to the chill quiet of the room. She looked up to find Farnham staring at her.

"That man..." he started.

"Is a banged devil."

Blue amusement sprang into his eyes and his shoulders relaxed. "You don't like him either?"

"Could anyone?" Vivi wrapped her arms around herself, still quivering. "No, don't answer that question. At one time I thought I could, but that was before I'd done more than look at him from across a crowded room."

"He does look a fine effigy cut in stone."

"And about as warm-hearted and pliant."

Farnham extended a hand, and Vivi put hers into it, surprised to feel its gentleness.

"I had a small fear you liked the man till I saw how you quaked at the sight of him," he said.

"How many suspects are we allowed?" Vivi asked.

She watched Farnham's eyes flicker and intensify as he caught the scent of this reynard. "Michael Maynor, a murderer. As I said: a man of alliteration. Call a counsel. In the kitchen, mind you. We haven't eaten."

That sounded rather unlike him. "Are you...hungry again?"

An officious hand waved in her face. "Nothing like, child, but you've got about as much spunk as a plucked chicken. Protein: isn't that what they prescribe for this sort of breakdown?"

"I'm not broken down." He'd tell her she needed to be sensible, and she was not woman enough to hear it again without flinging something at his head.

Farnham narrowed his eyes and put two fingers against her throat as if checking her pulse. "No. You're wound up. Same symptoms. Cure? Protein: a good egg or meat or something."

"I don't feel up to meat. Shall I make scones?"

"Fine. Scones, suspects, and a pot of tea." He offered his arm and picked up the candle-tree, lighting their way down the passage and into the hall. "I want to hear what has been fermenting in your brewery. Tell me everything."

"I can, now that Michael is gone."

Farnham cast his eyes heavenward and closed them with a thin smile. "And God bless Breen."

Chapter Twelve
Self-Preservation and All That

Long shadows ran in ribbons away from the candlelight as Farnham moved through the Manor. He was glad Vivi had condescended to take his arm tonight. Not that it mattered so very much, but he was getting rather fond of having a human thing to look after. Sir Toby Belch was all right and as far as hounds go, spectacular, but he wasn't this woman-thing clinging to his arm as if she *needed* him. He noticed that she seemed to perk up a bit when he joked, so he groped about mentally for some witticism he could present. The topic of murder could wait till the scones were in the oven and the tea steeping in the pot—liquid courage, tea.

"Were you able to decipher my chicken-scratch?" he asked. Oh, that hadn't been clever at all. That wasn't even remotely interesting *and* it was related to the murder.

"On the map you mean? Yes. You have good handwriting...for a man."

Should he take offense at that coy tone? No, Vivi cut her eyes at him in a sly, merry way as if waiting for him to puff up like a hoighty cock-robin. They had come to the dining room, so Farnham shook off her arm and set the candle-tree on the table. The flames gleamed in reflection on the glassy wood like the whirring golden beetles one could sometimes find in the back garden in summertime.

"Look," Farnham said before he could stop himself. "Titania has lit her lamps."

He felt the red rush into his cheeks. He ground his jaw. He'd not anticipated how silly it would sound aloud.

Vivi wrenched one candle from its socket and the golden beetle belonging to it moved down the table with her. "Let's make more," she said.

He was far too embarrassed to look at his niece, but he heard the gentle smile in her voice and in his mind could picture how the smile tipped the corner of her mouth in that pleasantly skeptical way. In a few moments, the table-top was inhabited by a dozen floating orbs from a dozen candles dispelling the stony gloom.

"Quite festive," Vivi pronounced. She took two candles into the kitchen and set them on the back of the stove.

Farnham followed.

Vivi opened the stove door and poked about in the coals. "And quite cold. I suppose you are too ancient to have been a boy scout as a child but tell me: are you any good at setting fire to things?"

"Well I'm certainly not yet the palsied eld," he snapped. "Give me some matches and some tinder."

"Where do you keep these witching implements?"

Farnham squeezed past her and rummaged in the cabinet over her head. The tinder box was empty. Beside it was a box of ammunition for his pistol, and a tin of old Darjeeling. He hated Darjeeling. Would that work as tinder? Probably not. Never mind, then. He'd use the old back-stage method. He grabbed a package of stale saltine crackers—he assumed they were stale; he hadn't eaten them for a solid month—and crumbled two in his palm. With Vivi looking on, Farnham dumped the handful of powder into the belly of the woodstove and struck a match. He held the match to the pile of crumbs and watched with childish satisfaction as they kindled and a few fine curls of smoke snaked upward.

Vivi tied an apron around her waist and pulled a bowl onto the table. "Couldn't you have used paper?"

"You didn't like my conjuring?"

"Very clever, uncle-mine, but it's hardly necessary."

"Pageantry is always necessary. Would lighting paper have the same effect? No." He stalked to the other side of the kitchen and flicked a switch, sending a flood of naked, electric light into the room. "Would electricity have the same effect as candles? Never. Always pageantry."

Vivi's eyes were round, disbelieving, astonished. "You have *electricity*? This whole time you've had it and made me go groping round like a chambered mole? It's indecent."

"My dear child, were you in the habit of noticing your surroundings like a proper detective ought, you would have noticed there were light bulbs on the ceiling." Farnham thought perhaps he shouldn't feel quite so pleased with himself. Oh, but he was savouring the tease.

She scooped flour and sugar into a stoneware bowl. "And every night? Going to bed, eating supper, hosting that vile Michael Maynor in your study...none of that needed candles?"

"Were you in the habit of noticing your surroundings like a proper detective ought," he repeated, most definitely enjoying it, "you would have noticed there were light bulbs on the ceiling *only* in the kitchen. You can't have a telephone without electricity, though I don't expect you to have noticed or cared. We had to have at least one room lit up like it was Christmas every day of the year to be able to have a telephone. I prefer candlelight. I told Allen to decide which room he'd like to scalp in so bald a way and he chose his own abode: *le cuisine*."

Farnham watched his monologue take effect.

Vivi rolled her eyes at him. "First you're a detective, then you have a telephone, now electricity. What next? Next you'll be telling me you run a prison in the secret passages beneath Whistlecreig and fill it with all the criminals you catch red-handed."

"That was a neat pun," Farnham said. "Red-handed."

Her face fell, and she cut butter into the flour in her bowl as if it were he under the blades.

"To business?" he asked.

"If it isn't too much of an effort."

The tick of the butter knives slicing the contents of the bowl sounded maudlin in the quiet kitchen. They wanted Allen home, that's what. A third would make things so much more comfortable. The noise, like miniature rapiers, continued and Farnham knew Vivi waited for him to speak. Knowing her, she'd probably want to know where he'd been all afternoon. He wanted to know about the map and about what Breen knew. Bang it. He wished that Michael Maynor wretch hadn't butted in and spoiled their scheming.

But, then, they'd not have their fourth suspect.

"Why do you suspect Michael Maynor?" he asked. "I mean, over Mr. Owens or the possibility of a woman...or... Jimmy."

Vivi's cutting slowed, and she ran her fingers through the buttered crumbs. "He said he knew Jimmy Fields and had been planning this visit for some time."

"Why is that so curious a thing?"

"Jimmy was headed to Crowborough three days ago. Why would he have left town for an undetermined length of time if he expected a reunion with a college friend?"

"Perhaps he knew he would return in two days," Farnham suggested.

"Then why leave at all? Why make a whole story about going off for a wander since his father didn't need his help on the farm so much? It's silly."

"Yes, it is."

Vivi dug in the icebox for some milk and sniffed it. "Just a bit sour. Perfect."

She poured a creamy stream of liquid into her bowl, then mixed it with her hand. The dough clung to her slender fingers in clumps, but she didn't seem to mind. Farnham found himself transfixed by the repetitive motion of her hands as she flipped and mixed the dough. All at once, Vivi tipped the bowl upside down with a clank.

The noise startled him from his reverie. Bang the girl! "Won't you continue?"

"If Jimmy didn't know that Michael Maynor was coming, why is Michael here?" she said. "Why did he make a point of telling us Jimmy had been expecting him? The easy answer is that he just arrived—perhaps for the second time this week— and has not forewarned Jimmy. He did not know that Jimmy had gone out of town, or his story would have been much cleverer. Jimmy doesn't often leave Whistlecreig, so Michael didn't think to confirm that his story about a long-awaited visit would fit."

She smoothed her palm over the dough, thoughtful, then continued: "Why would Michael be here now? He committed the murder and fled town, hoping no one would discover it. His hopes were unfounded, however, and the news hit London today. Obviously, he would like to be on hand to confound the investigation wherever he could. What better time to enter the melee than now? He conveniently has a 'friend' in Jimmy Fields so there is, at least, an alibi for coming here at all. In fact, were I not here, he would have been quite safe. You have no reason for knowing Michael Maynor from a toad in the garden. I have, and I know he is not the kind of man to take a holiday at a farm with some obscure country boy. He has far too high an opinion of himself."

Farnham sucked his bottom lip and turned these things over in his mind. Vivi's reckoning impressed him as being sensible, calm, and definitive. The appearance of this young man in town was an unfortunate accident *if* he happened to be innocent. Farnham was a reasonable man and liked to think of himself as unprejudiced, but the aura of happenstance hung about Michael Maynor's head like a spotlight, pointing the way to his being the guilty party. It seemed probable. Not absolutely final, of course, for the most obvious candidates were sometimes the least guilty. But, without argument, he smelled a rat.

As he did with Phillip Owens.

As he had with Jimmy Fields.

As Dillon had with Genevieve Langley.

As he would with a half-dozen more folk.

The flaw in Michael Maynor's alibi, Farnham mused with a wry smile, was that Genevieve Langley had been in town. As she said, no one would think it an odd story that one of Jimmy's college friends had come visiting; no one ought to have recognized him as a man from higher society.

"Setting Michael's guilt or innocence aside," Farnham said, "Did you find any likely places for the murder to have occurred?" He watched Vivi pat the scone dough into a lumpy circle and punch out fat circles with an empty jam jar.

She arranged the discs on a baking stone and slid them into the oven without speaking. Not that she wasn't going to speak, Farnham thought, but she hadn't quite decided what she was going to say. He liked that about Vivi: so many women rattled on as if words didn't cost something, as if people actually had time to listen to three sentences where one coherent thought would have done the job.

"I think," Vivi said at last, "that the murder could have been committed somewhere north of the Manor. What was the farm?"

"Holly Triad?"

"Yes. We determined that the murder occurred within a short period of time after the train arrived, as Miss Langley did not check into the hotel as expected. The people who found the body found it relatively soon afterward—and we must speak with *them* tomorrow. Assuming it was a man who was the killer—are we certain on that point?"

Farnham narrowed his eyes and followed her train of thought. "Reasonably."

"Right. Well, assuming it was a man, he would not have been able to get very far within our time constraints. My train arrived at three-thirty, more or less. Let us assume Lillian was familiar with the terrain and hurried to her meeting place. Cross-country, how far is it to Whistlecreig?"

Her mind was fascinating. "Not but a mile and a bit."

"So she flits a mile and a half over to the rendezvous point somewhere near Holly Triad. Give her fifteen minutes for that. She arrives breathless and worn out but manages to make the man furious. Presumably the rendezvous was less 'come hither, lover' and more, 'I demand recompense now' which would explain our murderer's humor.

"Perhaps he summoned her and did not let her know what variety of tryst he hoped to keep. She makes him angrier than ever, he kills her. Seeing what he's done, he knows he's too close to civilization to leave the body where it is. Lillian was a tiny thing. He flings her over his back and works his way through the woods behind the farm and begins to come South."

Farnham felt winded with the rapid-fire answers. "Hoping to dispense with the body...?"

"There is a marshy section of land just west of where the body was found," Vivi said. Farnham thought he heard a distinct ring of triumph in her voice. "I assume her killer was headed there when interrupted by the couple who found the body."

"Interrupted. And how would a murderer *not* be seen carting a body like a sack of potatoes across a hillside field?"

"Certainly he would have heard–Dickon Moorhen and Jane Grey, was it?—before they could see him. He deposits the body on the ground in a bit of a hurry–that explains the trampled ground—and hotfoots it up the hill where there is a fringe of brush, if I remember aright."

It was some few moments before Farnham thought it prudent to speak. Vivi's mind raced at a grand clip, and he wanted to be sure she had not overlooked some vital clue. "Tell me again the timing?"

Vivi ticked the count off on her floury fingers: "Fifteen minutes for Lillian to get from the station to the rendezvous point, assuming she was hurrying. I didn't think to tell the inspector this, but our train was held for fifteen minutes at a stop before Whistlecreig; if Miss Langley was to meet with someone at, say, three-forty-five, she would be extremely pressed for time—late, in fact; perhaps she knew the man was easily annoyed."

Farnham strode to the wall near the door where hung Allen's grocery tablet and a pencil on a string. "Fifteen minutes you say?" He scrawled the figure beside Allen's genteelly penciled notes of *"one dozen eggs, brown"* and *"sugar, two pounds."*

"Fifteen for Lillian to arrive at Holly Triad. What would you give him...five minutes to kill her?" Vivi's face turned red. "I mean, let us presume she was a bit late, and he was already in an ill temper. She does or tells him something that sets him off. It mightn't even take that long."

"Five minutes, let us say," Farnham agreed. "What next?"

"Fifteen minutes for carrying the body the half mile between Holly Triad and its final resting place, do you think?" Vivi asked.

"I've never lugged a dead body cross-country," Farnham admitted.

Vivi crossed her arms and eyed him. "Half an hour total. Give him fifteen minutes or so of his own for skulking away while Dickon and Jane find the body....at tops, fifty minutes from our arrival. Only half an hour if you count the passage of time until the body could have been found without the murderer...it quite fits in."

Farnham tallied his marks and dropped the pencil. It flung against the white wall with a small click and because he liked the sound, Farnham did it again but a bit harder this time. The little pendulum made small marks against the wall as the graphite struck. He watched this idly and thought. It was spreading logic thin to accept Vivi's scheme; the police would never agree. But then, the police had their theories about the murder being committed in the field itself. Farnham would not say their idea was impossible any more than he would say Vivi's was ridiculous. Was either correct?

"The silent foot will tell," he said at last.

Vivi turned and opened the oven. A beautiful smell of fresh scones flooded the kitchen and scooted aside every thought of the murder. Farnham's stomach, even, was calmed by the buttery fragrance.

"What silent foot?" Vivi wrapped her apron around her palm and reached into the oven, pulling the hot stone out and setting it on the counter.

Farnham stared at the perfect golden scones and the steam curling in laurels above them. "'The inaudible and noiseless foot of Time,'" he murmured, trancelike. "*Alls Well That Ends Well*, if you must know."

Vivi closed the oven with a backward kick and wiped her palms on the apron. "While on the subject of chronology, what on earth were *you* up to all this time?"

"What?" Farnham broke his stare from the scones and squinted against the electric lights, feeling bewildered somehow.

141

"Oh, where was I? Smoking in my fencing-parlor. Helps calm my nerves, you know."

Why that scornful look on her face? What had she against smoking? Or did she think he ought to have been working? Ahhh, that was more like it. She lifted the golden scones onto a plate, leaving moist, oily rings against the stone where they had been, and shook her head at him in a way half fond, half reproachful.

Farnham broke off the tip of a scone when Vivi wasn't looking and popped it into his mouth. Well, he had his health to look after. Self-preservation and all that.

Chapter Thirteen
All Bloody and Mangled

Morning, in all its lazy cordiality, blinked down on a blue bicycle and its girlish rider and cast a few lazy lances on her trailing shadow. The morning, however, got very little notice from Genevieve Langley. She had other things of which to think and not even the sight of a flock of grackles shooting up from a field like a handful of black paper shavings could pull her very long from deep introspection. From Farnham, she had got the names and addresses of the two people, Dickon Moorhen and Jane Grey, who had found the body. She meant to look them out promptly. Farnham had sent her off with instructions to meet at The Quagmire at noon where they would hold a consultation with Breen and off she'd gone.

Jane Grey and Dickon Moorhen. She tried to picture the two in her mind, picture how it might be to take a walk in the dusk with a lover and to stumble upon a murder freshly committed. The difficulty was to imagine a walk with a lover; bodies seemed easy enough to come by these days.

Steering with one hand as she used to when a girl, Vivi stretched her spine tall and with her gaze raked the flanking fields. There, behind and a bit to the left, was the ridge coming

143

South from Holly Triad; she had traversed this way often enough in the last several days to begin to recognize that it was the same ridge upon which she'd stood, staring at the cold, bruised body of Lillian Bertois in the heartless embrace of a November fog. For a moment, Vivi fancied she could see a form, resting motionless upon the bosom of the hill. She blinked, and it was only a grey, twisted trunk from some long-fallen tree.

Pulling her mind with some effort back to practical musings such as the fact that Jane Grey lived on Fellkirk Street, Vivi was annoyed to realize she would have to ask directions from someone in town. Too bad she had left Farnham's precious maps at home.

"Vivi!"

The shout turned her attention from the fields with a glad thrum. Ahead, Vivi saw Jimmy cycling in her direction. She stopped and waved. Jimmy flung up an arm in greeting, came even with her, and turned around so they rode side by side. Her skirt brushed his pants leg; he jerked an inch to the side.

"Don't want to catch m'lady's hem in my wheels," he said in reply to her somewhat startled look. "You're out nice and early this morning."

"Mightn't I say the same about you?"

"I was on my way up to the Manor on an errand," said he.

"Oh? For my uncle?"

"For his niece."

"Aren't we gallant this morning?"

He winked. "Would you, my dear Miss Langley, like to spend the evening at a dance?"

She tossed her head, laughing too. "Do you cut the caper, Mr. Fields?"

His grin jerked. "I'm not a bad foot."

"Well, that's a relief. I'm fond of my own feet and don't like them trod upon. Are we to waltz or is it to be American jazz which, I own, I am fond of? In either case, I'm sure I don't have anything suitable to wear; I didn't come to Northamptonshire expecting to attend parties."

"Actually, a grass skirt would be more appropriate if you have one." Jimmy's eyes snapped with that roguishness born of pleasant banter. "It's Fiji cannibal dancing. Learned it from an islander himself after narrowly missing having my scalp done in with his skinning knife."

His laugh was infectious and simple, oddly suiting him.

Vivi pedaled a bit faster, loving the fingers of wind that stroked her cheeks with the motion and lifted her hair recklessly. "And where do you keep your islander friend who is to teach us the dances?"

"In a cell down Harbinger alley. Oh, never fear—I give him plenty of coconuts and a raw beefsteak every night." He winked. "I'm fooling. We're having a céilidh."

"A...a cay-lee?" Vivi faltered over the odd-sounding word.

"An Irish tradition." Jimmy rolled his "r's" and grinned. "And a grand lot of fun. There's a band playing and you reel the night away."

"Like the country dances they used to have at Brighton in the summers."

Jimmy tossed his head. "A bit—only much *much* jumpier and a complete batch more fun. Say you'll come!"

With all that was in her, Vivi wanted to agree, but she was unsure on what footing she stood with her schedule while in Farnham's house, not to mention working on the mystery. He mightn't enjoy her making plans for a pleasure-evening; she doubted he ever did so himself.

"There's lots of people at the dances—pretty near everyone in town who isn't a stiff bore or too ancient to kick up their heels," Jimmy pleaded.

145

Laughter bubbled through Vivi's breast. "Are you *trying* to look like a lost puppy? All right; I'll join you."

Farnham might complain, but Vivi had an idea he'd come round when she explained it was a prime research opportunity —who knew what clues she and Jimmy might stumble across? People were always too ready to gossip at social functions, as she knew from experience. And on that thought: "Will your friend, Michael, be there?"

Jimmy pedaled a few rotations. "Michael?"

"Yes, Michael Maynor. I mean, naturally I assumed he'd join us, being your chum."

"Oh, yes, *that* Michael—we called him Norrie at school. I'm sure he'll be there in good will. Always a one for pretty ladies, Michael Maynor."

"Are there many beauties in Whistlecreig?" Vivi blushed and feared Jimmy might think she fished for a compliment.

Fishing or not, Jimmy gave her a lop-sided grin. "None I like so well as you, m'lady."

"I am only glad there are other women! I'd begun to fear I was the only female in the land."

A good fifteen minute's cycling had pushed them fully into town and Vivi pulled off beside a bed planted in rose bushes. Russet branches clawed at the grey fence dividing the road from the garden of the house on the other side. In the summertime, it would be lovely. Today, it looked sullen and pale like a snappish old woman.

"Do you know Jane Grey?" Vivi asked, eyes trained on the wavings sticks, thin and wizened as the arms of any octogenarian.

"Janie? Aye, she's a sweet girl—engaged to marry my old chum, Dickon Moorhen. Her sister's a right pretty lass, too."

"Yes, Farnham has told me. 'Thus runs everyone in the world but I, and I am sunburnt. I must sit in a corner and cry heigh-ho for a husband'."

Jimmy snorted. "Come, now. It's not as bad as all that."

"No," Vivi agreed amiably. "It's not. I am quoting Shakespeare—Farnham's influence, I'm afraid."

"Ahhh, his old game. Used to stump me as a lad. You've got a right tough man for an uncle, Vivi."

She reached out and broke a twig off the rose bush as if by that motion she could break off the overwhelming sense of frustration. Farnham's caprice staggered her, but for all that, she'd meant what she'd said to him last night: he was sweet, somehow. She snapped the twig into three pieces and refocused. "I know. I know he's tough as Northampton-made boots, but he's also good."

"Good is dandy but he's too rough for you. They don't know how to handle women up Manor-way."

Vivi looked into his eyes and saw he spoke what he felt; she admired him for it. Here, at least, was one man who spoke outright instead of saying anything but what he meant.

"But...I hope I am man enough to admit that Mr. Farnham has never been anything but good to my father and fair to all his tenants," said Jimmy.

She shrugged and carefully broke off their gaze. It was too much to see how he tried to win her approval. "I don't yet understand," she said in a very light tone. "Does Farnham actually own the land? Everyone behaves as if he's their feudal lord."

This statement elicited a chuckle from her companion. "Old ways die long deaths. I suppose Farnham is no one's real landlord, but he is a Farnham and they've headed the land from time out of mind. Folk still respect him for his bloodline and breeding."

"I'd rather they respect him for his decency." Vivi spoke in a low voice, wishing not to cross purposes with the one person in the whole of England who made her feel wanted, but feeling the need to defend Whistlecreig's heir.

"Pouting? Have I set you off your tea, Vivi?" Jimmy's smile cracked out white as white and he cast himself to his knees among the roses. "Farnham's an odd boy, but you won't hear me criticize his mettle. Give me a second chance, please Queen Genevieve!"

"Rise, knave." She put out her hand and drew him to his feet, laughing. "I didn't expect to lecture you."

"At your service, madam." Jimmy tipped his cap. "Perhaps you ought to go into business as a young ladies' finishing school marm. Now, Viv, don't get cross. Where were you off to? I can be your chivalrous escort before meeting Michael at the Lark & Eagle."

"I was headed to Jane's house right now." Vivi took the slip of thin paper from her breast pocket and handed it to Jimmy. "Do you know where Fellkirk Street may be found?"

"'Course I do. What do you want with Janie? Are you off to complain of your bachelor's existence up at the manor to a sympathetic female ear?"

"Hardly." Vivi pulled her bike upright and mounted it. "Unofficial detective work."

"Farnham's really got you working the case?" Jimmy's eyes laughed at her. "You constantly surprise me."

"I'm glad I can't be accused of being one-dimensional."

"Hardly. Might I watch? I want to see a lady Poirot; it's quite a novelty."

Vivi hung back as Jimmy took the lead. Again, Farnham's disapproving face rose in her mind and she knew just what he'd think of bringing company along for an official investigation. It would never do, however, to accept Jimmy's help in finding Janie Grey's home and then dismiss him at the door. Vivi could think of no reason why she shouldn't have company. After all, Farnham let Dr. Breen toddle after him up and down the county as if he wasn't capable of traveling a block without his personal physician.

They biked down Main Street, turned off on a side street, and made a right one block before The Quagmire; Dr. Breen's home looked different in sunlight; a bit more run-down but quite as cheery with a few stubborn red roses hanging to the stone walls and ringing like bells in the rough breeze. The Quagmire and its roses passed out of sight, and in a moment Jimmy had slung himself off his bike at a small brown house. Vivi followed his example and leaned her bike against a stone half-wall. Her breath snagged between her teeth as her knuckles scraped against the pitted stones.

"Caught your fingers on the rocks?" Jimmy took her hand and turned it to the light. "No blood."

"Which is really just as well," she said. "I've had enough arterial crimson to last me an eon, thank you."

Jimmy narrowed his eyes and smiled down on her. Her cheeks pinked under the fondness of that look.

"Is this the place?" she asked quickly.

The fondness stepped out for a walk and Jimmy was himself again. "Janie Grey's residence, madam. Have any further orders?"

"None. You may watch if you'd like. It's bound to be quite dull. I'm only inquiring as to what she saw from the road the night of the murder; likely she'll have told the police anything worth telling already, but one can always hope they've overlooked something."

It was a wry smile Jimmy next served her. "Dickon already complained to me over his pint last night. Said the police worried his Jane to a thread over it. Said she'd far rather have forgotten it entire than have to relive it a dozen times over."

Vivi felt a twinge of womanly guilt over bringing up a sore subject in conversation with a lady she'd never met. Every feminine sensibility rebelled, but she had committed to Farnham and she would not be thought silly. "*Then, brethren,*" she thought, quoting Spurgeon to herself, "*be not so polite.*"

149

Together, the two approached the low doorway. A tortoise-shell cat beside a red geranium regarded them from a window and a thrush hopped into the bare, faded garden. Jimmy rapped on the blue-painted door, then stepped back with his hands in his pockets so Vivi had command of the situation. In a moment, the door fell in, revealing a neat young lady with brown hair combed into a bun at the nape of her neck.

"Hello?" Brown eyes full of polite confusion studied Vivi's face.

"Hello. Please don't try to remember me, for we've never met," Vivi said. She put out a hand. "My name is Genevieve Langley. I'm Mr. Orville Farnham's niece."

"Oh, aye." Jane's eyes flitted over Vivi's shoulder to Jimmy. Her rigidity softened. "Well, come in, won't you? I wasn't expecting company, else the house should be a fair bit tidier. Cilla's gone out for a walk and left me with the tidying to do."

They were led into a combined living and dining room containing a red couch faded to pink and several old high-back chairs rather too grand for the small room. Sunlight danced on blue and white striped paper and the tortoise-shell cat swiveled her head and blinked greeting.

Vivi walked over to the cat and ran her hand down its back. The creature arched her spine and began a kettle-thrum purr. "What is her name?" Perhaps speaking of the cat would relax Jane.

"Mattie."

"She's a rare beauty." Vivi let the cat rub its cheeks on her fingertips and scratched under its chin. "I always ended up with orange tabbies as a child, but I always wished for a great, tawny Siamese; my mother was shocked and told me I was outlandish. She didn't like cats with blue eyes." Vivi laughed at the recollection, and the cat jumped to the floor, pointedly ignoring Jimmy's presence.

"Miss Langley," Jane's voice was quiet and measured as she spoke. "I might sound like a lummox, but I must ask: did you come to have a chat about Mattie or is there another purpose?"

"A woman who speaks what she thinks," Vivi said with a smile. "I like that. Well, the truth is, my uncle Farnham is working on the...murder." She winced mentally but managed to keep the smile, even as Jane stiffened.

"Mr. Farnham is working with the police?"

"No, Jane. He's not."

"Then why..."

"He has neglected to explain in full why he thinks it his duty to investigate these things. They are men; do they ever offer satisfying explanation for their motives?"

"Did he send you?" Jane asked. "Because I've already talked with the police, and I told them it weren't Dickon and me and it *weren't* Cilla."

Vivi found herself unprepared to meet this. "You mean to say they suspect you and your fiancée in the murder?"

Tears sprang into Jane's eyes, and she crossed her arms. She pinched her bottom lip between her teeth. "I...I don't know. I don't know if they suspect me and Dickon ..." Jane shook her head fiercely and swallowed hard, an obvious effort to keep from breaking down in front of company.

"Do you *think* they suspect you?"

"They...*Lord* in Heaven, save us—It's untrue."

"Do they suspect Cilla?" Jimmy's masculine tone smoothed like chocolate over Jane's pain.

She nodded, tears blotting out the wariness in her eyes, and dabbed at them with the back of her tan hand. "Miss Langley," Jane tried to appear cheerful and polite, "You won't know this, having never met my sister, but she's not quite without...feelings."

Without feelings? This made no sense in the context in which she thought they were working.

"Without feelings for...for gentlemen. More than one. She's a fair bit gadabout but she's got a heart of gold for a'that and I *know* it wasn't her."

"I'm afraid I don't..." Vivi said. "I mean, it was a woman who died, not a gentleman."

"I think what Jane means," Jimmy said, his eyes snatching from one to the other as he spoke, "is that the police reason that Cilla's motive would be—and correct me if I'm wrong, Janie-luv—that the actress had come to Whistlecreig to steal the affections of a man Cilla loved? And Cilla killed her for it?"

"And who's the man Cilla loves? Haven't the police asked him? I should think that a more likely place to begin," Vivi protested. "Who is he?"

"Which one?" Jane whispered. "There are...many."

"But surely the police could hardly expect—well of all the —" Vivi paused and put her hand on Jane's arm, wanting to comfort her. "I have some notion of Chief McMulligan's methods, darling. He hasn't a notion how to speak to women. Besides—I have never met a woman strong enough to kill and carry the body some distance, as we believe the killer to have done."

"You've never met Cilla." If Jane could have looked more miserable than before, she did so now. "She's a farm-lass. Stronger'n many men about town. Oh, she's *capable*...but it was not her."

"I believe you," Jimmy said. "I mean, if it's any comfort. And Miss Langley here does too."

"But the police won't because...because Cilla won't tell 'em *where* she was."

There was nothing to be said or done in the horror of the accusation that a woman had slain another—and not just any woman, the sister of this gentle girl—so Vivi did the next best thing and nodded agreement.

Jane sniffed and, though tears still stood in her eyes, she presented to Vivi a trembling smile. "I'm sorry to go to a puddle like this. It's just...it is such a *shock*." The tears almost began again, but Jimmy pressed a handkerchief into Jane's hand and she sucked her breath between her teeth. "Dickon an' me were going for a walk. I work as a teacher, Miss Langley, so there's not much time for courtin' between classes in the daytime and grading papers at night, even when Cilla helps out. Dickon swung by my place before going for his pint and asked if I'd like to take a walk. It wasn't a nice night, but a girl doesn't think of silliness like that when her man asks her sweetly, you know."

Vivi pressed her hand. "Of course not."

"We thought we'd just take about for an hour or so together before gettin' back for tea and all. Mr. Inspector Dillon quizzed me right good on that one. He said no one in their right minds'ud go for a walk on a night like that."

"Well, Mr. Inspector Dillon has likely never found himself in the good graces of any woman. He's not quite an authority on the subject, I'd expect."

Jimmy chortled behind her, causing Vivi to remember she had better take care in her discussion of the male race. "Pray, continue, Miss Grey."

"Dickon an' me just took a wander down the road up toward the Manor; it's our favorite walk, bein' so gentle and firm. We'd got about a mile up the road and the fog was thickening. I told Dickon maybe we'd better turn back toward town, seein' as it was dark by now and hard enough for motorists to see in the fog without throwin' people on the road in their way. Dickon laughed at me—he's a great one for laughin', my Dickon." Jane's lips quivered into a smile and her brown eyes gained composure.

"At any rate, just as I said that, he put his arm round my waist and we turned toward the field. A breeze was springing up and shreddin' the mist like it does now and then I saw a dark shape on the hillside."

"Excuse me," Vivi interrupted, "but why would that have aroused suspicion? Couldn't it have been a fallen tree or rocks or something?"

Jane tucked her chin humbly, but her words were firm: "Do you believe in women's intuition, Miss Langley?"

"I do."

"I felt something in that moment like a black hand down my neck. 'Dickon,' I said, 'what do you reckon that is?' Lovers memorize every little thing about each other, you know. And that being mine and Dickon's favorite walk, I know its face as well as I know my Dickon's. It was all wrong. Dickon called me a silly goose and said it was nothing, but I knew. He told me we'd best head back to town like I'd been badgerin' him for. I think I made him cross," Jane said, a spark of mischief kindling in her eyes, "but I told him I wouldn't leave till he'd gone for me up that hill to make sure no one was hurt. Sometimes people take a ramble through the fields this time of year and I thought it'd be easier than anything to fall and twist your ankle in a fox-hole on a night like that."

"I agree," Vivi said. "It was the very devil's night."

"Well, Dickon scrambled up the hill and the fog soon closed up behind him, but I heard him shout." Her voice trembled again and she cleared her throat before continuing. "He shouted my name like he'd seen something terrible, then he comes flying onto the road all wild-eyed and tells me we've got to run for th'police. It was a body, he said. A body all bloody and mangled."

Chapter Fourteen
Bull-Dog

"The Recreational Center, mind you," Jimmy called over his shoulder as he biked off. "Seven-thirty and don't be late, or Michael and I will forcibly drag you out of that racket of a mansion."

"I'll be there," Vivi called back. She waved until Jimmy turned down a street and out of sight. Jane Grey's testimony had been helpful in one manner: Vivi now knew that the police had taken Jane's sister as the lead suspect in the murder. *Why* the police would suspect her was quite another thing. Many women flirted—weren't some of Vivi's closest friends among the set?—and yet no one suspected them of murder. It seemed a long shot—a very long shot.

But then, the police had likely not heard of Michael Maynor in the way *she* had. They would know soon enough. A man like Maynor didn't wander about town without attracting attention for his liberality at cards if not for the way he commanded the female eye.

Jimmy had not let on that Michael's visit was a surprise, and Vivi had not felt it the proper time to inquire about it. Why was Michael here and why was Jimmy covering for him? This

155

was a puzzle whose answer Vivi was not keen to ponder. Why must the world always play her false?

She pulled a watch from her waist pocket and checked the time. Still too early to meet at the Quagmire. Why, she had as much as an hour before she'd even be politely early. She could return to Whistlecreig Manor, but that seemed useless and could only end in Farnham saying something that might annoy her.

There was work to be done in this case if she was man enough to do it.

She walked her bike away from Fellkirk Street and turned back to town. A stubborn spirit she barely recognized had crept into her heart since coming to Whistlecreig. It led her to do unconscionable things like attend murder scenes and explore the old Rowan Walk alone and carry secrets about in broad daylight—everything her mother and other Society women would have considered fast and heady. And yet Vivi knew she was still as much a lady as ever. At least, she *had* been up till now.

Willing herself to be sensible and forego the plan, Vivi turned the opposite direction into town and made for the hotel. She gained the porch and rested her bike against the posts where she and Sir Toby had waited for Farnham the day before. Vivi unpinned her hat and fluffed her hair, then returned the hat and smoothed the wrinkles from her clothes.

It was madness, this plot unformed, yet solid in purpose, fomenting in her mind. Where there was a murderer, there was a weapon and it seemed to Vivi that the course of action was to look in the prospective murderer's lair for that weapon.

She was a fool.

But fools often succeed where wise men flinch to enter.

Vivi opened the gilt and glass doors of the hotel. The action jangled both a bell and her nerves, but Vivi was not to be cowed by the several pairs of eyes that looked her down curiously as she entered. The man behind the desk with his shirtsleeves rolled up and the buttons of his vest undone had to be the proprietor, Mr. Burnes.

"Mr. Burnes?"

One eyebrow rose, and he fished for a cigarette from a box tucked in the garter around his sleeve. "Aye? Summat you need, miss?"

"Yes, in fact. My name is Genevieve Langley and—"

"Old Farnham's niece? Did he send you here to blather 'bout that murther thing, because if he did I fink the police have the main of it already figured out wiffout old Farnham's messing about."

Vivi blinked with all the innocence she could muster. "I am Mr. Farnham's niece, but I can't imagine what you reference. A murder? How horrible."

"Hadn't you heard, miss? Young lady 'bout your age had her head craunched in. An actress, she were. Pretty too."

His intonation suggested it a sorry thing that the actress had died instead of Vivi if it meant denying mankind a beauty, but she was not about to let herself take offense at an ignorant man such as this. She leaned her chin in the palm of her hand and tapped the tip of her shoe against the floor. Must it always be so hard to appear entirely natural and at ease? She wished the men seated at the back of the room might stop staring, but Time fled in his cinquepace and it was now long since the silence had become awkward. Must she declare her purpose to the entirety of Great Britain?

"Terrible thing, murther," Mr. Burnes said as a variation.

"Murders are wretched." She slid her palms along the counter. "I can't imagine why my uncle would bother me with it—*I* have come on no such errand. I'm here to visit a friend, actually."

"A friend, miss?"

"His name is Michael Maynor; he enjoyed your hospitality last night."

Mr. Burnes' eyes narrowed, and his wiped a grin off his face with the back of his hand. "Awww, you're friends with *him*? I can see how a gel like you'd be wantin' to see that gallus. He's your sweetie, is he?"

Vivi drew a breath through a clenched smile and felt the weight of her secret. "Certainly not. We're only good friends."

Mr. Burnes chuckled. "Shall I call him down?"

"Ah, no." Vivi took the key from Mr. Burnes's outstretched hands and tossed it with a wink. "I'll just go up."

A chorus of laughter followed this pronouncement, and Vivi's cheeks burned. So there was a certain amount of scandal associated with young women mounting the staircase to young men's rooms, but she would *not* have her conversation with Michael Maynor overheard by a band of country rooks who might or might not like a juicy dip into the world of crime solving. All the better if he was not at home, but that seemed quite unlikely; the best thing for which Vivi hoped was to catch sight of the murder weapon if Michael had been stupid enough to leave it about to catch the fresh air.

She followed carefully-penned signs glued over peeling wall-paper; followed them up a tobacco-stained flight of stairs and into a hallway. The carpet runner was bare in most places, garishly bright beneath the hall tables. Dim electric lamps clung here and there to the yellowed walls. The key given to her by Mr. Burnes possessed a paper tag denoting Room 117 as Michael's.

Vivi breathed a prayer and knocked on the door signified, hoping Michael would be out and she would be absolved from having to beard this lion in his den.

The knob turned, and every hair stood up along Vivi's arms as the door fell in a crack. Michael's face appeared some inches above her head. For once in his life, he didn't appear to have anything to say. Employing all her charm, Vivi smiled up at him.

"I've come for a visit, Michael," she said.

His fine mouth twitched into a catty smile and he held the door open valiantly. It was not until Vivi had crossed the threshold and entered the room that she realized he was in a state of some undress, wearing only slacks and a thin cotton shirt. She had obviously interrupted him in his preparations for meeting Jimmy at the pub. Michael shoved the door with one brawny arm, put his hands in his pockets and lounged after her into the room.

Vivi's breath snagged over her tongue, and her cheeks felt unpleasantly hot. She had never seen Michael in anything less formal than a dinner-jacket, and it frightened her. It had not struck her then how very muscular he must be to fill such a figure; how easy might it be for a man of Michael's build to destroy a woman—any woman—If he wanted to? She did not feel faint from admiration. It was brook-brown terror that rushed upward. He was a perfect Titan.

She was glad he had his hands in his pockets, for then she didn't have to see his strong, supple fingers—fingers that could close with ease on a woman's throat and extinguish the life from it. But would he? Michael Maynor was a rake, but was he a murderer? It struck Vivi as ironic that she'd put herself in a position to voluntarily find out.

"I can't imagine you've come just to bask in my fabulous presence." Michael dropped with the sultry heaviness of a panther onto the arm of the one chair in the room, leaving Vivi standing. Not that she minded—his head was now level with her own and he seemed less threatening seated.

"You're right, Michael, I haven't." She smiled again, spread her hands and shrugged. "I want to know why you came to Whistlecreig."

"To visit Jimmy."

"Untrue."

Michael narrowed his eyes at her, and she saw the muscles in his arms tighten. A flutter of nerves passed through her hands. She clasped her arms behind her back and made fists to still the panic.

"I don't know what you have against me, Miss Langley."

"Have I anything?"

"Well, you so plainly hate me and I've done nothing." He almost pouted in tone, and blinked lazy eyes at her.

"I'm wont to speak plain and to the purpose, Michael."

"I know you from days of yore, my dear Vivi. You've always been a bluestocking."

"That's hardly complimentary."

"Just following the lady's lead."

"Michael, I hope you realize you have come to town at a very unfortunate moment in its history."

Michael lit a cigarette and drew deeply of it, grinning. "You mean this murder. Are you still ruffled over that, biddy?"

"Wouldn't most people be?"

"You think I've got something to do with it," Michael said. This idea seemed to have no effect on him. He chuckled and winked at her. "By Gosh, woman, I like you in a topping rage."

Vivi released her clenched fists. "Really, Michael, if you're going to flirt, you ought to try to come up with a dazzler that *hasn't* been used since antiquity."

He pushed off the chair in one swift movement and advanced on her. "Something original?" Rough fingers swept through her hair, tangling and tugging it till Michael had brought her chin low. He stooped and put his mouth to her ear. "What can I say to you that you haven't heard before? That you're beautiful? You know you aren't. That you're intelligent? It's God-true. That I'd marry you if you'd ever given me half a chance?"

Vivi bent her head, willing him to release her hair from his fingers. The tension in his fingers eased, but he continued running them through her hair, his voice thoughtful now:

"I know you don't like me, Vivi, but we could have made shift of it, you and I."

"Not you," she murmured.

"Why not?"

"You chase after everything that wears a skirt, Michael. Hardly an ideal husband."

"You wouldn't have minded. I could have rescued you from becoming an old maid and you..." he let go of her hair all at once and forced her chin up with two strong fingers, "you would have kept me afloat with your inheritance, saving us both from Society bores who *will* gossip."

Vivi breathed through her nose and looked deep into Michael's eyes, hating him. He had proposed marriage once and she had refused, suffering her family's annoyance. The marriage would have been a social salvation, she knew, but it would also be a condemnation, and in the end the thought of living as the pageantry bride to a man like Maynor out-horrored the idea of celibacy. The old humiliation still stung, however, and Vivi hated Michael more intensely now than she ever had before.

She lifted her chin up and away from Michael's fingers and scorned him silently.

His lips moved as if to speak, then warmed into a statue's smile. "I suppose you didn't come to speak about *us* either."

"No," she said flatly. "We've exhausted that topic."

He stalked away from her and returned to his seat, arms crossed over his chest. Vivi closed her eyes to steady herself against the riot of thoughts as to why she had been stupid enough to enter the same room with him. The murder weapon, of course. *Idiot*, to think she'd find it.

"Will you answer three questions?" Vivi searched the room keenly, but it contained nothing on a cursory glance but a washstand, a bed, and a chair.

"Only three? Why not?"

"Answer them honestly or not at all."

Michael dropped his jaw and rubbed it, casting his eyes up at her in reluctant flirtation. "All right, Madam Barrister."

"Do you know Jimmy Fields truly, or are you making that up?"

"I know him truly."

"Did you know Lillian Bertois?"

He rubbed his jaw again. "The actress?"

"Did you know her, Michael?"

Their glances clashed, and Vivi took custody of Michael's gaze, silently commanding him not to look away. A pulse of several breaths shuddered between them, ghastly, livid, terrifying. Michael rolled his shoulders in giant, powerful undulations that somehow reminded her of a wild horse preparing to stampede. He tugged his chin one direction and popped his neck, then pushed it back in the other direction with a small crack.

Then his gaze opened, and he nodded. "I knew Lillian."

Startled by this admission, Vivi lowered her eyes and studied a coffee stain on the carpet. She had one question left. She had expected Michael to deny all association with the actress. His answer took her off balance like a physical blow, and she felt herself incapable of logical thought for a moment or two. So many questions and she could only pick one. How and why did he know Lillian? How well did he know her? Was she the reason he'd come to Whistlecreig? What would he think of Vivi's secret?

But the same stubbornness that had led her into this squalid room, alone with a man she did not trust, stiffened against the challenge. There was really only one question to which she sought an answer.

"Did you kill her?" Her clipped tone fell politely on the ear.

Laughter, low and disbelieving, rumbled from Michael's chest. "Are other women such Jezebels as you? Damn, Genevieve Langley. Why have I always found you irresistable?"

"I'll thank you not to curse."

Michael sprang up and shoved Vivi against the wall, leaning down into her face and pressing her against the wallpaper as if he would pin her there forever. Intensity twisted his features and when he spoke, his face was to Vivi that of a rabid creature.

"You have gone too far if you accuse me of murder, Miss Langley." He whispered the last words close to her ear and when he drew back, his eyes were too bright. "You come to my room without provocation. You insult me. I agree to answer three questions, and you accuse me of murder. And what do I get from this, O purity? What gift will you lay at my feet for my cooperation?"

"Nothing."

"Nothing?" he hissed, grabbing her face between shaking hands and pressing her head harder against the wall.

Vivi slipped her hand into her pocket and brought it out again with the utmost care, her secret weighing heavy in hand. "Release me now, Michael."

"Why? You aren't terribly persuasive."

"No, I'm not. But I have a bull-dog." She pressed the barrel of her secret in the center of his broad chest and smiled.

He froze and stared at the snub-nosed pistol she held against his torso, spat a curse. "Where did you get that?"

"Release me."

"You don't know how to shoot."

"No? I hardly think it matters at point blank range."

Their gazes collided again, but this time Vivi felt no fear. She had helped her cousins clean their pistols numerous times and knew that the gun she had found in Farnham's map box was quite intact—had loaded it herself, in fact, with ammunition she'd found hidden in a kitchen cabinet.

She brushed hair away from her face, impatient of a sudden. "Did you kill Lillian Bertois? No, I'm tired of being pressed against the wall like a butterfly on cardboard. *There* you are. Thank you."

Michael stepped backward, away from Vivi's pistol. She kept the barrel trained on him and felt confident he would make no more trouble.

She smiled again. "I could go crying to Farnham and Breen about this and they'll make your life absolute hell. But I won't if you just tell me it was you. The *police* will have the pleasure of consigning you to the devil."

"You little..." Michael growled and stepped forward.

"No, stay there. Thank you. I prefer to admire you from a distance if it's all the same."

Michael slung off toward the window and jammed his hands into his pockets. "I do so hate to satisfy you," he said.

Was it going to be this easy? Vivi swallowed and followed his pacing with her gun. She was tired of this interview and quite ready to be in the clean air of the outdoors. Farnham and Breen would expect her soon, and she had no intention of confessing her errand to them. This was no great detective artistry, she was aware, but she was no great detective. She was very simply a tired woman with a gun in hand and a murderer in her presence. Michael had slipped up and showed he was capable of great violence and possessed a passionate, cock-trigger temper. If she could get him to confess, she would have

—

She saw him make a swift move in her direction. "*Don't* move a step closer. You think to disarm me?"

His eyes shone venom at her. "I don't think to do any such thing, Genevieve Langley. You misunderstand me woefully. About us—about the actress. Everything. I did not kill her. I had nothing to do with it."

He placed a hand on her back. Vivi flinched from him, but he shook his head and drew her toward the door.

"I've no desire to *hurt* you, Miss Langley. That isn't my way. You don't see *me* pulling guns on people." He jerked open the door and made a bow. The hall light gleamed dull on his arms and cast grave shadows in the hollows of his cheeks as he looked up at her. The shadows fled when he straightened. "Take care with that thing." He gestured to her pistol as he closed the door. "One of these days *you* might become a murderer."

The door closed, and Vivi was alone in the dank hall again. She stared at the stubby bull-dog in her hand for a moment, shocked at her own courage. Then, with a pallid smile, she pocketed the weapon and turned down the hall toward the staircase. She'd defended herself with a loaded gun. Wouldn't Farnham be outraged?

"Miss Langley?"

Dash her stupidity. Phillip Owens, scarred and quiet yet, mounted the staircase with an expression of barely-concealed surprise.

"Mr. Owens!"

"Got a message for me from your uncle?" the agent asked.

"No message." Unable to think of any good excuse for being in the dim hallway of a strange hotel, Vivi went ahead with her confession: "I was visiting a friend, actually."

Rather than passing, Mr. Owens paused before her and chuckled. "Gosh girl, you sure do get around."

"Yes. Well, I'm afraid I must continue to 'get around' as you so eloquently put it, for I'm already late for another meeting."

That scar. She drew her eyes from it, but they descended again and yet again until she felt peculiarly drowned in the guilty mark. "If you'd excuse me."

"Of course." The agent stepped to the right and let her pass, but his words a moment later caught on her ear like a cuff. "You tell your uncle to keep me updated. I want to know what anyone hears or thinks or knows. Fool police can't solve anything."

Angst like stones weighed Vivi's feet as she descended the stairs, for Mr. Owens had spoken his parting glass in a loud tone terribly easy for anyone in the hotel to hear. Not only had she not found the murder weapon, but she'd alerted one suspect to the other's presence. Oh, that she'd left well enough alone!

Chapter Fifteen
Council at The Quagmire

A bluff of filtered sunlight accompanied his niece as she slipped into The Quagmire. Farnham looked her over and offered a mildly observant sniff as substitute for the greeting he was loathe to make. Genevieve Langley, paragon of all things mannerly, was late.

"Such a gorgeous morning for a ride." Vivi's smile was bright, hurried. "Weather so obliging. Barely needed my tweeds at all, which is nice because in London I'm always tweeding and one does get tired of looking like a graham biscuit. And—what is more to the point, gentlemen—I'm convinced that Cilla Grey is as innocent as I." Vivi, pausing only to silently inquire where to put her coat, continued: "It isn't Dickon and Jane the police are after. I left my bike in the garden, I hope you don't mind. It's Cilla, Jane's sister. The police are ridiculous."

"*You* seem to be vying for that honor," Farnham mumbled. From the moment his niece had stepped in and shed that brown coat, Farnham had sensed she was false. How, he wasn't sure, but there was a reason for the bright red in her face and the way she chattered along like a hiccuping blackbird in a manner ripe for plucking nerves.

Dr. Sir Lancelot Breen conducted Vivi to a seat on the battered red couch. "It is a pleasant day for cycling, isn't it? And I agree entirely that Cilla is a dear girl, albeit a confirmed flirt. Had an awful time with her lungs as a teenager. Got to know her family quite well."

Farnham greeted his niece dully from under half-mast lids. "You're late. You tread upon my patience."

Breen took up a native pose near the hearth and smoked a haze of exasperation in Farnham's direction—a humor decidedly uncalled-for in the latter's opinion. What did Breen know about the matter? His niece was late and his patience veritable cheesecloth. Next Breen'd be saying Vivi ought to be given a royal treatment for having arrived at all. Ridiculous man.

Vivi seemed as unconcerned as a crocodile sunning himself on the River Nile. "I thought you said I was to come at noon."

"It's twelve-fifteen, madam," he snapped. None of this Cleopatra in his presence, *s'il vous plaît*.

"Oh dear. A whole fifteen minutes. Have I kept your tea steeping too long?" Vivi was not at *all* penitent. "What is it they say? 'The British like their tea stiff enough to trot a mouse on, the Irish like it stiff enough to trot a cat on, and the Australians boil it all day long till it's stiff enough to race horses on?'

"Have I made you Australian tea, dear uncle? What a pity! They say it affects the accent first. You begin to have a twang." She drew the word out wallaby-wise and gestured with her little hand.

The tea *would* taste absurd by now and it was all her fault. He had no interested in drinking penal-colony brew or losing his manicured accent. *Women.*

The doctor rubbed his palms together from where he crouched near the fire which, incidentally, was stuck in a most dubious stage of infancy.

"Shall we officially begin?" he said. "Mrs. Froggle promised to send up a tray with sandwiches presently so there's no need to stand upon ceremony."

Farnham jutted his chin at Vivi, too lazy and peeved to move further. "Sit down, won't you? I expect you'll have much to tell us about how you spent a perfectly ripping morning with Jimmy Fields. That being, of course, the most likely reason you are so unconscionably unaware of the clock."

The color mounted in her cheeks, and Farnham was gratified. There, at the very least, was a bit of the truth.

"Don't give me that knowing look, uncle. I met Jimmy on the road and he offered to show me Jane Grey's house."

"You mean you let him know what you were about?" His stomach took offense at the news, crossed its proverbial arms, and churned.

Vivi tossed her head in a gesture singularly defiant for her. "Someone was going to have to tell me how to get to Fellkirck Street."

He bristled badger-like at this blatant contradiction of his personal methods and all modes of common sense. "I hope you realize he is still a suspect. I hope you aren't one of those readers of mysteries who forgets to suspect a person because of their superfluous chutzpah."

Vivi smiled a queer little smile as boxed up and secret as a jewel-casket. "I won't quarrel with you about Jimmy."

"Truly, no need to crack crowns over the matter, Farnham." Breen poked at the young fire as if Farnham was there among the coals. "She's done naught wrong. She's only made a friend and that's a thing you were never a good judge of anyway."

Farnham manufactured a placating smile, reflecting on how offended he was at everyone wanting to reprimand him.

Magnanimity. Your Leonine head. He'd heard someone call his head thus years ago and the description always came back to comfort him in moments of consternation. It was a steady Gibraltar in the straits of domestic woe.

"I shan't quarrel with you, Vivi," said he. "I know you're a clever and wise girl and left Jimmy at the door, so what harm could he do? Please, proceed with your tale."

Again, his niece's face flushed. "I didn't leave him at the door—he asked to come in and see me 'Poirot-ing' and I didn't see a reason not to let him."

"Are you in earnest?" The old stomach took a bally jog up his spine and cheered as it passed the finish line.

She tossed her hands. "He's friends with Janie and Dickon. Truth be told, I think I got more from Janie with Jimmy present than I would have if I'd sent him packing. Jane is convinced of her sister's innocence, but Cilla won't say where she was the night of the murder. And Jane is still awfully upset about the police."

"And good reason when they're a lot of turnip-headed bureaucrats."

His faithful doctor groaned. "Really, Farnham. You're in a foul mood."

"Do you have a pipe, Doctor Breen?" Vivi inquired. "I think a bit of smoke would choke him up nicely."

They both laughed at him. He hated being laughed at.

Farnham reminded himself to keep calm. Bang his ulcers. And bang this growing sensation of coziness; in faith, what a cozy, antagonistic party they made! With a bit of blue sky sliding in at the window, the bare clutter of The Quagmire made an ideal background for their tri-cornered ill humors and made it almost quilt-like.

He had been in a perfectly marvelous mood before Vivi's entrance, and she'd gone and poured verbal ice cubes down his spine. Ice cubes are quite chilling to the tropics of a warm heart. Vivi couldn't be expected to make a very accomplished detective her first time round and knowledge of her deficiencies was probably the cause for this horrible humor of hers.

He could be gallant. Gallantry, Orville Farnham could do. Indeed, perhaps by the next time she'd—next time? Oh heavens, no. She's be gone in a couple weeks. As soon as he'd convinced everyone he needed no help with his dodgy stomach.

"Seeing as it is your errand about which we came to talk, my dear, would you be so kind as to tell us about the police?" Farnham took a pencil and notebook from his breast pocket and flipped to a clean sheet. *Superfluous thoughts, away!* "This little council needs someone to take the minutes down properly. I've never held a three-person investigation. I can see why now: too many bang details."

"The police do not think Jane and Dickon committed the murder," Vivi continued. "Or at least, they aren't the primary suspects."

Breen nodded. "Got that much from Inspector Fawnwicke when I met him at the Crossing this morning."

"It's Jane's sister, Miss Cilla Grey, whom they suspect."

Farnham tossed an eyebrow. "What motive?"

"Jane was understandably vague," Vivi answered. "She gave me no concrete answer."

Breen nodded. "Nor did Fawnwicke."

"It seems Cilla is one of those girls who makes it her business to make her family ridiculous," Vivi said.

"Cilla Grey is not a bad sort." Farnham dug his pointer fingers into his temples and bore their blindness. "She's a butterfly. She plays with hearts and flies away, but she *isn't* a bad sort."

Vivi shrugged. "The police seem to be going on a motive of jealousy: Cilla has a lover here in Whistlecreig and killed the woman who was going to come between them."

"Drama. Theatricals. Tragedy in two parts. Oh, the *pathos*. And she won't tell the police where she was? Probably taking a moonlit walk with this week's flame. How suspicious."

"The whole thing is a wretched mess, Farnham." Breen sounded a bit disgusted and it niggled Farnham's temper. "I hope you realize you've only got three days to try solve this thing before I win our bet."

"Don't preen, yourself, my good fellow. You haven't won yet." *Not at all.*

Breen fixed him with a curious eye. "I've been doctoring and speaking with the rival investigation, Vivi's been rummaging up the woeful secrets of a *femme fatale*. What have you been doing, Farnham?"

"Besides smoking, you mean?" said Vivi. "He finds it beneficial to thought patterns. Let us hope he came up with something brilliant from his efforts. I could swear he burned through half a box of Cubans after dinner last night."

"I did, rather," he said. "Come up with something brilliant, I mean."

"Let us hear," Breen said. "Fair play: we told you our schemes, you tell us yours."

Farnham slung himself forward in the chair, the thrill of the chase coursing through his veins again. "Not just yet. It needs to marinate." There were a few points yet unclear. He didn't want to announce any of it aloud before he was certain. But oh, how dear old Allen had set the sun rising on the case! He was a butler of all butlers, a champion of all domestic servants, a brilliant adornment to the intellectual kitchen. But Farnham was not ready to tell anyone any of this. He could play Vivi's game better than she. They would see.

Breen jumped to his feet and brushed off his hands. "Right. Well. We seem to have all had delightful mornings of productivity. Shall we anticipate Mrs. Froggle and meet her sandwiches in the kitchen?"

"Just a moment," Vivi interrupted. Her face had gone red again and Farnham took notice. "Might I offer one bit of advice?"

"Go on," Farnham said.

"Don't believe the police for a moment. Michael Maynor is a man capable of much. Follow him, and I believe you will find your man."

Farnham steadied his gaze. "Speak you from experience, or are you merely angry with him for living?"

She met it gentle, humble. "Experience."

Was there a shade of deception in her eyes? No. She told the truth. There was more to the story than Farnham knew, but she had not presented any false information. He honored her for that piece of honesty. The whole of it would come out eventually. She was a strong girl; he, a persuasive man.

"Also," she continued. "I am going to be at the ceildih this evening. Jimmy invited me."

"The ceilidh?" Farnham asked, startled into a question by the announcement.

"Yes. Anyone want to come with me?"

His jaw sagged and his stomach clenched "You can't expect me to go to a crowded party and hop about like a savage. It's unconscionable. It's unhealthy."

"I *always* go," Breen confessed. "Rather fun. Keeps me in shape and my foot on the native heath. No one reels like a true Scotsman."

"You *would*," Farnham said, feeling the bitterness of his best friend's betrayal. And, because he could think of nothing better to say, followed it up fiercely with: "Dash it all! And dash *you*."

Chapter Sixteen
Ceilidh

Twilight spoke outside the Recreation Center, dark purple but for window-slot commas colored bright as pumpkin moons with electric light. These grace-marks gossiped to brilliant Venus their illumination and breathed into the dusk with a color like foxes. Such visual conversation calmed Vivi, who felt awed of a sudden by the prospect of descending upon the entire township at play and felt the lights a nearly-audible welcome.

"I'm glad we're a bit late," she said to no one in particular.

The door to the Center stood open, though the night was chill, and shadows flicked across the square of brightness one after another. It was a moment before Vivi realized the shadows did not move senselessly but whirled in rhythm with the faint skirling of an Irish band. Something flipped in her belly, but it was not apprehension. It was the prospect of dancing that set her trembling like Babel's tower; she was terrible at Society, failing at attempts to play nursemaid, but she *could* dance and it is a precious sort of self-controlled human who denies himself the pleasure of displaying his talents in public.

Breen had picked them up in his car and brought them here. They parked in the lot near the Presbyterian Church and strolled up the lane now toward the large, well-lit Recreational Center. It was a newish building—probably the newest Whistlecreig possessed. Big and white and box-shaped, Vivi thought it quite ugly, but ugly or not, this was the place where she would get have amusement for heaven's sake. For that she would forgive its austerity.

Farnham dragged along behind her, severely dreading this occasion as he had more than once announced. She slowed until he came abreast of her then slipped her arm into the crook of his elbow. Again, his arm felt skinnier and frailer than she would have assumed.

Recognition of his frailty aroused an almost motherly feeling in her breast which she was swift to press back. Even so, a warmer feeling toward Farnham took up residence, and it seemed she was not an alien in a foreign land: Farnham's eye travelled the length of her arm as if he didn't quite know what to make of this voluntary display of trust and affection but was not displeased by it.

"Yes, this is an apology," she said with a laugh. "I'm sorry I've been cross."

Farnham didn't speak, but his shoulders eased back, and she knew he'd accepted it in good faith. Gravel crunched under their feet and Breen's, who walked a bit ahead, as they neared the building.

"May I claim the first dance?" Vivi asked. "Or will my audacity in asking you drive you off from me as a 'fast' girl?"

Farnham put his hand over hers and squeezed. "As you request."

"Good."

"Hurry, old man," Breen called with a laugh as he squeezed into the hall and the orange light swallowed him up wholesale.

On the stoop, Farnham straightened his cardigan and brushed Vivi with an accusatory scowl. "You've rumpled me, hanging on my person like a clothespin."

"I can't possibly rumple you more than you'll be rumpled, presently," she said, feeling blithe. "Dancing is not conducive to tidiness, you know."

"You are rash," he grumbled.

"Am I? How charming."

They paused a moment to purchase tickets from a large, bosomy woman with grey-streaked hair.

"Ay yup," the woman warned. "Room's a fair bit crowded tonight. Small, brown eyes scurried over Vivi. "This your niece, Mistah Farnham?"

"Yes, Mrs. Froggle," Farnham said, "Miss Genevieve Langley."

Vivi shook the woman's plump, sweating hand, and the keen eyes again fled up and down.

"Woy up, then!"

"How do y'do?" Vivi answered, figuring the woman's odd words were a like manner of greeting.

"Well she don't look like a fiz-gig and ent that a relief!" Mrs. Froggle said with a wink at Farnham. "Lord knows we've got enough of 'em in the world."

Something had been decided in that mention and a shred of tension dissipated like mist in an early sunbeam.

"Miss Langley certainly is *not* a fiz-gig." Farnham offered Vivi his arm and drew her through a knot of damp, sparkling-eyed young people toward a table draped with bunting.

"I take it I'm to be glad I'm not a 'fiz-gig'?"

"Quite." Farnham smiled at a young girl behind the table. "Two glasses of lemonade, if you please. Thank you." He handed one glass to Vivi and raised the second in his left hand. "To my niece, who is anything but a wild, brazen flirt."

177

"May I always avoid such censorship," she agreed, and drank the pleasantly too-sour liquid.

The band had suspended music for a moment while the crowd of flush-faced, damp-haired dancers caught their breath. Now, a lone fiddle scraped a few wild, hovering notes and descended into a rollicking melody with the accordion, second fiddle, and drummer scrambling to keep up with its intricacies.

"Rather a deafening noise, isn't it?" Farnham remarked drily. He set his empty glass on the table in front of the waitress and eyed Vivi. "Ready?"

"Are the dances terribly hard?" she asked with sudden misgiving and a wild look to see if Jimmy might rescue her.

"It's more a case of goodwill than correct footwork," Farnham answered. "Bob about with enough spirit and they'll think you the best reeler as ever lived."

He pulled her to the foot of a line of dancers. A tall man in a green shirt beamed at Vivi. His forehead glistened with sweat, and his shirt stuck to the center of his back in a long dark oval; one more indication that there was perhaps more exertion involved in these Irish dances than even the jazziest of clubs Vivi had graced with her presence.

"Dip in," Farnham yowled over the cacophony. "You'll have us trampled!"

A caller shouted directions at the head of the room, but his voice was so muffled by the tread of a hundred feet as to become useless in aiding Vivi's comprehension. She stared at the next couple down the line and tried her best to mimic the intricate movements made by the girl.

"I don't quite have it!" she protested as the man in green grabbed her elbow and swung her the opposite direction to that she'd headed.

"S'okay, miss," he puffed, shoving her the other direction now, back toward Farnham. "*Right,* then left."

She ended in Farnham's arms, and the wild Irish beat quickened. He spun her out, and she collided with the girl beside her.

"Ay up!" the girl said with a laugh. "Join hands and go left *then* right."

"But that gentleman said—"

"Just listen to the music!" the girl called over the green man's shoulder as he swung her.

Farnham's arms were around Vivi's waist again, and he picked her up and forcibly pirouetted with her. An ache formed in Vivi's side, and she realized she was frowning at her feet as she spun, focusing too hard on the steps and paying no attention to anyone in the room but the grinning, glistening couple to her right. If they would *stay* on her right. Half the time they ended up on her left or in front of or behind her. What the *devil?*

A firm hand tapped her shoulder, and Vivi looked up, startled, to see the girl. "Get a move out of there," she warned. "You'll be trampled."

It was then Vivi noticed the couple at the opposite end sashaying down toward her region of the Poles. She backed up until she was beside the girl.

"It's a fair jumblement, ent it?" the girl laughed. "My name's Cilla."

Cilla! Though dense as a Yorkshire pudding with the confusion, Vivi perked up at this. Cilla Grey? She was dancing in the company of a murder suspect?

"I'm Vivi," she answered with a smile. A dozen questions hovered on her tongue. *What is your defense?* seemed like a good place to start. Even, *So the police think you killed Lillian Bertois?* But the music was relentless: in a sudden burst of openness, Vivi asked instead, "Do you think I'll ever get the hang of it?"

The girl threw her head back with a laugh. Light caught on her black hair in blue ripples. "Most do. All the couples work their way up the room and when they make head, come gallopin' back down to make room for another head."

"Sounds easier than it feels." Vivi fisted her hand and tried to rub out the cramp beginning under the left side of her ribs.

"Where do yah hail from?" Cilla asked, eyes on Vivi, then darting up the line to keep track of the other dancers.

"Darlington," Vivi answered. "But I spend a deal of time in London during the Season."

"Did you go to the theatre?"

Suspicion crawled into the atmosphere of their end of the line. "Sometimes."

"Ever been to America?" Cilla asked.

"Not yet, but I have a wish to go."

When Vivi next caught a glimpse of her face, it appeared perfectly natural in its curiosity, but she had prophesied the next question and was not at all surprised when Cilla asked:

"Knew you Lillian *Bertois*?"

Farnham chose this moment to execute a wild and rather breathless spin so that Vivi had a beggar's chance of formulating any sort of answer overtop of the accusation which filled her mind.

"I didn't know her before the train coming to Whistlecreig," she answered carefully, "but she seemed to me a...quiet girl."

"She was ikey, that'un," Cilla said with decision and met her partner's hand with a merry laugh and outstretched fingers.

Vivi stopped a moment in the dance, and Farnham tripped over her feet.

"Vivi! The dance, woman!"

"You had met the actress?" Vivi asked. "You knew her?"

"She weren't a nice-un. Ikey, hoighty *and* a fiz-gig." Cilla seemed to consider the topic finished. "And what're you doin' here?"

"She's come to stay with me and nurse me back to apple-pie-order, Miss Cilla," Farnham offered. "And she's helping me with some business."

Cilla laughed again—she seemed a great one for laughter, Vivi thought. Whenever Cilla tossed her head, her braids glistened, and Vivi saw the eyes of many young fellows steal wistful glances at her. She remembered what Jane had said about her sister and the gentlemen. Cilla was a coquette and a half, it was true, and this coquette was trying a bit of charm on the great Shakespearean actor himself:

"Don't see you at many dances, sir! What kind of business can a great man like yah have here? You wouldn't be workin' on the murder now, would yah?"

"But of course," Farnham said with a smile for Cilla and his right hand for Vivi as it came time again to begin another series of reels. "Who wouldn't want to help bring a murderer to justice?"

Again, that saucy toss of her head. Cilla and her partner wove through the dance with a rustic sort of grace, Vivi and Farnham hauling after them.

In any dance at any assembly, Vivi could not remember feeling quite so winded. The music stopped mercifully when the head of the line was still four couples ahead. She had dreaded sashaying down the line with the eyes of two dozen dancers bent upon her. It was not the sort of notice Vivi enjoyed in a roomful of strangers.

Farnham elbowed Vivi round to the lemonade table again. They each drank a second glass and Vivi took a third. It was some moments before her breath had slowed enough to allow her to look around for anyone she knew.

Chiefly, where was Jimmy?

The young man in the green shirt stood in the opposite corner with his arm around a young woman whom she recognized as Jane Grey. Cilla stood near them, and Vivi smiled over the resemblance, though Cilla was in all ways a brighter, bolder copy of her sister. The same cupid's bow in their lips, the same gloss in their hair. A sister was a thing Vivi had never had in close proximity. Claire and Maria were only seven and nine respectively; hardly the sort of ages to count as companions for a grown daughter.

Vivi would go talk to the trio. It wasn't for the pleasure of dancing she'd agreed to come to the ceilidh.

"Are you planning to quiz them in front of everyone?" Farnham murmured in her ear.

Vivi flushed. Could Farnham read her thoughts so easily? "I suppose not."

"Leave Dickon to me," he said. "Where is that swain Michael, anyway? He's your responsibility."

"Yes." She felt small and hot with the admission. Michael was her responsibility and Jimmy's friend. If she was going to spend any time this evening with Jimmy, she would not be able to shake his guest from her thoughts and sight.

"To the hunt, then," Farnham said with a salute.

He wove through the pressing crowd, disappearing from sight in the crush of bodies. He resurfaced at the far end of the hall and made a courtly bow to the two young ladies. Cilla tossed her head, and Jane smiled, more reserved than her sister but pretty, after a fashion.

Vivi grinned over the pleasant tableau and returned her attention to her own surroundings and the pulsing heat of a room over-filled with active bodies.

Where was Jimmy? She wanted him. She wanted a jolly anchor in the ocean of people to whom she was unknown.

"Miss Langley."

The low voice was almost a growl it was so deep, and Vivi jumped what felt like a yard into the air. "Mr. Owens!"

"What *is* this?" he asked, flinging a hand to the dancers. "I'll stick to jazz. Maybe even a little tap."

The idea of this frightening person clicking his heels on a parquet floor made no sense. "You...tap?"

"Why not?"

"Mr. Owens, I feel as if I ought to explain about—"

"About the reason you were visiting that guy? Listen, Miss Langley, in the line I'm in, ain't nobody going to cry home to Mommy about a daytime visit to a cutie's hotel room."

Indignation passed like Death's angel over Vivi's heart, and there was no crimson mark to spare Phillip Owens. "I would have you know everything that occurred in that gentleman's room was perfectly decent!"

Actually, she had pulled a gun and he had nearly kissed her. The decency was imperfect at best.

"Oh, I believe you," Mr. Owens said. His eyes, which were inclined to a watery blue, were even glassier when he stretched his lids wide open.

"Thank you."

"I believe you just like I believe that little kitty-cat in the corner didn't commit the murder." He glared in the direction of Farnham and the shimmering apparition that was Cilla Grey.

"You've heard the rumours then?"

"Heard 'em."

"And you know what motive they assign to her?" Vivi asked. "Jealousy? Isn't that a little far-fetched for a motive in real-life?"

Phillip Owens took a glass of lemonade and downed it in one gulp, his face bitter. "You ever read the Bible, Miss Langley?"

The irony. "But of course."

"Ain't nothing too far-fetched for jealousy."

"I...I see what you mean."

"Adults are just kids. You want something, they have something, you take it or smash it. Or smash them."

"Mr. Owens, have a heart!"

"Can't afford to. Lil didn't have one, that Cilla kid don't have one. And if you don't care a red cent for anyone else, killing 'ems easy. I know."

"You..."

"I know what it's like not to have a heart. It's nice. But I don't go killin' people. It'd be easy," he jabbed his pinky finger in Cilla's direction, "but I don't go doin' it."

In that moment, Vivi could not decide whether her panic or sense of the absurd had the upper hand. None of her suspects were playing fair. Did forthrightness and blatant announcements of murderous feelings count for or against a man's innocence? If Phillip Owens had committed the murder, he'd steer clear of the subject, wouldn't he? Or could he be employing a double-bluff? Bang clever people.

"Well, if you'll excuse me." Phillip Owens stuffed his hands in his pockets and stalked to the opposite side of the room where he struck up conversation with the Black Roe's Mr. Burnes.

And a jolly good-riddance to him.

Where *was* Jimmy? She'd give him a right good scolding when he ever came round again.

"Vivi, my dear thing!"

"Doctor Breen, I was wondering where you'd popped off to."

"The claims on a doctor's time are never finished. Little Tom Sharpley had a splinter in his hand from crawling about on this villainous floor. I extracted it to the tune of a lusty howl. A dance, Vivi, for the old man?"

Truth be told, Vivi little felt like entering that mayhem again, but the doctor looked *so* hopeful.

"All right, but do let's choose the obscure end of the line."

"As you wish."

He led her into the frayed ends where the tiredest dancers clustered. The dance began, but this time Vivi knew her business and was able to somewhat keep up with her partner. For a while she felt that the moment for Genevieve Langley's dancing abilities had finally come, but a particularly quick spin clouded her mind. She tripped once, twice, and Breen pushed her through the next movements at double-time with a:

"Blast, blast, blast," uttered between clenched teeth.

He needn't snap like an old pug dog. It wasn't her fault, this odd sensation of falling to sleep while standing. "I'm sorry I've—"

"Back to work, Vivi! You can't just stand there."

"I'm sorry I've got to..." Another wave of disconnection severed her from the ability to feel Doctor Breen's hand on her arm. "I'm so thirsty."

She peeled away with an extremely vague sense of regret to leave the Doctor in the middle of the dance, too vague a sense to bother following.

At the drinks table, Vivi's eyes flickered over every face one by one but there were too many people. Far too many. Faces that had been familiar before were lost in the flickering. A hundred grinning mouths became two hundred, two hundred smiling eyes became four-hundred. All five of her senses protested against the overload. The living heat, noise, and colors swirled in a twist of confusion.

A fluid, disquieting sensation of falling asleep and rising above the rest of the room filled the front of her head, and she struggled to make it back to the shore of reality. Fresh air. She wanted it as a thirsty man craves water. She moved toward the now dark square of the doorway, flickers of alarm shooting through her chest at the idea that something might impede her freedom, or that she might stumble head-long into the crowd before she made it to the salvation of the outdoors.

A hand grabbed her elbow. "Miss Langley?"

The voice was wool-edged and distant. She willed her eyes to focus on the face belonging to it. "Ji—Jimmy. I...I don't feel well. Please help me."

He put a warm hand against the small of her back. It was hot and the heat crept through her dress, but it was steady. She leaned into the curve of his strong arm and allowed him to lead her through the dark portal into another, cooler world. He steered her to the white side of the building and helped her lean against it, but he kept her in his arms.

She drew several draughts of the fine air and tried a smile. It wobbled pitifully, and she pressed fingertips to her forehead, willing the floating sensation to drop her back to earth. "I am sorry. I...I don't often feel so..." Her words came with difficulty, and the wooliness gathered in the corners of her mind. She dug in with her heels. "So *dense*. The crush was suffocating me."

Jimmy's arms loosened a bit around her as if he feared he added to the problem. "Should I get Dr. Breen?"

"Oh, no. I will be fine presently. It's just a...silence..." she frowned and bent her head, "*silent* migraine. I get them now and then when a small is too room for a...a crowd. Or when I've been sp-spinning."

Humiliated, Vivi gave up conversation and dropped her head, pillowing it against Jimmy's chest. She had not realized he stood that close and every sense of propriety told her to stand up straight again. But she had no will, no energy left. The wooliness continued and, were it not for Jimmy's chest under her head and his arms around her waist, she knew she would be prostrate on the ground. His arms tightened around her waist, and he rested his chin on top of her head. "No rush, Vivi. I'll be your leaning post."

A few tears pooled in the corners of her eyes and ran down her cheeks. She had just enough coherency left to wonder why she was crying. That thought brought three more tears. She sniffed and felt Jimmy draw away.

"What's wrong, luv?" he asked in a gentle voice.

"I...I don't know."

He tilted her face toward him and brushed away her tears with one work-hardened finger. His smile was soft in the orange glow of the window. "Is the murder upsetting you?"

"No, but my...head," Vivi managed. "I feel....sleepy."

Jimmy's chuckle rumbled beneath her cheek. "Did you bite a poisoned apple, Snow White? Now...what *was* the remedy for that? Ah...I remember."

Before Vivi was quite sure what he was doing, his lips were on hers, gentle, inquisitive. She was too surprised to protest, too astonished and pleased to wish he wouldn't kiss her like this. He pulled away and smiled, the uncertain light playing off the well-built planes of his features.

"Feel any better?" he murmured.

She drew a shaky breath, which he cut off halfway with another kiss. She pushed her wrists against his chest, and he released her gently.

"Please...don't." It was pleasant—very pleasant. But she knew she didn't have her wits.

"You don't like it?" he asked, his face suddenly red with embarrassment. "I won't if you'd rather not. I'm sorry I didn't ask before."

"It's not that," Vivi said, feeling even more muddled with the flare of her first kiss adding to her fluff-filled thoughts. "I'm not...I'm not *well*. I don't know what I'm doing."

The smell of cologne filled the small space between them, mixing with the spice of the autumn air. She felt cold and wanted to lean into his solidity again, but it would not be wise. She needed to remember who she was, where she was. *God, destroy this migraine. I cannot think. I cannot—*

"Do you want me to ask Farnham to take you home?" he asked.

"I just need a moment to collect myself, I think," Vivi answered. His kiss had towed her back to a new, vivid reality which was dizzying. Quite as dizzying as the former mist.

Chapter Seventeen
Cheap Peace

Farnham moved with what he considered feline grace to where young Moorhen and his bride-to-be stood. To interrupt a tête-à-tête between a couple seemed boorish, but what could be done? Vivi had not left him much choice in the matter, pushing him to come to this godforsaken ceilidh. And not a place in which he could stow away in a corner. There were people everywhere.

He resented being assigned to trawl about like an unmoored row-boat looking for weeds in which to tangle. But tangling in the police force's murder suspects was not unsuited to Farnham's particular mood. He slunk through the disgusting press of hot bodies and managed to make it to the lovers and Miss Cilla without being trodden down in the mob.

He pulled the edges of his jacket into order and mopped his forehead with a folded silk kerchief from his pocket. "How are you this evening, Miss Grey? Dickon, looking hale as usual."

Dickon's handshake was forthright and dry—a thing for which Farnham wished to commend him in a room crowded with sweating bodies. What people found to enjoy in an assembly such as this was far behind the borderlands of his expansive comprehension.

"Have you seen Inspector Dillon?" Farnham inquired. "I wished to speak with him." Beneath the handkerchief with which he dabbed at his face, Farnham watched what effect the request would have on Dickon. The young man tensed with a look of annoyance rather than fear.

"Ent here," Dickon said, tilting at Farnham with a proud glance. "But you might find him uwer at th'station. Ah've got pleasanter company t'bide my time." He pulled Janie close with a hand on her waist and looked straight at Farnham. "Ah suppose you've heard. Whaddyer do about it? They'll think what they think. Ah've no desire t'widdle 'bout it till they realize they'd got the wrong person."

His voice barely carried to Farnham's ear over the din of the company, but Farnham heard the staid defiance in Dickon's tone. He was polite but unflinching and more than a dab cutting. Over Dickon's shoulder, Miss Cilla eyed Farnham as if sizing him up.

"You, Miss Cilla."

"Yes, Mr. Farnham?" Was Mab's gaze a jot prouder than the dark beams bent on him from those eyes?

"What do you think of the matter?"

"You're th'first to ask me direct. I think her agent done it. You seen him? Great hulking-strong chap with a marred face. Police want a bit of what they're keaching, they need look no further'n Phillip Owens. Nastier chap I never hope t'meet. I'm tatered with talking about this murder."

Tired she *must* be. Farnham liked Cilla in the way he liked the capricious East wind and the crabapples that gave off a bellyache to those who over-loved them. He wanted to be shown her innocence but be shown he must.

"Do you mind if we step into the card-room for a moment?" he asked.

Cilla pursed her red red lips and looked exasperated. "What would I be wantin' to slear off with you for?"

"I want to hear your story from your lips. Give you a chance to tell it straight."

"I told the police already."

"I am not Chief McMulligan. I don't bang your head with a kettle-drum if you happen to repeat yourself."

She laughed at this, and immediately after Farnham was a man with arm burdened by the pleasant weight of this Rowena.

"Truly, Miss Cilla," he said in her ear as they squeezed by the rows of dancers and made an escape into the no-less-crowded card-room. "I want to see the truth come out. Only the truth. That's all I'm after."

The sharp glance sent toward him rested a moment with uncommon gentleness on his face. Cilla squeezed his arm against her blouse and smiled.

"Truth's all anyone deserves," she said.

"May I speak with you directly?" he whispered. There were only a lot of elderly folk in this room, including Farmer Garridy and Jimmy's father, Mr. Fields, but he'd rather not risk being overheard.

"No sense rootling round. Ask me."

"Man to man, as it were?"

"Ask me and I'll tell you."

Farnham drew an uncertain breath. It offended all his sensibilities to pry into the personal life of a young lady. "I don't suppose anyone doubts you were *not* at home the night of the murder. It is understood you are almost always away from home—in company—in the evenings?"

She lifted her shapely chin. "It is understood."

"Is it true that the police think you committed the murder of Lillian Bertois?"

"That's what they've been thraping into me head day and night, yes."

"And you won't tell them what you were doing?"

Down the curve of her cheek strode a deep shade of rose. Girls could still blush! Fascinating. He'd thought it died out with modesty some years back.

"I was...with a fellow."

"Where?"

Her head snapped up. "Next you'll be asking what I was doing."

"Where, Cilla?"

She drew a breath through her nostrils and turned a killing look on him. "At the Black Roe."

"What man?"

"He's a friend. He's not in town anymore."

"Oh, Cilla." Farnham muffled his frustration in his damp palm.

"'Fore you look at me like that with your nose all ikey and high, I'll have yah know it was a fireside visit. All proper'n right."

"And Mr. Burnes would be able to tell me this."

The blush came again. "Mr. Burnes had gone to th'Lark an' Eagle."

"Cilla, Cilla. If you're going to deal in scandal at *least* have witnesses. I believe you were at the Black Roe with a man. I even believe you to have had *semi*-honorable intentions but *bang* it, girl, the police won't believe you if you cannot produce a witness for your story or—better yet—the murderer for theirs."

"What am I to do?"

Farnham patted her arm. "Keep an eye out for me. Tell the police what you told me. McMulligan may be the very devil when it comes to manners, but he's no slack-jaw. I think you can trust him to keep your story to himself and his men."

"Then y'do believe me?"

"I do. *Heavens*, girl, I wanted to believe it. I'd hate to see anything happen that would cause your sister pain." He looked her over a bit severely and deemed it a good thing for her. "You'd do well to think of how your gadding about affects her because a better or more patient person has never walked this earth. Walk a bit circumspectly and *try* to be a lady."

"And now I get a lecture." Cilla pouted her rosebud mouth playfully and before he could prevent it, kissed Farnham's cheek. "Get along, old fellow. You've made me sit out two dances and I won't have all me fun spoilt!"

"'I would to God thou and I knew where a commodity of good names was to be bought.' Good evening, Miss Cilla."

Farnham exited the room and hid himself among the assembly. He prided himself on his abilities for theatrical effect, as well he might. It was one of his many talents. His agent, Barth Melchior, had even intimated once that it was his *only* talent.

He was a talented man, if anyone cared to notice—and not just as an actor. Why must humanity be so very one-dimensional? The world assumed he was good at nothing but acting. He was good at many things. In fact, put a man like him beside a man like Michael Maynor and—

"Bang, it's you!" Farnham said cheerily and put forth a hand to pump Michael's.

After this required civility, Michael withdrew his hand and pointedly wiped it on his pants leg. Farnham locked eyes with him and did the same, feeling that two stray dogs would have made a merrier greeting of it.

"You're here," Farnham said with a horrendously affable smile.

"As you see."

"Are you well?"

"I'm not ill."

They had silence.

"Hot room," Michael said.

"I felt a chill a moment past," Farnham lied. "Large crowd."

"Dinky compared to the clubs in London."

"In my day," Farnham offered, "there was a delightful practice called conversation. You ought to take lessons sometime—you'd enjoy it."

Michael narrowed his eyes at Farnham. "Where is your niece?"

"Isn't she with you? I thought you two were inseparable."

Michael laughed. It would have been a fine laugh except its heart was eaten away and it rang hollow on the ear. The band struck up yet another skirling, screeching tune like a soundtrack to Farnham's ulcers. He clamped a hand over his belly and joined in Michael's laughter as a way of further defaming the sham hilarity. Two men who never laughed, laughing together over something that was not in the least amusing. Unusual, but not unheard of. Farnham thought it likely Coriolanus and Aufidius laughed together now and again. Sensible, if you thought about it, for no one else would read malcontent in the sound. A man could have an entire duel under cover of laughter and ten to one, no would notice.

Farnham shot out a hand and grasped one of Michael's. "Thank you."

A quiver of interest and confusion sliced between them. "Why?"

"For giving me peculiar insight into the way in which I converse."

Michael only looked at him in reply. "I wonder, Mr. Farnham, what people enjoy about life in a small town?" The dancers crowded into their end of the room as they whirled, and Michael flashed a disgusted look at a young miss who trod upon his toes unceremoniously.

It was Cilla, and the recognition thrilled Farnham. Suitable. She *should* stamp the life out of his feet. He replayed Michael's expression in his mind and felt satisfied.

"A life in the country is a life crowded by disagreeable odors and ignorant people," Michael further complained.

Farnham shrugged. "We like our privacy." He was surprised at his own answer, for it was not often Farnham voluntarily sided with the rural people of his ancestral home. He liked to think them quaint and himself intelligent. But he would not stand for a cocky city fellow to trample over their reputation.

"Privacy? Yes, you do." Michel eyed him with a look which Farnham was at odds to decipher. "Your niece, however, stands far more upon London fashions. We had a nice visit in my room this morning. Quite cozy."

Vivi had been with Michael? In his room? Then she was no different than Cilla, whom—for all her virtues—he would hate to have as a niece. Fury wrenched in his gut and Farnham was again placid. "London manners do great credit to the buoyant spirits of young women, then. A country girl would never feel so...liberated."

The last word came out with difficulty, and a host of bitter things he planned to say to Vivi pooled in his throat. She had spent the morning in Michael's room. Cheap, like Cilla.

Michael's eyes traveled to the doorway and focused on something. Farnham followed the look and watched Vivi slip in from the darkness without, Jimmy Fields behind her. His hand was on her shoulder as if he was her escort. Who was her paramore: Jimmy? Michael? Or did she prefer keeping a line of beaus on a string? Was that the fashion in London? Perhaps she *was* a fizgig after all. Her eyes met his over the crowd, and she tipped her head to one side with a smile of relief.

In a moment she and Jimmy had joined him and Michael in their cramped corner, and she grabbed Farnham's hand and clung to it. Her fingers trembled where they rested on his wrist and Farnham studied her face. Something was off.

"I got a migraine," she explained. "Jimmy caught me right before I fainted dead away in the middle of everything."

"Heavens," Farnham said. "Wouldn't that have been exciting?" He flipped her wrist gently and pressed his fingers against the white underside. What had Jimmy been about? She obviously trembled not from fright but excitement: color heightened, pulse erratic, eyes looking anywhere but at the two young men.

"Miss Langley," Michael said. "I do hope you're better now."

Vivi focused on him, her eyes somewhat glassy and overwhelmed. "Yes. Quite. A bit wooly still, but nothing like before."

"You're a lucky man, just happening to be present when a damsel is in distress." He slapped Jimmy's shoulder with a chuckle which his friend echoed.

"Fate seems to be making a tossed salad of us," Jimmy said with a laugh. "First I rescue her from the train station, then from breaking her head on the unhallowed tile of the Whistlecreig Rec Center."

Jimmy rested his hand on Vivi's other arm and smiled. Under Farnham's curious fingers, her pulse raced again. What *had* the rake been doing to make his niece twitchier than a brood mare?

"None of us are gallant enough to think of Miss Langley. This press shall certainly bring on another headache if we stay any longer. Shall we repair to the Lark & Eagle? It's mainly deserted on social evenings," Someone said.

Breen bounced up just then, blowing hard through his cheeks, hair standing erect in spines all over his head. "*That* was a reel!" he panted.

Farnham noticed the music had stopped again—mercy of mercies—and the crowd milled about. "I had just suggested to the young people that we leave this hovel and have a visit at the pub. Vivi felt faint and I've quite enough of rattling up against sweaty bodies."

"Excellent idea, my dear Farnham." Breen saluted. "I'll just grab my coat and swing the car round."

In a few moments, they were installed in a comfortable corner at the Lark & Eagle. Farnham wrapped his hands around a mug of hot cider and leaned into the leather embrace of the booth. Too long since he'd been at this pub, which never failed to remind him fondly of a certain back-alley establishment in Oxford. A fire growled and snapped in a wide hearth and threw orange and yellow lances at the dark wainscoting of the walls. A gentleman's place, Farnham thought. A place wherein the cares of the world at large and the cares even of Whistlecreig seemed forbidden. All was peaceful, all hallowed in the way a favorite corner often is...he remembered now why Breen spent half his life here instead of at The Quagmire. Breen sat in a chair pulled up to the end of the booth and drained his second pint of bitter.

"That," he remarked, "is a better chase than any reel."

Jimmy raised his matching pint and winked. "Far better."

Vivi tipped the bowl that had held a quantity of soft, hot rolls made by the fair hand of the proprietor's wife. "What I wonder is, where did all the bread go?"

The cider slid warm and kicking down Farnham's throat. "'O, monstrous! but one half-pennyworth of bread to this intolerable deal of sack!'"

With one eyebrow screwed up, Breen massaged his forehead. "Oh blast. *Henry V?* Am I right?"

"Fourth," Farnham corrected. "The intake of sack considerably slacked off when he'd reformed. You'd do well to try the principle, dear sir."

"I'm a doctor," Breen answered. "I happen to know a bit of alcohol is beneficial to the digestion. Just a *bit.*"

Farnham slipped Vivi one of the rolls he'd taken and forgotten to eat. "My dear Breen, I'd hate to be your horse and wear a bit that size."

"Then be glad," Breen laughed, "that I don't *own* a horse."

The plump daughter of Haskins, the proprietor of the Lark & Eagle, approached the table. Michael hailed her with his empty tea-cup. "Another cup, please. And this time, *brandy* with a splash of *tea*. Afraid last time you got it backward."

The girl giggled and took his cup behind the counter where she filled it and returned, still giggling.

"Thank you, Ambrosia," he said. "You do Dyonisis proud."

She blushed and curtsied, and Farnham waited. When at last she moved off, Farnham stretched till the ropy muscles in his back and neck ached. This evening had been unpleasant and he felt not much-advanced in the case. Of *course* the bet was not what drove Farnham, but it irked him to know there were only a couple of days before he'd be forced to satisfy Breen's ego and admit his first defeat.

"Michael, how long have you and Jimmy known one another?" he inquired of a sudden.

The company around the table paused at this sudden introduction of conversation into their somewhat dozy party. The young gentlemen shared a darting look, one to another, as if unsure how they ought to answer.

"Since college," Jimmy said—a safe answer, Farnham thought.

"Eight years," Michael replied. "We were only poor, unpolished rubes of eighteen when we collided with one another at the university."

Farnham held the mug-edge to his bottom lip and smiled over it. "Spent your holidays in London together? As did the doctor and myself—thought it utterly the worst hell and best heaven earth could offer."

Michael sipped his brandy-with-tea and leaned back into the booth. "We had larks at the Atheneaum. Never a finer club in which to while away the jovial hour."

There were too many banged people at this table. Farnham wanted to watch Breen who tottered on over-full and study Vivi's reactions to Michael's words. He wanted to watch Jimmy, who had obviously done *something* to his niece and looked rather abstract, and Michael who had also done something to bring down Vivi's hatred. And through all this, he wanted to actually learn something about this murder. *Hellfire*.

He took a sip of his tea again and ran his thumb nail in a little circle on the table-top. "Surely you tired of the club—Breen and I did. One can only stand the company of the old faithfuls for so long before feeling the dry-rot creeping up one's back." He chuckled. "We shook things up with outings to the museums, the Opera...typical amusements."

Michael smiled. "The theatre was our distraction."

"And rambles in the countryside," Jimmy added, coming out of his lethargy. "Always more at home in the hills than crowded London streets."

"Exactly," Michael agreed. "You would have loved our rambles, Vivi. Lots of scope for the artist's eye."

"You know," Jimmy said, "We ought to plan a ramble here. There are plenty of good views round about, albeit not as fine as those up by the Lakes. Do you remember, Michael, the holiday we took in Cockermouth?" He whistled. "Prettiest place I've ever seen. What about tomorrow?"

"I have nothing better to do," Michael said. "As long as Miss Langley isn't occupied?"

Farnham drew back to a better angle at which to survey his niece's face and still be able to see that of the two young men. There was more to this suggestion than he could currently fathom. Were they both after Vivi? Two men after the same woman? Well, it had happened before, Helen of Troy and so forth as the probably-illiterate Phillip Owens had suggested. What did Breen think of it? He appeared to watch Vivi too, his color heightened by a few good pints.

With the eyes of all the gentlemen upon her, Vivi pinched off a bit of her roll and ate it with a shrug and a conscious smile. "If my uncle has no objection," Vivi said. "I'd love to see a bit of the countryside."

"Do you object, Mr. Farnham?"

Farnham ejected a dart of a glance at Breen and another at Vivi, and his mind whirled like a cog that would not catch on the other cog and move the machine. What had he missed? Instinct told him the answer to a riddle was flinging about in the rafters of the Lark & Eagle, right over his baffled head. What was the bang clue? Nothing seemed out of the ordinary. It was all perfectly right and normal...except somewhere he had missed something.

Cursing his distraction, Farnham created a benign expression. "Mind? Of course not. I'd rather like to go myself. But," he added, deciding his course all at once, "I'll let you young folk enjoy the day without me."

Jimmy cast himself back in his seat and settled against the leather. "All settled then. Gosh, but I'm tired. What time is it anyway?" He stifled a yawn and twisted in his chair to find the tavern clock.

"Half past eight." Vivi snapped her pocket-watch back together and tucked it in her coat pocket with another small smile. "Not so terribly late, but I feel it's bed-time."

Farnham watched Breen dig in the pockets of his coat. "What ails you, Breen?"

"Have we really only been here an hour?" the doctor answered. He brought forth a heavy, ponderous watch and opened it, then chuckled. "Ah, you'd best keep better care of your watch, lass. Lazy little thing; you're half an hour behind me. It's nine, and on that note, I've got to begin my rounds early tomorrow."

The legs of Breen's chair scraped across the floor as he pushed the chair out. "How's your head, Vivi?"

Vivi scooted out of the booth. "Better."

Breen lifted her eyelids one at a time and peered at her. "Sleep generally cures a silent migraine. Get some rest. These rambles the lads speak of are none too easy on the feet. A stroll for them's a matter of several miles. Call it a ramble and you'll be gone all day."

Farnham followed Vivi out their side of the booth. The young gentlemen had followed their example, and now the whole party stood in the center of the tavern with the golden lamps on the wall throwing a gentle cast of their faces. Peace like one of their grey fogs spread through the fivesome, and Farnham felt his unease slip away.

"'Truth hath a quiet breast,'" he quoth, and shook the hands of the two young men.

"And by that, he means what most people mean when they say, 'farewell,'" Breen said with a laugh. He clamped his hat on his head and escorted Vivi out the door toward the car.

"Cheers." Farnham followed his old friend and niece, leaving Mr. Maynor and Mr. Fields standing tall and young like Spartans in the center of the pub.

Outdoors, the cold shocked him out of his lethargy. He'd been at peace when enveloped in that musty leather booth that smelled of books and cigars and October ale. But here, in the air as cold as reality, that peace tasted *too* warm, cheap.

Farnham stuffed his fists deep in his trench coat and balanced on the edge of the curb.

Something had transpired back in the Lark & Eagle, and he'd missed it. He couldn't afford to miss a bang thing. What had he missed? His stomach flipped like a pod of dolphins merrily executing gymnastic feats for a large crowd. God grant him a chance to find out. Another few nights like this, and the investigation would be undone.

Chapter Eighteen
Take a Ramble

Sometime in the darkest hour of the night, Vivi awoke. Sweat pressed her silk nightdress to her body and pooled in the small of her back and on her belly where she lay half-buried in the feather mattress. For a moment, she thought she had been awakened by a noise, and she lay in the darkness, waiting to hear it again. Her heart pounded heatedly in her ears and moisture caught in the back of her throat. She would choke in a moment, choke in her own saliva. She sat up on her elbows, listening, too alert to everything. There were no sounds.

Vivi closed her eyes and saw Michael's hands coming at her throat again, pressing her head against the wood, leaning into her face, and she could not breathe.

She tore her eyes open, and there was no one in the room, no sound of anyone stirring...nothing. It was the terror that had awakened her.

All the flush of her triumph over him had died with evening's light. She had threatened Michael with a *gun*. Stupid woman she was, she had showed him her aces and told him of her hatred and now no thought of friendship would ever stay his hand from harming her.

"What a complete idiot," Vivi hissed at herself, and her chest heaved with frustration and terror combined. "A complete, total, entire idiot."

She climbed out of bed. Her nightdress clung to her calves, cold and reptilian like the wings of a butterfly that had not developed enough to fly. What exactly had she thought to gain by her visit to Michael's room? An enemy? Well she had certainly gained that, whatever else she might have lost.

He knew Lillian and had admitted as much.

Sleep had departed Vivi's senses, but a mental wooliness replaced the physical density, and her thoughts badgered one another and came forward in an overwhelming force. Vivi walked to the heavy dressing table that had belonged to one or another of the Farnham ancestors. Which one? The woman who'd been smothered by her husband? Had he done the deed in this room—In her bed? Severely, Vivi pulled the table drawer open and took Farnham's pistol from it. It weighed heavy and compact in hand.

As long as Michael remained in Whistlecreig, she would have to carry it. There was no choice. If he ever found her unarmed, she would no longer be the strong woman she claimed. She would be helpless...as Lillian Bertois had been helpless.

"I am such a fool," she whispered to her reflection then climbed back into bed with the pistol tucked above her headboard, close to hand if something or someone tried to enter her chamber.

As sleep continued to elude her, Vivi replayed Jimmy's kiss in her mind. So close, he was, so protective and gentle and coaxing...

No, that made things worse. She scrubbed her gritty eyes with a back-motion of her hand and sighed softly. Today's ramble boded nothing but complexities from one end to the next. Bang it, but she wished Farnham was coming.

"Halloo the house!" The warbled call came muffled and merry-toned through the thick walls of Whistlecreig Manor.

"Crumbs. They're early!" Vivi left her delicate arranging of a few rowan branches in a blue jug and trotted out of the kitchen. Midway through the hall, she found Allen on his way to the door. "You're back!" she exclaimed.

"That I am, Miss," Allen said with a bow.

Vivi came to him and planted a kiss on his cheek. "It is *good* to see you."

Allen stepped backward, eyebrows nearly meeting his severely combed hair. "Really, Miss, I'm not certain Mr. Farnham would—"

"Be a duck, Allen. He won't mind. I'm just very glad to see you. You've no *idea* how awkward it can be without a third. Well, I suppose you must have because until I came it was just the two of you." She stopped there, a bit breathless and eagerly glad for the surprise of a safely-returned Allen on this morning when her courage needed bolstering. If he could come back unscathed from London, certainly she could survive a foray into the wide wilderness of Northamptonshire.

"Right. Well." Allen straightened his shoulders and flicked a paw toward the entryway. "I'll just be answering the door then, Miss."

"Do." Vivi turned at the doorway and spoke to Allen over her shoulder. "Tell the gentlemen I am fixing sandwiches and they're to wait in the dining room for me."

The immaculate bow was aired again and Allen made for the doorway.

Vivi returned to the kitchen and finished fixing the jug of rowan. Unable to sleep, she had risen early and gone out to the Rowan Walk where the halcyon gold and red of the avenue had soothed her soul. Legend had it that where a rowan grew, bad things could not happen. Further, that secrets were whispered to those who would listen. Superstition was a thing alien to all branches of the Langley family, and Vivi did not linger in the golden avenue to take benefit from those legends. Still, remembering the fox, she had also taken Sir Toby Belch and was surprised to find that she enjoyed the companionship of such an aimless creature.

The jug being arranged to her satisfaction, Vivi trimmed the crusts from the stack of hearty sandwiches and stacked them onto neat squares of waxed paper then folded the paper and tied it with red and white striped string. A very satisfying stack of fat packages, they seemed. These she stowed in a deep picnic basket beside a thermos of lemonade and another of coffee, a tin of ginger biscuits, and a few green-throated apples. Over it all, she tucked a clean stable-blanket she had found in the back hall that had probably never seen the back of a horse in its existence. All the same, a few tenacious and mysterious white hairs were seen when one looked carefully; they would simply not look, then.

The picnic was now packed.

Vivi checked the room—no one was about—then removed Farnham's pistol from its temporary hiding place above the kitchen cupboard. She'd carried it carefully from beneath her pillow to the cabinet, having a half-amused fear that it would go off on its own and kill her dead on Whistlecreig's unpolished marble floor. In a deep inner pocket of her tweed jacket, she stowed the weapon then checked the laces of her walking shoes and tucked her hair under her hat.

All ready. All wound up and breathless and guilty-seeming when there was nothing to feel guilty about. Fugitives felt similarly, Vivi reflected, and somehow the admission failed to cheer her as it might have were not Michael Maynor at that instant on his way to escort her far afield.

At this moment, the sound of two strong voices hit upon her ear from the dining room. The gentlemen had come, then. Anxiety swelled in Vivi's throat and, though she was armed, a faint panic descended on her. She had committed to going with these men—alone—on a long country ramble. Farnham had sanctioned the plan, but it wasn't as if anyone actually *knew* where they were going. And she was reasonably certain one of the men was a murderer! In the grand school of stupidity, she was certainly winning the prize for model pupil.

She took up the picnic basket and carried it through into the dining room. "Gentlemen! This is a merry meeting!"

Michael lifted the basket from her arms and set it on the table. "When fair Athena bakes a cake, a pleasant time we soon will make."

"Was that your own poetry?" Jimmy asked.

"But of course."

"Shoddy stuff, isn't it, Vivi?"

In response to this, and perhaps gratitude for Jimmy lightening the mood, Vivi laughed. "Convenient rhyming can hardly be called poetry, Mr. Fields, in which case, Michael did quite well...for doggerel."

"Slain by the Fairest's tongue," Michael commented. "What have you packed in this thing? It's heavier than lead."

Her smile was sufficiently arch to boost her confidence. "Only a lunch which you'll be mad over when we finally stop."

"Yes, but who do you propose to lug it about *until* we stop," he countered.

"You're quite strong," Vivi said with a light, cutting tone one could almost mistake for friendliness. "I'm sure you can carry things cross-country without overmuch trouble." If not picnics, bodies.

"If your back wears out, Michael, I'm par for the course." Jimmy patted his pockets. "Well, shall we gang tae the heelands, Leezie Lindsay?"

Vivi shrugged. "I'm game. Allen, when he comes downstairs, will you please tell Mr. Farnham I've gone?"

"Of course, Miss." The man bowed, and Vivi's throat clenched with an awful premonition of tears. Why was she crying? About Allen, of all people?"

As she turned to the gentlemen, Vivi made a dazzler of a smile knit of terror and insincerity.

"Which direction are we headed?" she asked. "I mean, just in case I prove unworthy of your confidence and get blisters a mile or two in. I assure you, I weigh much more than that picnic basket, and I doubt even the gallant Mr. Maynor would enjoy carting me afield."

Jimmy pulled a map out of his breast pocket and pressed it on the table. "Thought we'd head cross-country toward the Mill. We'll make a broad sweep parallel to it, then run North, up toward Marlingford Farm, cut across at Ealsey Hollow Farm—maybe pop in for a cup of tea with my old man—then stop by the ridge up at Holly Triad and....come back through the Rowan Walk. That is, if Farnham won't mind us trespassing."

Allen straightened from bending over the map. "Not at all, sir. He would be glad to know someone has been using the old Walk."

"Wonderful. Then, shall we?"

Jimmy extended his arm, and Vivi took it while Michael followed along with the picnic basket in his arms. By the time they'd gone halfway down the drive, Michael was already puffing.

"This is the most awkward thing ever. Can't we pitch it in the grass and carry our sandwiches vagabond-style?" he called after them. "A bit of lunch done up in a hankie and slung over a stick would be loads easier to carry."

"There *are* straps," Vivi said. "Here." She took the basket from him and turned Michael about, guiding his strong arms into the leather straps so that he soon wore the picnic basket like a knapsack.

"Now I look like a boy-scout."

"But your arms are free," Vivi said. "Come, let's not spoil a lovely morning by quarrelling about lunch." *By quarreling about anything.* Recent circumstances considered, Vivi did not deem it advisable to annoy Michael in any way.

The picnic basket now settled across Michael's broad shoulders, the group could move off. At the end of Whistlecreig's drive, Jimmy slung open a gate and guided them into a field. The ground was covered in low, dark green grass, thatched over with the deadened stalks of nettles and daisies. Here and there are resilient stand of purple asters brightened the ground. The year's last songbirds flitted over the fields and swallows dipped low over the party's heads, wheeling off at the last second before colliding with them.

"Oh, Vivi," Jimmy said, "I almost forgot." He held out a walking stick to her. "You'll probably find this useful."

She took it from him and felt the weight of it in her hands. Simple and beautiful carvings of a flowering vine twined the length of the staff and the wood had been polished to a beautiful sheen. It was not a man's walking stick at all—rather too short for anyone but herself. "Did you...make this, Jimmy?"

He dipped his head in acknowledgment, and the muscle in his jaw clenched, making a dimple hover in his left cheek as if he was trying not to smile. "It's nothing fancy. I'd saved that stick of wood for a while...just didn't know how I wanted to work it. Till I met you."

An unseemly clank followed this rather tender declaration as Michael stumbled over a tussock of grass and the thermoses inside his basket collided. "Are you tired already, old man?"

The stick felt smooth as satin under her palm. "Such a light color. Wherever did you get pine?"

Michael snatched the stick. "It's not pine. Too greeny-grey. Pine's yellow. Rowan, I'd say."

"Now you really are a boy scout," Jimmy grunted.

Desperate to soothe the ill-humour swirling in their party, Vivi took back her staff. "Rowan? What a lovely thought."

"Charmed wood for the most charming of all." Jimmy's blue eyes dwelt on hers with fondness and something else.

"It'd also make an excellent bludgeon, Viv. Any gentlemen try to bother you, bash 'em over the coconut."

Michael's tone was teasing, but Vivi saw Jimmy tense as if he had already had as much of Michael's sullen arrogance as he could well stomach. She didn't blame him and wondered if it was not an accident they hadn't seen each other since college.

"You can stop being disagreeable anytime now," Jimmy suggested

"I'm the soul of congeniality. You're hogging the lady's affections."

Vivi hefted Jimmy's staff in her hands. "He was only giving me a gift."

Michael shifted the basket on his shoulders. "I'd think I was the one needing a staff. What did you pack in here? Sandbags?"

"Horseshoes."

"But of course."

The rising sun was a bit ahead and on their left as they rambled in the rough direction of the town and the mill. The fellows kept up a brisk enough pace and, before they had gone over a mile or two, Vivi found herself glad for the stoutness of her shoes and the aid of Jimmy's walking stick. The day grew warmer as the sun rose, but not so warm yet that she began to perspire. For that, Vivi was grateful. She cared not for the messy bits of a well-rounded life in the countryside. Sweating can never be considered dignified, whatever merits it might possess.

At the top of a grassy ridge, Jimmy paused and turned back to help Vivi clamber up the slope. Michael was close behind, a tinny-sounding, clanking addition to the party. They stopped a moment to catch their breath and survey the land. Jimmy cupped his hands around his eyes and faced the glare of the sun.

"There," said he, taking his hands down, "is Whistlecreig."

"Manor or town?" asked Vivi, who had begun to be confused about where exactly all the tramping had taken them.

"Manor's behind and to the right, town's *ahead* to the right." Jimmy pointed down the gentle undulations of the land. Following the direction of his finger, Vivi could see the spire of the church tucked behind a long ridge, and the neat scar of train-track running across the land's otherwise unmarred face.

"And which farm are we crossing?"

"The Southern bits of Marlingford and some miscellaneous land owned by locals. See those low buildings over there?" He pointed toward a stand of farm buildings without a house to the right. "That's Hilton's pig-styes."

"Where are Garridy's?" Vivi asked, remembering fondly her altercation with Farnham over where they would buy bacon.

Jimmy looked at her, brows upraised. "Quite the local expert, aren't you?"

She tossed her head with an arch laugh. "I like to know from whence my food comes."

"Garridy's bacon runs more to the fat. It's better."

"When I buy bacon, I prefer meat. Hilton's."

"Garridy's," Jimmy laughed.

"*Pax Romana?*" suggested Michael in an impatient tone. "This talk of bacon is making me cursed hungry."

"Want me to take a turn with the pack?" Jimmy asked.

"No," Michael said with a nice smile. "Then Miss Langley would no longer be indebted to me and we all like ladies owing us favors."

An awkward silence followed this remark, and Vivi wished upon her life that Michael was not present. He made the worst third she had ever encountered. It struck her that if ever a man was to fight a duel of honor, he could not do much worse than choose Michael Maynor as his second. What a cheering spectre he'd be on a misty morning at twelve paces. Quite bolstering to the courage, his spartan good-looks.

"We'll head off to the left a bit more," Jimmy said, consulting his map. "Can't see terribly well 'cause of that hill, but you can see the river where it runs across the road? That's the stream that feeds into the mill-pond. You remember, don't you, Vivi?"

"Of course."

"I don't," Michael butted in. "I've never been here, remember?" He drew the map toward him. "Is the water drinkable? I've got the devil of a thirst."

"Yes."

"By the rood, *mein* host, that is good to hear. Well, off, shall we?"

And so the ramble continued over a few more hills until the final, gentle descent onto the main way just where it engaged with the Kettering Road. They walked in the soft dust kicked to the sides of the road by automobiles, and a pleasant, hazy aroma rose to join the morning sun that now beamed down with great goodwill on the adventurers' heads. It was a mild day, extraordinarily mild for November, and Vivi soon wished she could remove her coat and walk along, like the gentlemen, in her shirtsleeves. Michael had removed his jacket on the first hill, and Jimmy's jumper had long been slung across his shoulders as if he'd been a matador in cable-knits.

Her coat stuck in damp patches to the backs of her arms and around the soft curves of her waist. Vivi was past the point of gentle perspiration and far past what her mother insipidly called "glistening." But she had the fact of her pistol to reckon with. If she was certain she could be the only one to handle her coat, she might risk removing it, but there was no guarantee Jimmy might not act gallantly and insist on carrying it for her, which would only be disastrous.

"Someday you might end up a murderer." Michael's foreboding words jangled Vivi's spirits as she imagined Jimmy dropping the coat, or the trigger of the bull-dog catching on the fabric and ejecting a bullet into his brain.

"You all right, Vivi?" Michael trotted up till he came even with her and peered into her face.

"Fine." Vivi breathed through her nose, trying to disguise the fact that she'd begun to pant a bit and wish for cooler attire.

"Your face is red."

"I'm *fine*, Michael."

Jimmy turned about at this exchange and walked backward a few paces. The sun lit his face from behind with a dusty halo. "He's right. Why's your face red?"

"Exercise? Fresh air?" she snapped.

"Contemplating that kiss?" he offered with a roguish grin.

Michael twitched almost imperceptibly. Vivi saw it.

"You kissed her?" His tone was measured with wartime blockade accuracy.

"Yes, my dear Maynor. 'Stolen sweets are always sweeter' and so forth."

Vivi wished to high heaven Jimmy had said nothing. What was it that made men require to always boast about their exploits to one another? If there was one thing she hated, it was the conceited air some men carried about with them, as if every conquest they made was by their prowess alone and had nothing to do with the lady's decision. It showed a decided lack of delicacy and Vivi was put out with Jimmy for it.

Michael rubbed a hand over the back of his neck. A hot, sweaty smell like that of a horse gone for the running rose up around him, masculine and active. "Redder than ever now, Jimmy. I don't think Miss Langley appreciates our rough-housing."

"Not much," she admitted.

"Sorry, Viv," said Jimmy, quite gently.

She waved her hand to dismiss the conversation and willed everyone to forget it. To this end, she quickened her pace and reached the mill a step ahead of the others. She spread her hands on the broad-beamed rail and stared into the water. The cool depths beckoned her with a delicious, chuckling murmur, and she felt hotter than ever. Almost panicked with the heat, Vivi dug her fingers into the buttonholes of her jacket and threw the garment open. Cooler air embraced her, sweet relief to her galloping pulse.

"I wish I could take a swim," she murmured.

Michael slung his burden to the ground. "Why don't we?" Sweat painted a wet square against his back where the picnic basket had rested on his skin. He flapped his shirt and blew air through his cheeks. "I feel like a blacksmith's furnace."

Jimmy threw his jumper across the rail and leaned on his forearms. He nudged Vivi with his elbow and spoke quietly: "I am sorry for bringing up the kiss. Honest."

"I know."

"Do you? You look awfully angry and hot."

"I am hot," she conceded, before realizing her error.

"Then take off your blasted jacket, silly girl. I'll carry it for you." Jimmy moved to ease the coat from her shoulders, but Vivi stopped his wrist with her hand.

"Please," she said, feeling his tendons shift under her palm. "Don't."

He gave her a close look which she met with as much honesty and forthrightness as she could muster. "I will be fine, presently. I'm so hot and damp right now, I know I'll get a chill if I start removing clothing."

"Wouldn't that be a sight?" Michael muttered, coming up on her right side. "Britain's most circumspect debutante removing her clothing along a country road."

"Shut up, Michael," Jimmy said.

"I'm only making conversation. It's not like Vivi'd actually *do* it. More's the pity." He finished in a mumble, but Vivi heard.

She flushed crimson with fury and, for the third time that morning, consigned Michael Maynor to someplace hotter than anything offered by this earthly realm. *Oh God, get me through today,* she breathed, and for the first time in her life felt she could understand how a person might commit murder.

Chapter Nineteen
Feinting

Allen looked to be plucky this morning—well, what of him Farnham could see from his reclining position among the pleasantly suffocating folds of his feather bed.

"Allen, what time have you?"

"Half-eight, sir."

"Wonderful. Miss Langley gone off, I presume?"

"Quite early, sir. In the company of two gentlemen."

From the disparaging plunge at the end of his sentence, Farnham could tell his butler did not quite approve of this method of deportment. Why Allen should take exception to something Vivi did was beyond him. Unless Allen disapproved of his niece's companions. Maynor was an unfortunate addition to the party, Farnham would be the first to admit, but Jimmy was a decent local lad whom they'd all but cleared of suspicion.

Sudden misgiving stirred near his ulcers. "Do you think there's any *danger*?"

"If I may speak bold, sir?" Allen cleared his throat. "I think Miss Langley is a capable woman. Not likely to have the wool pulled over her eyes. She's clever enough to be on her guard."

Farnham picked at the covers with his fingertips. "Yes. Yes, I know. I could have gone along with her all the same. Do you think I ought to have?"

Allen's eyebrows beetled gently at him, and he placed a tray with two crust-less pieces of toast and cup of coffee on his employer's lap. "Not much sense in 'ifs' and 'shoulds', sir. She'll be right as rain, I imagine."

"But I don't even know where they've *gone*. Those are two young men who have both been suspects in a banged *murder*, Allen. I can't imagine what I've done in letting her go off. Her mother would kill me if Vivi got murdered too. A triple murder —wouldn't that be case for the Courts? The actress, Vivi, and old Orville Farnham inside one week."

Farnham shoved the tray to the side, sloshing tea onto the toast, and sprang out of bed. Allen stared at the carnage sadly, probably contemplating the sad state of affairs the country had come to when men didn't recognize the merits of a butler who would toast bread to the heights of perfection.

Farnham had his banged niece to thank for this new breed of thought. He slipped into his bathrobe and cinched the ties savagely.

"Get my pistol, Allen."

"Your pistol, sir?"

"Yes, Allen."

Allen picked up the tray and moved the teacup to the side with a frown for the now-soggy toast. "The one in the box of maps, sir?"

Farnham's stomach bit him at his butler's abstracted tone. "Yes, of course, Allen."

"What do you propose to do with the pistol, Mr. Farnham? Nothing rash, I hope, sir."

"You know me. I'm never rash. Prompt," he flicked his palms outward and bent his knees, "decisive, cunning, quick, but *never* rash."

"Just so, sir."

"Well, the pistol, man. Get it! I haven't all day."

"I believe, sir, that would be rather difficult." Allen placed the wrecked tray on the nightstand and removed a folded handkerchief from his pocket with which to dab at some tea that had escaped the plate of toast and landed on the bed-spread.

"Why? God and His saints be praised, *why*, Allen?"

"Because, sir," Allen said, patience seeping into his voice, "I think your pistol went along with Miss Langley."

Farnham aborted a real live curse that had made it halfway through his lips and stalked, shaking, from the room. He turned on his heel at the doorway, livid and in a topping rage. "Allen," said he, voice quaking with suppressed emotion.

"Yes, sir?"

"All hell shall stir for this."

"*Yes*, sir."

It was quite noon by now, if she was any good at reading the sun, which talent she felt inclined to doubt. Vivi reached into the deep front pocket of her coat and found her watch. Beneath her palm, divided by a thin wall of fabric from the inner pocket, she could feel the small bulk of Farnham's bull-dog. This encouraged her, for as long as she had a loaded pistol, she could not be as helpless as she now felt. Removing her watch, Vivi clicked open the golden lid and read the numbers. Half-nine? That couldn't be so. It must have entirely stopped working sometime last night after Doctor Breen discovered it lagging.

"Does anyone know what o'clock it is?" she asked. They reached a rough sort of turnstile and climbed over, finding its funny iron arm quite rusted in place. There had been a variety of gates and stiles to allow their passage over the walls and fences dividing one field from another; this had been the oddest yet, reminding Vivi of the queues at an amusement park. Only, there were no carousels beyond this, just another field. And another, and another and another. Would they ever end or had they got entangled in a sort of Sinai in which there was no egress, no, not unto forty years?

"What o'clock is it?" she repeated.

Michael rubbed the back of his neck and hitched up his sleeve to look at his wristwatch. "Fifteen after eleven. Your watch dead?"

"Yes. It was slow last night, you'll recall." She shook her watch and listened for a tick. None came. "Afraid it wants a funeral."

"We ought to get Doctor Breen to sign the certificate of death," Jimmy joked. "We'll hold off the burial till we've consulted him."

"What a funny thing it must be to be a doctor," Vivi said, reflective of a sudden. "Your services are required everywhere...death-beds...birthing rooms..."

"Murder sites?" Michael offered.

"Yes," Vivi said slowly. "I should not like it."

"I should not care."

"Oh, Michael, don't be insensitive." She pocketed her watch again and looked away, pretending to admire the view.

This little shenanigan they were playing was so false it fair chilled her. She knew that Michael knew she suspected him of murder. If he *was* the murderer, he would want to get her out of the way. Surely the police would be able to trace his trail and arrest him in the end...but perhaps she'd be dead by then and it would not matter. The only thing she could do was what she had *been* doing ever since she had aggravated matters by barging into his hotel room—stay close to anyone who was *not* Michael and pray never to be unfortunate enough to find herself alone with him.

"Ealsey Hollow is just around that copse of trees." Jimmy offered his hand to Vivi and led her away from the fence, onward once more. "You'd be able to see it if there wasn't a rise of land just beyond. If you want, we can rest up a bit and have a cup and a chat with my Dad."

"And a game of horseshoes?" she inquired.

"Two games."

"Why not? Michael, do you mind?" She was making an effort to include him in conversation. What more could he want? He had better not still be furious with her, for she didn't know how else to distract him.

Michael turned dull, mocking eyes to her with a look that announced his perfect comprehension of her motives. "Tea would be fabulous. Maybe we'll lunch, then, too? I know it's a bit early, but I'd love to shed my turtle-shell. We could leave the hamper there and have someone deliver it to Whistlecreig later."

"Perfect," Vivi said.

They continued the ramble, and the prospect of a comfortable hearth at which to rest her feet put a bit of life back into Vivi. The ramble had become more of a trudge in the last mile, and she was glad for the thought of a respite. Breen had not been joking when he said their rambles were serious affairs. What had they walked, seven miles?

"How far have we gone?" she ventured.

Jimmy, who appeared to be in fine fettle yet, turned his chin over his shoulder and smiled. "Do you need me to cart you home pig-a-back?"

221

"I just wondered—I like to know my way."

"It's been a matter of seven miles, I'd say. We made such a broad sweep, and the detour to the fern glen wasn't necessary."

If the opinions of her feet were to be counted, Vivi thought the fern glen not worth the extra walking; in the spring, it would have been a beautiful, feathersome place, but now the fiddles were tightly curled in russet dreams and showed no sign of being anything but rather dead stalks someone had neglected to mow. But she was glad to have seen the place all the same. Perhaps, if she was—by some fluke—still at Whistlecreig in the spring, they would return.

"I'm all a-dither, Jimmy," Michael said from behind. "If a body was to walk straight from Whistlecreig to Ealsey Hollow, how far would it be?"

"That is rather the problem, isn't it?" Jimmy said with a laugh. "I'm afraid there's no walking straight from anywhere to anywhere in this part of the country."

"What a frustration it would have been for Napoleon, if he'd ever made it to Northamptonshire," said Vivi. "Marching an army through your wicked stiles one by one like sheep ready for the shearing. It would make it easy to count the enemy, now wouldn't it?"

Michael laughed—his first laugh of the morning. "I like your stratagem, General Langley. Know your enemy's numbers and knock him off one soldier at a time. Very neat."

"I bow to your superior knowledge of slaughtering. I'd be much handier organizing hospital beds."

Jimmy smiled and led the way onto a path winding through the copse of trees.

"Really? Hospital beds?" asked Michael. "I fancied you rather the Jael, assassin type—sneak into a man's room and blow his brains out—though I assume you'd use a pistol, not a tent-peg."

The laughter of the all three filled the small stand of woods and startled a few doves from the underbrush. She laughed—for what else could she do?—but inside, Vivi shuddered and her hand involuntarily crept toward her thigh to feel if her weapon was still there.

Michael Maynor knew far too much.

Farnham stalked into the little-used parlor and pulled one of his fencing swords from the rack holding a variety of antique and contemporary weapons.

He was a failure. How could he, a man well-versed in life, have allowed his own niece to go off alone with two knaves? *He* was old enough to count the cost; *he* knew what thoughts occupied the minds of men; *he* ought to have been her protector!

Still in a rage, Farnham made for the straw man at the far end of the room and, with a quick thrust, lunged at it. What had he been thinking, letting Vivi go on a banged ramble with two banged murder suspects?

He groaned and, with a swift *flèche*, toppled the straw mannequin. Farnham growled and hauled the thing upright again. He didn't want to fence with a dummy—he wanted to perform a derobement on the weapons-thief and retrieve his pistol before she did herself harm with it. Women could not shoot—well, today's women. Farnham had always fancied the fair Beatrice would have carried a pistol about with her—*and* been a crack shot—but it seemed doubtful of Genevieve Langley. What did she think to do? Protect herself? She'd probably end up blowing out her own brains in an effort to save someone's life.

One life lost on Whistlecreig's sod was enough. The idea that she was going to accidentally add another—probably her own—to the account caused sweat to stand out along Farnham's forehead and sent him with an unusually forceful flunge at the straw man.

"Blast women!" he shouted, and stabbed the mannequin.

"Useless creatures!" he yelled with another stab. "Maddening!"

"Sir?"

The introduction of Allen's cool voice had an electrifying effect. Farnham turned about with ill-disguised impatience to find his butler standing in the doorway, stripped to his shirtsleeves.

"*What*, Allen? The smallest *worm* will turn if trodden on. I'm a very viper today." The flexible blade of his sabre trembled in hand.

Allen took one respectful step forward. "I fancied you might like a *live* opponent, sir. You seemed to be in the mood to have it out with a man. I am willing, sir."

His butler's offer of service disarmed Farnham. That any man would voluntarily cross swords with a furious Heir of Whistlecreig showed a sort of fealty he must commend. It was better than Crusoe's Friday or Ivanhoe's Womba. It was... touching.

With a low grumble that was neither denial nor assent, he turned his backsword basket-first to Allen and chose another for himself.

They positioned themselves in the familiar pose. "It's this bang murder, Allen. *Allez!*"

Allen darted forward in a *balestra,* finishing with a lunge which Farnham beat-parried. Allen attacked again, this time with a fierce agility Farnham had not expected from his ponderous butler this early on in the match. Farnham parried the attack, but before he had quite rescued himself, Allen played a deft flick and ended with his sword-point on Farnham's chest.

He stepped back and swung his weapon in a wide, aimless circle. "Very good, sir. Play a bit lighter. Less thrashing, more dancing," he instructed, respectful but firm.

Farnham flicked the lapels of his dressing gown with a frown. "I know, Allen. You don't have to tell me."

"Very well, sir. What was it you were saying about the murder?" He poised again with one arm thrown back over his head.

"*En garde!* I can't - figure - how - to - pin - him," Farnham said, underscoring each word with a series of feints at Allen which did not upset the butler.

Farnham extended his weapon and made little jabs and cuts at Allen. Steel rang on steel with a joyous sound, and he found his thoughts focusing less on his emotions and more on the murder. Allen held back for a while, simply parrying every blow. Good man, Farnham thought, for realizing his master was in the depths of a puzzlement. Then, swinging his rear leg over his front, Allen sprinted past Farnham in the neatest *flèche* Farnham had seen in an age. It surprised him so he stood rooted to the floor. Allen made to score a touch, then let his arm fall when he saw that his opponent was not in the humor.

"That was bang neat of you," Farnham said. "I didn't know you could move so fast."

Allen grinned, a lopsided, jowled affair. "Thank you, sir. Chasing mice from the kitchen has its merits, sir."

"I'll say it does." Farnham dug in the pocket of his dressing gown for a handkerchief, only to find it empty. Allen saw his predicament and proffered his own on the end of his sword.

"Many thanks." He patted his forehead dry and folded the kerchief again.

"You were saying, sir, that you couldn't find how to pin him. I gather we are discussing our suspect?"

"Correct. I am certain of my man—more so because of the facts which you, my *dear* fellow, were so good as to upturn."

"I was honored," Allen answered, and poised for the attack again. "*Allez?*"

He slid forward on his front leg in a lunge, fast and perfectly rigid, but Farnham was ready this time and threw himself into a *passata-sotto*, pressing a hand to the floor and lowering himself under the thrust of Allen's blade in one fluid movement.

Allen broke off with a laugh. "Wasn't expecting that from you, sir."

"Neither was I," Farnham puffed. Allen extended a hand and hauled him to his feet. Farnham dusted off his robe and tossed his weapon into the air.

Allen watched the gesture. "Do you have one particular thing that is hanging up the investigation, sir?"

"Proof," Farnham conceded. "I'm not an official detective, unfortunately. I can't perform arrests, and the police will not listen if I have no proof."

"Did the medical advice not help?" Allen asked. "I thought for sure—"

"No, it will help. It will." Farnham clapped his faithful butler on the shoulder. "We'll get our chance. Presently, something will fall in our way that will put the thing together. All the pieces...all the lovely, scattered pieces."

Allen scraped a curlicue into the dust on the wood floor with the tip of his sword. "You have only till tomorrow before you've lost your bet with the doctor. Your *first bet*, sir. I wouldn't like to see that happen."

Farnham cast his eye out the dim, front window. "I know, Allen. Me neither."

"Then *when*, sir? Time isn't our ally."

"I know."

"Is there anything further I can do?"

"Nothing. We must wait and trust Providence to bring us a chance."

"When?"

"Soon, Allen, soon."

"No, sir."

Farnham snorted. "What the blazes do you mean by telling me 'no'?"

One corner of Allen's reluctant smile quivered. "Not 'soon,' sir. 'Anon'. It's more Shakespearean."

"Oh. Quite right, Allen. We shall catch our man. But when?"

"Anon, sir, anon." Allen returned his sword to the rack. He stayed a moment, toying with the handles of the weapons.

"What is it, old man?"

"If I were you, sir, I should go find Miss Langley."

Farnham's heart fell like a dove shot from an autumn sky. "Why?"

"I don't like her being off with him. sir. I know she'll never be with one gentleman without the other, but you never know what might befall a girl alone in the countryside. Even if she does have our pistol, sir."

The double meaning of Allen's words hit Farnham in the gut. You never knew indeed; Miss Lillian Bertois had not known, and they were now investigating her death. "Leash Sir Toby Belch for me."

Allen bowed. "Yes, sir."

"Will it be useless, trying to find her?" Farnham asked nervously.

"Not entirely, sir. Miss Langley took the liberty of asking Jimmy, in my presence, where their walk would lead, sir."

"Blessed girl!"

"I fancy by this time you will find them on the ridge behind Holly Triad, sir."

"Oh *God!* Holly Triad?"

"Was that a prayer, sir, or ought I to look at you askance?"

Farnham smiled in a spasm of annoyance and fear. "A *prayer,* since you ask. The murder was committed near Holly Triad. I have the most awful feeling...Oh *God*, it's awful. Stay his hand, most merciful Lord," Farnham mumbled, fumbling to insert his weapon in the rack. "Call Breen. Tell him to meet me on the road between the Rowan Walk and Holly Triad with a car and his dueling pistols. And call the police, too."

"Quite right, sir."

"And you'll get Belch for me?"

"In a trice, sir."

"Good man. Oh *fire and flame*, if only she hadn't taken my banged pistol."

Allen smiled sympathetically. "I can imagine the annoyance it would cause a man to be stripped of his weapon in so cheap a manner, sir. But if you don't mind another observance...?"

"Of course not. Go ahead, Allen."

"At this moment, Miss Langley is ironically the one in need of a firearm. I'm glad she stole your pistol."

He passed a hand over this thinning hair. "Bang it, Allen, you're right."

"Thank you, sir. I'll be getting Belch."

"And I'll be getting dressed. Pray God no one kills her before I get there."

"Come in, come in, come in!" A pale, rumpled, dear old man opened the door of Ealsey Hollow Farm in response to their steps on a flagged walk lined with marigolds.

"Da, this is Miss Genevieve Langley and Mr. Michael Maynor." Jimmy pocketed his hands and grinned at his guests.

"I seen yah," old Mr. Fields said with a trembling, spotted hand for Vivi's. "I seen yah at the ceilidh."

Elderly people always left Vivi at a loss for conversation. Their routines never varied, their health only worsened...what was one to speak about?

At last, she settled on: "Thank you for letting us stop by."

It was the right choice.

"Come in for some toast and tea," Mr. Fields said. He shuffled back over the worn stoop of the cottage and into the dimness. "Come in. Don't be shy. Li'l Jim's walks aire fiercer than fierce."

"That they are." Vivi obediently stepped into the cottage and looked about the hall, taking in a fleeting, warm impression of wine-red papering hung with old calendars and tiny family portraits, bits of cheap porcelain and a dusty clock.

"Sit in that chair," the old man said, indicating a walnut rocker.

Vivi complied and watched Mr. Fields shuffle to a copper kettle on a hob. He poured water over tea-leaves into an ivoried pot that looked as if it had seen Babylon in its youth and looked at her side-long. His smile was gentle as summer honey.

"Do you know my favorite thing? Com'ny on cheery days. Best fun an old tater like me ever has. Gives me summat to do."

"Da, don't be chattering Miss Langley's ears off."

Vivi glanced up, jarred by the introduction of Jimmy's voice. He leaned his weight on his forearm against the low doorframe and dipped his head into the kitchen-parlor. Michael was nowhere to be seen.

"I ent chatterin'," his father nipped back, sending a look over his shoulder that made him almost uncannily resemble an arthritic little terrier deprived of his owner's attention.

"I don't mind," Vivi interposed with a giggle.

Mr. Fields poured a stream of amber liquid into a red willow ware cup and handed it to Vivi.

"Thank you."

"No trouble! Do y'know my favorite thing? Comp'ny on days that are cheery. Gives me summat to do. Best fun I get."

At this near-exact repetition, Vivi's smile became slightly fixed, slightly confused. She looked at Jimmy and met his shame-faced answer: his father's mind was no longer keen.

"Do you want to play horseshoes in a bit?" Mr. Fields inquired. "Milk or sugar?"

"Thank you, sugar. I would love to play horseshoes."

The old man sipped his tea, his crabbed, earth-stained fingers wrapped round the cup like a kindly badger's claws. "Best fun I get. Comp'ny's my favorite thing. Gives me summat to do."

Jimmy stretched his back. "Da, Michael's setting up a picnic on the walk. How 'bout we head outside and play horseshoes right now?"

Again, the terrier-like bristling. "A'right, a'right, Li'l Jim. Stop ditherin'. I'm just enjoyin' summat to do."

Quietly, so as not to chip the fragile red teacup, Vivi set it on the register and put her hand over old Mr. Fields'. "I bet I'll win," she said.

A youthful mischief kindled in the farmer's eyes. "Not if ah've aught t'do with it."

Chapter Twenty
I'm a Gentleman

An hour after lunch at the farm, it seemed to Vivi that they had passed all reasonable bounds of distance in their walk. The fragrant cup of amber tea at Ealsey Hollow seemed leagues in the past, the 'summat to do' a distant dream. The sandwiches seemed dreamlike too, now that they had gone on. Even the horseshoes were but a distant ache in her right arm.

"How much farther?" Vivi groaned as they slogged up yet another hill. Her blood buzzed in her fingertips and feet and mottled in her palms. She was not used to this much exertion, and goodwill had finally bent to weariness.

Jimmy took her hand and hauled her up the incline. "Holly Triad's just ahead. Best view in the county, I'd say. We'll see it up there, make our way back through the Rowan Walk, and you'll be home."

Almost done.

Home could not come too soon for Vivi. She hurt; blisters carved severe paths through her heels, making the work of walking a literally bloody affair. She would not, however, admit the greatness of her pain. She knew she was a small girl: the gentleman would only insist on carrying her. *That* she would not stand for, even if the idea of pillowing her head against Jimmy's shoulder and being carried in his arms was not entirely repugnant.

"Tiring out, Miss Langley?" Michael asked from behind. Before she could protest, he looped his arm through hers, causing her to lean against his bulk as they walked.

"No more than you, I'm sure," she fibbed, and tried to remove her arm from his grasp.

"Valiant words, darling, but I know you. Let me help you." He turned his head to look in her face as they walked and whispered, "Don't be stupid, Vivi. You and I both know you're worn out. Just use my arm. I don't mean anything by it but to help you. I'm a *gentleman,* remember?"

As much as Vivi hated the idea of being indebted to Michael Maynor for anything, she had to admit that her heels hurt less when she could use Michael for support on one side, her walking stick on the other. So on they went, and the land unfolded in gentle hills and valleys as it had all day, and still they walked on. Since leaving Ealsey Hollow, there had been no houses, no buildings of any kind. Just hill after hill of farmland, and copses between.

"Jimmy?" Vivi called ahead.

He turned, his handsome face flushed with red, shirt-collar thrown open against the heat of the walk. "What?"

"How far is Holly Triad?"

"Only a bit more."

"What do you mean by a 'bit'?" Michael asked. "If you take your bit of a walk like the doctor takes his bit of drink, our feet will go to shreds."

Jimmy stuffed his hands in his pockets and swaggered back to them, grinning. "Have I exhausted you entirely?"

"Entirely? No." Vivi let go Michael's arm and smiled, tucking her hair under her hat again and wishing she didn't look quite so blown.

"Good. It's not much farther. We're almost there, in fact. Will you take my arm?"

Vivi walked up to him and put her hand through his crooked elbow. He smiled down on her, and they made to go forward.

"Wait," Michael said.

Jimmy turned, and his arm tensed like a rod in Vivi's grasp. His gaze seemed frozen over his shoulder. Vivi rotated to see Michael with a pistol aimed at Jimmy and a cruel smile on his face.

Confusion broke against her like waves. What did Michael mean?

"Michael, what sort of joke do you think this is?" Jimmy asked. He pulled Vivi closer and threw a protective arm around her waist. "You'll frighten Miss Langley."

"I seem to find that hard to believe." Michael removed his scathing glare from Jimmy's face long enough to bestow a sympathetic, knowing look on Vivi.

Jimmy shifted from one foot to the other. "What is this about, Michael?" His eyes sparked a dangerous blue Vivi had never before seen, and his jaw bulged. "Are you serious about this?" He waved a hand at the gun, at Vivi, and the fields around them.

A distinct, odd sense of detachment filled Vivi's mind, much as the fog had on the morning they saw the actress's body. She felt as if she looked on their group from the vantage point of one of the swallows, and was not really there at all.

"Are you going to kill us both? Make it a total of three people you've killed in the same town?" Jimmy asked. His voice hauled Vivi back to the flickering reality of the fact that she was caught in the middle of a stand-off. "Really, Maynor, if you wanted to kill us, you'd have far better luck not doing it in my hometown, within reach of *her* uncle."

Michael seemed unmoved by this argument. "Let her go, Fields."

Jimmy's arm tensed around Vivi, and she wondered if Michael would shoot if he kept hold of her. Who would he shoot?

Both of them?

Her?

Jimmy must release her if her pistol would be any use whatsoever. *Oh,* how she hated Michael Maynor. To Vivi's temporary relief, Jimmy obeyed Michael's demands and threw Vivi from him, whipping out a gun he had concealed.

"Stand there," he said.

For a second, Vivi thought Jimmy spoke to Michael, and it pleased her to see straight horror imprinted on Michael's smooth countenance. From the corner of her eye, she saw Jimmy raise his hand—to shoot Michael?—then a sharp spasm of pain drove through Vivi's ear and the world reeled in a black tumblement.

"I said stand *there,*" Jimmy's voice shouted from afar.

Jimmy shoved Vivi in front of him. She stumbled forward, dizzy and dazed from the blow. Her sight was dark around the edges, and Michael wavered in her vision, now distant, now close, like a dancing marionette. Why had Jimmy struck her? What had happened? His arm went around her waist, and his fingertips dug into her soft belly, cruel and vicious, pulling her against him.

"You shoot me, Maynor, I'll shoot Vivi."

Something cold pressed under Vivi's curls, right at the base of her head. Horror, shock, anger flooded through her body and edged out the pain of the blow to her head.

"What are you doing, Fields? Let Vivi go!"

"No," Jimmy said. His voice was calm. A playful kiss landed half on her temple, half on her ear. "I rather like her. I don't want to *share.*"

"Is that why you killed Lillian?" Michael stepped closer. "No, *don't* look at me like that. Is that why you killed her? I know you did it."

"Jimmy?" Vivi struggled in his grasp, and he drove the barrel of the pistol closer to her head.

"You are dead if you move, Viv." His breath puffed hot and moist against her cheek. This was madness. Michael was openly declaring Jimmy had killed Lillian Bertois. Why, how could Jimmy have even known the actress? Farnham was right? Michael was *innocent?*

No. The pain of the blow shot through with fear nauseated Vivi. She would vomit, presently.

Fighting for consciousness, Vivi tucked her head. "You don't have to kill us, Jimmy."

"What are you talking about, woman?"

"You didn't know Lillian. You didn't commit the murder."

Michael's laugh jarred them all; Jimmy clung to Vivi more desperately than ever, pulling her backward so that she felt his knee in her thigh and his heart pounding against her shoulder blades.

"Didn't know *Lillian?*" Michael laughed again, the movement jarring shards of sunlight off the gleaming metal of his weapon. "Faith, you're an *innocente.*"

"What does he mean, Jimmy?" she whispered.

The fingers of Jimmy's left hand ran up her cheek and lifted her hat to play in her hair. He bent his head close. "Lil and I had some good times. She was fun. Like you. Strong too —bruised my jaw with her little fist."

Disgust rose like bile in Vivi's throat, and she had a job to keep from uttering a choice host of battle-worthy curses against him. In playing with her curls, Jimmy's grip about Vivi's waist had loosened an increment. She gathered her courage for a few seconds, then thrust her elbow backward, into his gut, and ripped away.

He grabbed for her, tearing at her coat. "Viv—I will shoot you."

"No," she said with a deadly calm in her tone and her pistol in hand. "You won't." She spent his initial spasm of shock cocking back the trigger. "This is Farnham's pistol. Hair trigger. I *tested*." She had not tested, but he need not know. "If you move one step from where you now stand, I will kill you."

"That would be murder," Jimmy said in a dead-level tone.

If he meant to scare her, he failed. "It would be self-defense. I'm a woman, Jimmy. I understand nuances."

It was an absurd trio, and the odd detachment came again and allowed her to see just how absurd. Michael's gun was trained on Jimmy, Jimmy's on Vivi, Vivi's on Jimmy. Two against one. Wasn't it? No, it was every man for himself; she could not trust Michael's loyalty. He had pulled his gun first.

God, give me strength.

"Is this going to be a stalemate?" Michael asked. "Come now, who will give?"

Silence.

"We needn't spill blood to settle our differences."

Vivi scoffed. "You spilled blood to *make* your differences."

"No," Jimmy said. "We had differences before. Lillian was the difference."

"Jolly word-play, all of us," Vivi spat. "What does it signify? Why kill Lillian?" She did not know to whom she addressed the question. She did not expect anyone to answer.

"Jimmy—" Michael began.

"Stop." Jimmy turned his pistol from Vivi to Michael, casting half a glance back on her. "Stop right there."

"There is no scenario in which we all get out of this, Fields," Michael said. "Someone is going to die."

"Well, it isn't going to be me."

"Trite. So trite. Come now, old fellow," Michael trilled taking a half step forward. "If we're going to kill each other, let's at least do it with finesse. We are wordsmiths, you and I. We ought to be able to insult each other cleverly."

"Yes, we ought."

"Would it have been so bad for you, Jimmy?" Michael asked.

Vivi realized they had relapsed to the subject of the murder. Would *what* have been so bad? She felt woefully in need of enlightenment. There was little doubt in her mind now that Jimmy had committed the murder. Still, she dared hope.

"Lillian didn't love you," Jimmy said defiantly.

"Well, she didn't love *you*."

Vivi's heart seized at the low growl in Jimmy's throat. "It was not my child, Maynor."

There had been a child? *Oh, God have mercy.* Wait till Farnham heard about this development...that is, if she made it out alive. Michael was right; there was no way they could all make it out alive. Someone would die.

Keeping his gun trained on Jimmy, Michael reached up with his other hand and reflectively flicked a bit of dust from his shirt sleeve. "I didn't know there was a child." His voice betrayed no hint of the steel she saw his eyes.

"You are welcome to the information." Jimmy's voice was dead and cold as a penny in a well. "It was your kid."

No. It could not be. Genevieve Langley was not standing in the presence of two men discussing which was the father of the illegitimate child of a woman of low morals. Her cheeks flamed, and her heart pounded against her chest as if seeking to find a way out. Necessity demanded she stay, good breeding and decency implored her to flee.

237

God, forgive me for being here.

Jimmy stepped forward, closing the gap between the two men. They seemed to have forgotten her presence. "Lillian came here to blackmail me. It was *your* child, Michael—and don't play dumb. You knew about it. But Society doesn't like little fatherless whelps, does it? After you refused to let Lillian have that little procedure, she turned to money.

"Oh, Lil's a devil all right. Should have gone into business. She told me her plan: pawn the kid off as mine, ruin my reputation, unless I *paid* her. But the child was your doing, Michael. She told me that, too."

"You can't prove that," Michael said through clenched teeth.

Jimmy shrugged. "I know. That was the whole problem."

"So you killed her?"

A breeze lifted the damp curls off Jimmy's forehead, and he pursed his lips as if considering the accusation. He nodded and shrugged. "Yeah, I did."

Michael's face went white, and a faint scar Vivi had never noticed stood out, livid against the paleness of his skin. "You killed a woman and child."

"It *would* have been a child, yes. Oh, come on now, Maynor. It was hardly anything yet. Just an inconvenience."

"It was a child, Fields," Michael repeated. "*My* child."

"You didn't want it."

"You *killed* it. And Lillian. What did Lillian ever do to you?"

Jimmy choked off a laugh. "Blackmailed me! What was I supposed to do? I didn't have the money to pay her off." He rocked back on one foot and motioned Vivi over with his pistol. "Of course I'm going to have to kill you both, now that you know. It's unfortunate, really. You're not at all a bad sort, Vivi."

"How did you do it?" Vivi asked, wanting to buy time before he put a bullet into her body. She could face death bravely, but she wouldn't refuse a few moments more of life.

"With your walking stick. Oh, you needn't look so horrified. It wasn't a walking stick beforehand. It was just a piece of rowan. I carved it especially for you, my love. And to think rowan used to be a symbol of healing and safety. You are clever enough to appreciate the irony, aren't you?"

A shudder passed down Vivi's spine, and her heart quivered. She imagined the thick green grass slippery with the struggle, the gold leaves trembling above, hiding berries as red as blood itself. There was no place in England more perfectly secluded or secretive. And she had walked there alone.

"You killed her in the Rowan Walk. My Rowan Walk."

"Where else?" Jimmy asked. "Quiet, lonesome, handy to the road. Lillian wasn't much bigger than you, Viv. Easy to carry. I would have hidden her in the swamp, and no one would have known. I was interrupted. I needed another plan."

"Crowborough," Vivi breathed.

"Right. Crowborough."

"That was quite stupid of you," she stated flatly.

Jimmy pursed his lips. "I realized I would raise suspicion, skipping town like that. So I came home."

Vivi said. "You lulled our suspicion with that foxy scheme."

His old smile quirked. "You suspected me?"

"At first. But your return cleared you in my mind, at least."

"Good. It worked."

Vivi stepped forward, wishing she did not have to believe Jimmy capable of killing her. Only, now she knew it was so. "After you've killed us, what do you expect to do? Michael and I will both be dead...you will be the only suspect."

"I'm leaving England forever," he said simply. "Tired of it. Old Lil's gone off. You'll both be dead."

"Your father?"

"My father is senile."

At the cold, heartless tone of his voice, tears sprang into Vivi's eyes. This was wrong. It was so wrong. The murder of the woman, and the tiny baby within her body for which no one had thought to check. The approaching murder of both she and Michael Maynor. The dismissal of Jimmy's sweet, aging father as a piece of nothing.

"You are dead." Vivi's voice choked with tears, and she swallowed hard to get over them.

"*I'm* dead? I can't imagine what you mean," Jimmy said.

"When this is over, you'll possess a body, but your *spirit* is poisoned and withered and *dead*." It was horrible, so horrible to see the man she thought he was unraveling gravecloth after putrid gravecloth. Two great tears rolled down Vivi's cheeks, and she fought to keep from sobbing. She edged closer to Michael, feeling that they alone shared some semblance of a common purpose. Never had she expected to ally herself with him.

Michael bent over her head. "Two against one, Vivi. We have him."

"If you think you'll kill me," Jimmy narrowed his eyes, "you can dismiss that idea."

Before she quite knew what had happened, Jimmy squeezed the trigger and Michael fell to the ground with the shot, writhing in agony.

Vivi paled but found the scream she meant to utter had bottled up under her lungs, making it impossible to breathe. Her hands shook as she looked in panic from Michael on the ground to Jimmy with his gun now trained on her. There was blood, a lot of blood. She did not know whether it was a fatal wound—there was not time to look. She knew she would soon join him on the ground.

"When do you want me to do it?" Jimmy asked with a polite smile. "Do you want to be facing me, or shall I let you walk away a couple paces? The choice is yours, darling. I'm a gentleman."

Chapter Twenty-One
Close Your Eyes

Deceptive, that's what. The brilliance of the day was insincere, a preamble to something rather miserable. He might have known criminal roilings would choose today to go on under cover of sunlight and high spirits. Farnham paced the road with Belch near the exit of the Rowan Walk and scowled. Breen had better hurry. With each passing moment, he felt danger rising like a great pillar of cloud going before him into the wilderness. He must find his niece before any harm came to her. For harm *would* come. That he knew.

Ah, there came Breen, speeding up the road in a cloud of goodwill and dust. The doctor threw the automobile into park and hopped out with his medical case and a concerned expression.

Inspector Dillon, that over-eager young man, jumped out after him. Belch wagged up and smelled the inspector's pressed trouser knees all round.

"Farnham, what is this? Allen said it was of some moment?" Breen hauled up next to Farnham and placed a conciliatory hand on his shoulder.

"Of some moment?" Farnham tried to keep the incredulity from his tone. "You're bang right it is; I have good reason to think my niece is in the company of the murderer of Miss Lillian Bertois and in some measure of danger."

"God have mercy," Breen murmured, obviously shaken.

"She's palling about with Cilla Grey?" Inspector Dillon scratched his head. "Seems unlikely."

Farnham stiffened like an old tom-cat. "Not Grey, no. Jimmy Fields. I can explain later, but I would appreciate it if you would arrest him when we find him."

The young inspector narrowed his eyes and stuffed his hands in his coat pockets. "On whose authority?"

Bang the devil himself. "On *your* authority, good man, and on my word."

This seemed to appease the young inspector, and he removed his hands from his pockets like a man suddenly awakened for the hunt. "Right, well where shall we find them?"

"Allen thinks they will be on the ridge up near Holly Triad, or close to it. That was the way they'd proposed to go."

"I thought Maynor was our suspect," Breen said.

"He's there too. The trio left for a merry day underneath the greenwood tree."

"Careless of you, Farnham. I'm surprised."

"And I'm ashamed. But time for regrets later—did you bring your pistols?"

Breen answered by bringing forth a brace of fine silver pistols—rather too fine to allow for him ever having fought a real duel in his lifetime. Farnham would have bet not a single bullet had ever exploded from the barrel of those fine pieces. Dueling was illegal, anyway and far be it from the good doctor to deface random regulations. Breen was such a mother's favorite—he hardly ever bent the rules.

"Loaded?"

Between friend and friend flowed an electric stream of indignation. "Always."

Farnham turned one of the pistols in his hands. "Are you certain this lady-trinket will even shoot?"

"Don't fie upon me because I like to keep my things polished. They work. I assure you."

"See here," Inspector Dillon protested. "What on earth will we be needing guns for?"

It was a rather mean joke, he would allow, but Farnham turned to the Inspector with the pistol held firmly in the man's direction.

"Murderers generally kill people, don't they? Which is why we're looking for him. And I don't know about you, my dear Inspector, but when a man has a habit of killing others, I like to be prepared to defend myself."

"Would you mind very much, Mr. Farnham, not waving your pistol in my direction? Do you even know how to shoot that thing? Have you a permit?"

"Yes, and yes."

"If you don't mind me saying so, Mr. Farnham, I would like to be sure you can shoot before I agree to accompany you on this goose-chase. A careless man with a firearm is quite as dangerous as an armed criminal."

The young man was beyond all bounds of reason. There was no *time* for this sort of silly qualification. Farnham ground his horse teeth and shot a keen, hard look at Breen. Breen shrugged and looked away. He never would enter quarrels. It was the one thing that annoyed Farnham more than anything. No wonder he'd never had occasion to use his bright, spangled pistols.

"Do you see that clump of rowan berries?" Farnham asked, pointing into the curve of the green-carpeted tunnel where a cluster of red shown blood-lusty against a golden bower.

"Yes."

"I'll shoot the bottom berry."

Inspector Dillon squinted. "That little one?"

"Yes." Farnham took aim casually, with one hand, and sent a bullet through the air. One moment the berry was suspended from the branch like a dull ruby; a hair's-breadth of a second later, it was obliterated. He transferred Belch's lead from his left hand to his right. "I *can* shoot."

"That you can and I'm sorry I doubted you." Inspector Dillon shook Farnham's hand and took out his own gun. "Shall we off, then?"

"Yes. Breen, I expect we shall be in need of your services." His stomach dug fangs into his skin, and he swung off at a tight lope with the other men behind him.

"It isn't like you to be this twitchy, old man," Breen said, drawing up to his elbow. "Why are you so certain you'll need me?"

"Because," Farnham confessed. "An instant before you pulled in, I heard a shot."

"Couldn't it have been someone hunting?"

"No," Farnham said. "Unless they've taken to using a pistol to hunt grouse."

Vivi stared at Jimmy. She was silent. She would not have wished to speak even if she had words instead of this bottled, horrible scream that burned in her breast. She stared at his face, searching for the man she knew—*thought* she knew—In all the heartless determination. She had never fancied she would become one of those women who fell in love with an imagining. It was not love, however—couldn't be, in an acquaintance of less than a week—but an infatuation. And the man who had charmed her did not exist.

It was a pity she would not live to take this lesson along with her in life.

It was a pity she should die. So many things were waiting.

Jimmy was waiting.

He shifted from one foot to the next and behind her—somehow distant and all the more tragic for it—Michael moaned in pain. Michael was still alive. Good. Her heart began to beat again instead of standing at a shock. When had she become sympathetic to Michael?

When staring down the barrel of a gun.

She had heard the threat of death changed people. She believed it now, when the knowledge was entirely useless and pale as death itself.

"Jimmy, please don't do this," she said.

"What? Don't give you a choice how you want to die? I can't let you go. You know everything."

"I don't know everything and you *could* let me go. You've wounded Michael—probably fatally and you've...killed Lillian and her child. What more do you want?"

"Shut up about the kid!" Jimmy shouted.

"No, I won't!" Vivi shouted back. She still held her pistol. "I will not let you kill me."

"If I see your fingers tighten, mine will be quicker. You will be dead before you've squeezed the trigger." His face spasmed in the ghost of a smile. "And your aim is probably terrible."

"You misjudge me." Vivi's voice was so cold and pricked through with determination, she hardly recognized it as her own. "I am a perfect shot. And quick."

It was a bluff, but *pray God* it was not a lie. She might have a precise aim and she might very well be swift. It was just a pity she might test that bluff for the first and last time of her life all at once. If it failed, she was a corpse.

"Give me the choice to leave now, Jimmy."

His eyes were too bright, shining with a crazed, desperate expression. She wondered if far down, further than any of his crimes, he was a nothing but a shocked boy staring at a windowpane he'd broken and wondering how he'd ever pay to mend it. The idea drove a stab of tearful pity into her heart.

"Sorry, Viv." His voice sounded choked. "Can't do that. I can't let you live."

Vivi hefted her pistol in hand and shrugged, tears pooling in her eyes. "You *could*."

"I can't." The finality was chilling. "Just close your eyes. I'm going to shoot. *Please*. Close them."

"No."

"Do it, Vivi."

"No!"

"Close them!" he barked. His hands shook as if palsied, and a tear ran down his cheek.

Vivi prayed peace over Michael and forgiveness for the wrecked soul before her with the now familiar detachment deadening her senses to all but the idea that, in a moment, she would die.

"Will you close your eyes, Viv?"

She bit her lip, shook her head, and fixed her eyes on Jimmy's.

From the road near Holly Triad, Farnham heard a second shot.

Chapter Twenty-Two
Leaking Wellies

Farnham let go Belch's lead and sprang over the stile barring field from road. The shot was close and filled him with a terror alien to his daily calm. Shards of pain splintered in his side with the fear, and he ran faster toward the direction of the gunshot. *Vivi! Oh God, Vivi.*

Beside him, Breen ran. His friend was fitter, but Farnham still outstripped him. Breen's happiness did not depend on the girl being alive. His did. *Oh, merciful Lord,* his did. He knew it now and the overwhelming terror stole his lungs.

Let her live.

He despised the ground under his feet. Legs thrashing, arms pumping, Farnham forced himself up what must certainly be the final hill. The shot had been too close to allow otherwise. He gained the ridge, and his heart drummed all hearing from his ears. There, down the slope, were three bodies.

"Bang it!"

Farnham half tumbled, half-slid down the slope and ended on his knees next to the small, still form that was Vivi. He pressed two fingers under her throat and felt for her pulse.

249

It was there—God, it was there—faint and small and steady, like herself. He sat back on his heels and covered his eyes with one hand. She lived. She was unconscious, but she lived.

The sound of Breen's trenchcoat slapping the grass informed Farnham that the doctor had thrown himself to his knees beside him. "Is she—?"

"She lives."

"Thank God."

"Whoa-oh-oh. Look at this mess." That was Inspector Dillon's voice and, at its introduction, Farnham whipped around with a fox-humored snarl.

"Have you no shame?" he asked. "No delicacy?"

"I'm a *policeman*, Mr. Farnham. I deal in facts first." Inspector Dillon's sedentary, chap-reddened face sorely tempted Farnham's fist. "Which one did you say I was to arrest?"

Farnham got to his feet, ignoring Inspector Dillon, and watched Breen prod Vivi's abdomen, her arms and legs, and her back.

"Where is she hurt?" he asked.

Breen glanced up and shook his head. "That's just it: I don't think she's hurt at all. The dear girl only fainted." He nodded at Farnam's bull-dog pistol lying in the grass nearby. "And from the look of it, did us all bravely too. Inspector, will you please administer these salts to Miss Langley while I inspect the other two? There's a man. Thank you."

With a Niagara's portion of reluctance, Farnham resigned his niece to the inspector to watch as Breen squatted next to Jimmy Fields.

"Hello there, Mr. Fields," he murmured. "Playing rough with your friends?"

Jimmy, who had only been lying still and was not, apparently, mortally wounded, looked past Breen to Farnham.

He had his palm pressed to his arm and winced as Breen pried it away, releasing a fresh, pulsing flow of blood.

"Vivi shot me. The little vixen shot me," he hissed.

"Before you could shoot her? I confess," Farnham said, "I am impressed. Where'd she get you? A wound to the upper arm. Neatly done."

Breen prodded the skin, and Jimmy bit back a curse. "Sit still, Mr. Fields. I want to stop this bleeding. Pinch your armpit. There. Now sit *still* while I check Mr. Maynor."

Not that the man could run while his artery was spouting blood like a whale spouts water, but Farnham stood over him while Breen checked the condition of the other behind him.

"Still alive..." Breen said, his voice musing. Farnham didn't need to watch to see how Breen's gentle hands would be handling Michael, pressing firm but careful where the wound lay. "Shot to the abdomen...through the gut and out the back, it appears. He's lost a lot of blood..."

"Will he live?" Jimmy growled. Blood dripped through his fingers onto the grass.

"Most likely," Farnham said, staring down on the young man. "If you're tired yet of losing blood, you ought to elevate your arm." He jerked Jimmy's arm over his head and re-clamped the fellow's hand over the artery in his armpit.

Jimmy cried out in pain and uttered a curse.

"You think that hurts? Good. No, keep it above your head." Farnham ground his heel in the grass and glared at Jimmy. "We want you hale and hearty for your stay in prison."

Inspector Dillon took Jimmy away to the station with an almost comical nonchalance considering the ten-penny crimes more often committed on the sanct turf of the Creig.

Breen managed to make Michael as comfortable as possible before he drove back to the village to get help. He left Michael, still unconscious, to Farnham's care and Farnham sat crouched on the hillside, watching his niece. He cast an occasional eye over at the prostrate form beside Vivi, but it was she who consumed his attention, and she whose every breath he watched with the jealous care of a tiger.

She had not responded to Inspector Dillon's brief ministrations with the smelling salts but Farnham did not care to awaken her yet.

His heart still felt a fishnet over the ordeal, and he thought he could not cope with her upset and his own if she happened to go into hysterics upon waking. Belch flopped beside him in a flashing, panting pile, having finally wended his way thither after—by the look of it—having taking a detour to the brook for a bath. A bath, when Genevieve Langley was laying there unconscious and only just out of the greatest peril?

Together, man and dog watched the two unconscious figures as the sun plummeted behind them. In a few moments, Vivi began to stir.

It started as a quiet moan; her fingers crept toward her pistol in the grass.

Farnham watched this movement with approval; she remembered the danger in which she had been before fainting and was not entirely certain she was safe. Such behavior showed a sort of spirit Farnham was pleased to commend in one of his relatives.

Her fingers closed around the gun, and she brought it up with a shaky hand, following the motion by drawing herself into a halting, tentative sitting position. She passed a hand across her forehead and squinted at Michael, lying with a bandage around his bare abdomen, and the space where Jimmy had lately been. Then she turned in Farnham's direction, and her pupils contracted against the light flung like a mantel about his shoulders. Seemingly confused by the shadows surrounding her, she trained the gun on him with unexpected fury.

Farnham dodged and threw his hands into the air. "Vivi! It's me!"

"What?"

"Me, Farnham! You knocked off Jimmy with your shot. You're safe. He's gone."

"I k-killed him?" Her cheeks were paler than Michaelmas daisies.

"Just aerated his jacket a bit. It'll cool his blood. No real harm done."

She lost a bit of the wild look and tipped the point of the gun toward the grass. "Hello, uncle." He watched the color mount in her cheeks, and she gentled the pistol into the grass at her side and passed over it with a dismissive gesture and hazy sigh. "I...borrowed your gun."

"Yes, you did." His mouth bent in a grin. "I'm infuriated."

She lifted her eyes to him, doubtful, until he knew she had seen the laughter behind his words. "It came in handy."

"Appears so." Farnham stood and ambled to her side, taking both her hands in his. "I'm rather glad you can shoot."

She accepted the pull of his hands, a bit wobbly but stronger than she looked. She ran her hands down the skirt of her walking suit and rumpled her hair. "Poor Michael. Is he...dead?"

"Poor Michael? I thought you hated him. And no, he's not dead."

"I do hate him," Vivi murmured. "But he tried to save me and got shot for it. First noble thing that cad has done in his piece of a century." She pressed slender fingers to her temples. "Horrible."

"Your afternoon?"

"How could he have committed a murder?"

Farnham bit off a laugh. "And here I thought you referred to your own predicament. He isn't the first man to have done so."

"But to kill a woman *and* her child—wittingly."

"Bang it, woman. You knew about the child—how? I thought to reveal that cleverly at the tell-all."

Vivi gave off a shred of the old arch smile. "When he still doubted I could—and *would*—shoot, he told us mostly everything. On the condition, of course, that he get to kill us afterward. How did *you* know?"

"Allen," Farnham said with a vocal smirk.

"Dear Allen. Is that what business he had in London?"

"But of course. No, you are not strong enough for questions yet. We'll have a regular moot when things are settled. Tea, coffee, cakes, and full disclosure of everyone's movements."

The sun settled lower behind the hill, and long blue shadows stretched their fingers down the land in cold stripes. Vivi shivered, and Farnham guessed her coat was not the warmest thing a person could desire after a shock.

He had never had shock himself, he reflected. Not, at least, until he'd seen Vivi lying lifeless in the little scoop of valley and thought her dead. *That* was a shock he never hoped to repeat in the lingering years of his lifetime.

Farnham shrugged out of his trench and draped it over Vivi's shoulders. "Bang it all, woman!"

She tilted her head with a curious look in her eyes. "I frightened you, didn't I?"

"What on earth would make you think that?"

"You're angry."

"You stole my pistol."

"Your pistol is still lying in the damp grass, and you haven't looked at it. That isn't the matter." Her dry lips cracked as she smiled, and she put a finger up to dab away the stinging blood. "*You* thought I was *dead.*"

Her eyes held him, daring him to disagree and attempt a lie. The shadows stretched longer and threw half of his niece's face into a dim, blue color like the salient shadow of an archangel's wing.

Michael still lay on the grass, senseless. Soon the dew would be falling. It would not be good to leave him on the damp ground. Where was Breen?

"*I* thought I was dead," Vivi said in a simple voice. She shrugged. "It seemed the only possible outcome. I didn't have the element of surprise as I did with Michael."

"With Michael?" Farnham glowered at her. "What mischief is this?"

Vivi shrugged again, and her thin shoulders lifted his trenchcoat like a kitten burrowing under a blanket. "You'll find out at this moot of yours. Does...Doctor Breen know I'm all right?"

"He discovered it himself."

"Were you both terribly frightened?" Her smile was just a bit wicked.

Farnham didn't want to puff her head—goodness knows he'd hear enough in the days to come about how he'd mistaken her worth—but the question required some answer. He drew a deep draught of the damp, chilling air and made fists with his hands to keep his fingers from going numb with cold. He stared at Belch's red tail thrashing the grass.

"We were both concerned. As concerned as anyone might be to hear gunshots and find three bodies on the ground."

When he chanced to look up again, Vivi was grinning at him with a bit of a devil in her eye. "Admit it, dear uncle: if I had been dead, you would have been miserable."

"It would have been a very sorry thing, of course."

"No, uncle, *miserable*. You would have missed me, wouldn't you?"

He rocked on his toes and thought how to refute the charge.

He balanced on his heels and wondered if he would be able to make a general and philosophical statement about the sadness of a life cut short in its prime.

Where was Breen when he needed him? If *ever* Scotland Yard needed a leader for their missing persons lists, they ought to give him a ring. He was past-master in the art of disappearance.

Vivi's smile was still fixed on him with that knowing look, and her green eyes glinted.

At last, he shrugged gruffly and kicked Belch's tail out of the way. "Oh bang, Vivi. I'd be miserable as a leaking Wellie."

Chapter Twenty-Three
No Bedside Manner

"Ting! Cling! Ting!"

The rough tinkle of glass beleaguered by silver drove through the relative din in the Manor dining room. That would be Farnham, summoning them all to silence. It was only the sheerest delight in actually finding herself alive after that fateful ramble that kept Vivi chattering on to Breen in strict defiance of the improvised bell.

The fork on glass sounded again, this time more of a clatter than anything else. She would listen in just a moment, as soon as she'd finished telling him about—

"*Will* you be quiet?" Farnham roared.

Such a roar would break off Winston Churchill mid-sentence. Vivi turned to find her uncle standing on one of the upholstered dining-room chairs with a tumbler of cider and a silver fork in hand. He clanked them together once or twice again. His eye twitched at the discordant sound of his own making.

Vivi risked a merry glance at Breen—It had been unwise and the splutter that followed could hardly qualify as respectful.

257

No matter. Respect, let alone rational thought and gainful conversation, had avoided the dining-room this night.

Allen, sitting at the head of the table and looking essentially tragic, stared at his employer with a look that spoke of great loyalty and deep discomfort. He was not accustomed to sitting with his master at table, poor, dear soul. Vivi handed a companionable smile down the table and wondered if it would be poor form to hug the butler as she'd already done once.

"Mesdames and messieurs," Farnham said. "We have eaten, we have drunk, and now, we divulge!"

"How vulgar that sounds," Vivi observed.

Breen laughed behind her, and Farnham glared. "I will thank you, Miss Crack-Shot, to keep a civil tongue in your head."

"But of course, dear uncle. For it is a well-known fact that I am lucky to have any breath with which to speak. I shall save that breath and thank God for it."

Farnham shook the fork at her. "You do that."

"I will."

He glared, but Vivi categorized it as a fond sort of glare. She wasn't accustomed to glares being of the fond nature. Here, things were different. Lots of things. She liked different. Different trotted well with her moods.

Candlelight jinked through Farnham's cider and cast amber speckles of light on the wallpaper behind him. He caught Vivi looking at them and turned around, tilting his glass this way and that to test the play of the light. She wondered if he was remembering 'Titania's lamps,' too.

"Farnham, conversation?" Breen said with a yawn. "It's been a long and harrowing day for us all."

Farnham whipped around, and the light stopped its jinking. "Harrowing? For you? None of your patients died and they bally well *could* have, being riddled with shot like so many pheasants. I would hardly call that harrowing."

Breen cracked his knuckles. "And the little child in India ate lunch three days ago. *You'd* hardly call that starving."

"I exist off of a like diet," he mused drily.

"Fie on you."

Breen tossed his legs up on the table as he had done in her presence earlier in the week and gave Vivi an exasperated smile. She returned it with good will and thought what a comforting group they all were. Had it been only a week? She ran her mind through the previous days at Whistlecreig as a person might run their hands through a scoop of grain, feeling the kernels with interest as they passed rough and agrarian through her fingers.

Five days—or six? She had difficulty separating one from another.

Few times in her life had she ever felt such an intimacy with a party in so short a time. At home in Darlington, things were slower...less deep and violent in their pleasures and terrors alike. Life was much gentler at home, much more vivid here.

She liked vivid; it kicked like mustard.

"First on the list of ceremonies," Farnham drawled, bringing her attention back to the group, "I would like to publicly recognize Genevieve Langley for her entirely inappropriate and courageous behavior. To shoot a man in the arm cannot possibly stand in Darlington but, for her willingness to do so, a murderer is now in police custody. Whistlecreig commends your lack of propriety. Your health, madam."

They drank to this, and Farnham raised his hand to still any thought of departure back to their individual conversation. "Secondly, I believe the good doctor has a presentation he would like to make."

Breen twitched. "What the dev—oh. You sneak-thief!" He twisted to reach into the pocket of his coat and drew forth a broad leather wallet. This, he flicked open and from it drew a ten-pound note. "I think I have been treated rather ill in all this."

He rolled the tenner into a cigar and tossed it across the table to Farnham. Vivi watched the careless journey of the note as it traveled airborne, in serious peril of candle-flame and cake-icing alike.

"To Farnham." He flicked his hand in his friend's direction. "Who never can make a bet but he's too wretchedly stubborn to lose. What does that make...eighty pounds you've won off me?"

Farnham stuffed the note in his cardigan pocket. "Ninety. I chalk them up on the parlor wall."

"Next to our fencing scores? Is that what that is?"

"But of course. Gives me something for which to fight. Murders are tedious. Beating you once more is the sport in the thing."

"To the fiery lakes with your sportsmanship," Breen grumbled dozily.

"Shall we drink to that?"

Breen raised his mug. "With a vengeance."

The glasses clanked together with the merry cider-sound of liquid companionship. Now that he had their attention Farnham seemed none too hurried to finish the business and relinquish his audience.

"If you don't mind me asking, sir, what is it you wanted so particularly to discuss?" Allen's gentle, sonorous voice settled around their shoulders like domesticated snow, and it struck Vivi how the man seemed to run Whistlecreig on the force of his steadiness alone. He never usurped her uncle or lorded over him, but she did wonder in a passing way what a pretty mess Farnham would be in without him.

"The dishes won't wait forever, sir."

With a conscious smile, Farnham got down from his perch and settled in his chair like a normal creature. "Forgive me, Allen. The main of what I wanted to say is that now is the time to slay this many-headed monster. Each person represented here must enlighten the rest as to his movements. We already know the main points and where they lead, but I'm never satisfied till I know the minutiae. You first, Allen."

"As you wish, sir." Allen got to his feet and clasped his hands in back, pursing dry lips together before beginning: "Shortly after you came to Whistlecreig, miss," —said with a deferential smile and a quiver of the ponderous forehead— "Mr. Farnham called me into his study and asked me to accomplish an errand. He explained to me that the unfortunate actress, one Lillian Bertois, had been in London before coming here. As the police didn't have much of an idea what motive anyone might have in killing her and what motive *she* might have in coming here, Mr. Farnham thought it might behoove the investigation if I was to go up to town and see what news I could find of one Rhona Clay."

"Excuse me," Vivi interrupted. "Rhona Clay?"

Farnham pressed two fingers to his forehead, shadowing a careless smile. "Miss Bertois's given name."

"Never does he fail!" Breen shouted. "Always a card up his sleeve. Remind me, Vivi, never to allow myself to play poker here."

"Nonsense." Farnham seemed to resent this allusion the more dubious side of their history together. "Research is hardly cheating."

"But how did you know that her real name was Rhona Clay?" Vivi asked.

"I know that Americans are a terribly vulgar people with an aptitude for knowing everything about a person's history. More, sometimes, than the person knows himself. Uncanny, but helpful on occasion. A telegram from New York was all I required to set me off. Rhona Clay was the actress' birth name, and I figured that if she was to do any underhand thing while on our glorious Isle, she might try that moniker first."

"So Allen went."

The subject of this conversation bowed. "Yes, miss, I did. I started by inquiring at various practices in London."

Farnham speared a bit of cake with his fork and poked it in Vivi's direction. "*That* was where the boy did us proud! A doctor's office! I confess, I had not thought of the matter in that light."

Breen twirled his coffee cup so the handle pointed toward the center of the table and idly clinked the back of his spoon on the rim. "Chalk one up for Allen. What gave you the idea to prowl about the medical files?"

Victory's red herald crept into Allen's face. He tipped his chin a tidge downward so a third chin ringed his refined dewlap. "I tried to think like a lady, Doctor Breen. That is," he said, the red deepening, "to think of where I might have occasion to use an alias. Someplace I might not wish my public to know I had visited. When better to obscure a matter from the press, thought I, then on a question of a medical nature?"

"You are fount of inspiration, my dear man," Farnham said affably. "Pray, continue."

Allen shrugged round shoulders and bent his chin deeper. "There is little else to tell. I went to a half dozen doctors before finding one who had admitted a Rhona Clay. He would not, naturally, tell me what was the nature of her predicament, but through conversation with the receptionist, I was able to gather a description exactly fitting Miss Lillian Bertois. Really, Doctor Breen, there was little enough to it."

"And the child?" Vivi asked quietly. "Was it a guess?"

"An educated guess, yes," Farnham answered in the same tone. "I thought it the only explanation for a young woman of note coming to this rather hard-scrabble bit of the world."

They fell silent, remembering that one uncelebrated life that had been taken, never to be publically mourned like its mother who was being sorrowed after on both sides of the Atlantic. A terrible thing. Vivi's hands clenched with an involuntary movement as she imagined reaching out to hold the little baby that would never have its chance to live...killed by a man not his father for a fault not its own.

She had to know one answer. Her chest bulged with a latent stone of rage. "How did you know it was Jimmy? I was so certain of Michael...so stupidly certain. I even demanded at gunpoint he admit his guilt to me."

"You did what?" Breen snapped.

"Held him at...gunpoint."

"Idiot child," Farnham said tenderly.

If he didn't stop speaking to her in that paternal croon... "I didn't think of the consequences. And then, of course, I know him from of old and regarded him more as a horrible family ghost than a threat. And yet he was innocent. Laugh if you will...but I was wonderfully sure."

The quiet courtesy of a glass refilled scented the room with apple-tones and Farnham rolled his arm behind his head. "I tended to agree with you about Michael. He has such a terrible self-assurance...in fact, I hardly thought to question his proposed guilt till last night."

"What happened last night?" Breen asked.

"What time is is, Vivi?" Farnham answered, evasive.

She looked hard at him and shrugged. "Haven't a clue. My watch died this morning."

His glance was as good as an 'Aha'. "And it was lagging last night and, I would imagine, ever since your arrival."

"I don't understand," said Vivi. "How did this clear Michael of guilt?"

"Well, it didn't—not exactly, anyway. What it *did* was to cast Jimmy back in the field of possible suspects. I had all but cleared his name because of our time-constraints. We determined that the whole wretched ordeal was over within an hour of her arrival—but Jimmy was at the station with you in *half* an hour from the time in which you pulled up. No matter how accustomed he is to hauling burdens cross-country, he could hardly cheat our pinched time-dispensations. He could not have committed the murder."

"Slower, if you please, sir," Allen grumbled. "You'll have my intellect paralyzed."

"I begin to see." Breen had not stopped tapping the side of his cup with the back of his spoon. "Vivi had been alone on the platform far longer than she thought, and her watch was too slow to notice. Waiting in a strange place always feels like an eternity, so she would not notice if an hour or even *two* had passed. It all felt like the wrong end of the corridor of time."

"Exactly."

Half-forgotten, the blue jug of rowan showed garish to Vivi's sight where it sat in the center of the table. He'd killed Lillian in their own Rowan Walk among their own growing-gold and dangling rubies. A ball of loathing, reeking through her insides like sour milk, and she felt like smashing the jug and the rowans besides. Jimmy had defiled things.

She drew a sharp little breath through her teeth. "It is strange, I think."

No one spoke. The silence grew warm and full of their hearts beating in the glad assurance of being alive. Through this warmth of this moment, the thought of recent evils ran cold for Vivi.

"It is strange," she began again, "that the man I most feared was *not* the one intent on harming me."

"Come now..." Breen purred, soothing as a great, sun-soaked cat.

She held up her hand in a gesture imperious. "And to the man intent on harming me I gave credence on proof of charm and good humor. I hate that. I hate being womanly."

"*Come* now."

Allen rumbled in his chest. "Now, now, Miss Langley."

The gentlemen, save her uncle, were being such dears. Farnham merely stretched like a bony version of the doctor's cat-impression and closed his eyes at her.

"'Cry no more, lady, cry no more...men were deceivers ever.'" He rubbed his knuckle against his closed lids, and a yawn escaped, heavy as August. "We will all be called upon to testify in court—I do hope you know that."

At the idea of standing before that hawkish Chief McMulligan and again descending into obscurity beneath his savage eye, Vivi's jaw clenched. The hunt was over, but they had the hunting to pay. It was not like the books. After the murderer had been caught, things did not go back to their complacent thrum and bustle.

Not yet, anyway.

Not for some time.

Perhaps never.

Vivi rose softly. "If you'll excuse me, I am going to be somewhat scanter of my maiden presence."

It was full night by the time Vivi came downstairs again. She had heard Breen leave by the large front door and thought fondly of his passage from the house.

Dear man...she liked him so well, but his continuous high spirits did not match her present humor. Later she would be glad for him, glad for his merry, booming laugh and his chivalric way. But now, tonight, she wanted...what? An image rose before her mind's eye, gaunt and hunch-shouldered and skeptical. The sardonic eye turned on her with an expression half-grimace, half smile.

She wanted Farnham's company.

Vivi pulled a puce-colored afghan from the chest at the foot of her bed and draped it around her shoulders. It was an awful color—a fact which she thought likely to have sealed its fate as a thing belonging to an obscure back-bedroom—but it was comforting and peaceful in its ugliness. Trustworthy. Plain.

She had sat in darkness for some time, groping for the peace which seemed to elude her grasp. *Harrowing* was the right word for the day. She could not recall another time in her life in which she had felt more like crying and yet been entirely unable to conjure tears.

With quiet, steady fingers—for as she failed to scream when Jimmy shot Michael, her body still disdained to betray emotion—Vivi lit a match and held it to the stub-end of her bedside candle.

The courageous flare summoned an answering blaze from the taper, and the two bobbed beside each other in fantastical form on the wall.

She blew one out, and there was a single thumbprint of light in the room.

With this thumb-print to guide her below-stairs, Vivi exited her bedchamber. The stairway was dark and cold beneath her thin slippers, and an eerie wind whistled round the eaves and tried the roof with feverish hands. It was not a pleasant night. Somewhere nearby a rook scraped its raucous call over the wind. Vivi pulled the ugly blanket nearer her throat and took the stairs on the balls of her feet, careful not to awaken the slightest echo.

Electric light and a damp sound suggestive of pot-scouring spilled out from the dining room in a homely flood. That would be dear old Allen, attending to his very un-butler-ly duties with that air of resigned determination that made him such a darling. She found herself smiling even as she passed through the great, heartless hall and down the crooked way toward Farnham's study.

Solitude was not good for the soul. Even the knowledge that, while downstairs, she was near Allen's dish-washing was enough to lift her spirits. She came to the study door and the round knob in its center. Her candle picked up an ancient winking in the brass. She twisted her flame to the right and left and watched the play of light on the metal then collected herself with a silent laugh.

Eccentric habits.

She had begun to act odd, like Farnham. Quickly now she twisted the handle and admitted herself to the quiet throne-room where, but a week ago, she had trembled on that bit of scarred carpet in the presence of the great Laird of Whistle.

Tonight, there was no trembling.

Farnham sat in his chair, nursing one knee over the other, cheek cupped in the palm and fingers of his right hand. His left elbow crooked on the arm of his great chair, and his hand dangled off the end. Softly, slowly, his fingers clenched and released, clenched and released. He was lost to thought. Whither his mind wandered, through the halls of philosophy or his beloved Bard or some frontier on which she'd never stepped, she little knew. The scent of pipe-smoke filled the room, sweet and familiar.

"Hullo," she said softly, so as not to startle him.

He moved not, but his eyes lifted at Vivi, and the back-lighting of the fire hid their expression from her. "Hullo."

She stood with the candle in her fist for a moment, watching, then moved close to him. He stared at her flame, and she could see that he too was full of troubling visions.

A log fell to crumbling in the fireplace, and the reawakened flame nipped at her calves. She set her candle on Farnham's side-table and crouched near the fire, knees wrapped in the warm hollow of her arms. The wretched, mossy blanket slipped a few inches down her arms. It did not bother her. Here, in the glow of the fire and her uncle's company, she was warm enough.

A gentle tug on the blanket brought her head around to find Farnham jerking it back in place over her shoulder. When he had finished, his hand went back to its clenching and unclenching.

"Lonely?" he asked, abruptly breaking the silence.

She smiled. "A bit. And cold. And disheartened."

"Mmmm."

When the silence had lasted too long, she inquired: "You?"

He did not answer for a moment but picked at the arm of his chair. "You once said I thought of solving murders as a game." His tone was quiet but heavy as if it took quite a lot from him to bring up his failings. "That isn't so, you know."

Vivi tossed her head with a laugh. "I know."

"You do?" He raised his head. "You aren't convinced I'm a heartless creature who likes folk to die so I might amuse my intellect?"

She reached behind her and patted his hand. "You are not quite so psychopathic, my dear uncle."

"I suppose I must thank you for that sentiment," he said. More coals fell. "Do you really understand?"

"I think...I do. Now." She watched the coals like dragon-scales writhe and wink in the belly of the fireplace. "You see the crimes and you must away. To sit by without doing anything...that would break a man's spirit. Evil must be hunted down and justice paid. It is the warriors' way."

He hummed to himself. "The warriors' way. I like that. 'Why should a man, whose blood is warm within, sit like his grandsire cut in alabaster?'"

"*The Merchant of Venice*," Vivi murmured. "Am I right?"

"You are."

"I'm good at this."

Eyes still on the coals, she heard the sizzle strike of match and smelt the pungent sulphur following. The sound of

Farnham's lips opening and closing over his pipe stem filled the space between them, and a soft grey cloud curled from behind her, floating toward the invisible lure of the chimney.

"What now?" she asked. "What does one generally do after solving a murder? I know I shall have to stay in Whistlecreig to testify."

"You shall."

"And after? When your stomach is less dodgy and I've been quizzed again by our *dear* Inspector McMulligan?" Her tone was light, but inside her heart had stopped beating as she waited for an answer to this worst of inquiries.

He stretched his legs forward till his shined shoes were even with her knees and cracked his knuckles. "I imagine," he said in a flawlessly lazy voice, "that I shall always have these bang ulcers."

Her heart flipped. "Always?"

"Breen says there isn't the least probability they will go away with any sort of expediency. Waited too long before beginning treatments. It appears the banged things are here for good."

"I'm sorry to hear that," Vivi lied. "I suppose you will be needing a qualified nurse?"

"It's not as hellish as all that just yet. An amateur will do."

"An amateur nurse?" She readjusted her legs so they stretched before her and the tips of her slippers brushed the hearthstone. "That sounds risky. She'll probably poison your water with arsenic tablets, mistaking them for bicarbonate."

"God forbid! Do you mean for her to murder me?"

Vivi turned back to look at him, eyes snapping mischief. "It would let Breen win his bet, for you could hardly solve your *own* murder in a year's time, much less a week."

He scowled and shook his head, but the corners of his mouth curled in a smile. "You are a witch. But you haven't discouraged me. I'd find a way."

269

"Bet you would."

Another long silence—longer than before. "It isn't an amateur nurse of which I stand in need."

"It's not?"

"No. *You've* shown me it is utterly useless to expect anyone to oversee my health but myself. And Breen, of course, when he insists on butting in."

"Unfair, sirrah!" she protested, laughing.

"On the contrary, my dear Vivi, since your arrival we have been kept out odd hours, submitted to the most inclement weather and crowded assemblies, rattled about on bicycles, and been assaulted by the press. I can hardly call that useful, prudent behavior for a young nurse and her charge. I must give you a shabby reference."

"Your generosity is unequalled, uncle" she answered. "The last patient gave me no reference at all."

"Good. You deserve none. You make a rather horrible nurse, Genevieve Langley. No bedside manner at all. No, as an amatuer in *that* profession, you're a thorough failure."

Her vanity fluffed under the raillery. He *liked* her. "What profession would you suggest I enter, then? My family will hardly want me to hang about their necks as a prime example for my sisters of How Not To End."

"Naturally not. I needn't tell you it's hardly a flattering state of existence. Visiting at a children's hospital pays very little."

"Indeed. Have you any suggestions? I am glad for any bit of direction for my rather wandersome life."

He steepled his fingers and looked at her keenly over the points. "Detective."

"What?"

"Amateur detectives."

"Us?"

"Vivi and Farnham. Northamptonshire's best-kept secret."

"You make us sound like a back-alley inn," she said gaily. "Do you really think I'd suit?"

He regarded her for some moments with his head to the side. "Probably not. But it seems you attract villains. We can hardly call your reputation *innocent* at this point. You've taken to carrying pistols and shooting men, my dear. You've become..."

"Fast?"

"Odd."

"How chivalrous of you!"

"I try."

"Vivi and Farnham," she mused. "A precarious partnership enough."

"Nonsense." Farnham rose with a groan and stretched out a hand to help her up. "Blood binds us together, goose. That is anything *but* precarious. Can't get away from family."

She took his hand and hauled herself up, leaving the puce-colored blanket in a disgruntled heap on the floor. "I'm to be an amateur detective?"

He grinned down at her. "That or have Mrs. Froggle tell the world you're naught but another fiz-gig."

"Oh dear," Vivi said with mock astonishment. "We can hardly allow that. I don't think I would like to be a fiz-gig."

"In that case," Farnham said, handing back her candle with a savage wink, "Tomorrow you'll start lessons."

The End

Books By Rachel Heffington

Fly Away Home

1952 New York City

Self Preservation has never looked more tempting.

Callie Harper is a woman set to make it big in the world of journalism. Liberated from all but her buried and troubled past, Callie craves glamour and the satisfaction she knows it will bring. When one of America's most celebrated journalists, Wade Barnett, calls on Callie to help him with a revolutionary project, Callie finds herself co-pilot to a Christian man whose life and ideas of true greatness run noisily counter to hers on every point.

The new friendship sparks, the project soars, and a faint suspicion that she is falling for this uncommon man grows in Callie's heart. When the secrets of Callie's past are exhumed and hung over her head as a threat, she is forced to scrutinize Wade Barnett and betray his dirtiest secrets or see her own spilled.

Here there is space for only one love, one answer: betray Wade Barnett to save her reputation, or sacrifice everything for the sake of the man she loved and the God she fled. The consequences of either decision will define the rest of her life.

Five Glass Slippers

One Beloved Story - Five Exciting Writers - A Collection to Cherish!

THE WINDY SIDE OF CARE: Rachel Heffington

Alisandra is determined to have her rights. She knows that she is the king's secretly dispossessed daughter, the true heir to the throne. Prince Auguste is an imposter, and if she plays her cards right, Alis will prove it to the world! That is, if charming Auguste doesn't succeed in winning her heart before she gets her chance . . .

Available where books and ebooks are sold.